THE BEAST IN THE LAKE HAD CLAIMED ITS FIRST VICTIM.

A young girl had been hideously destroyed by something that lay hidden deep in the lake near the shores of Chicago.

No one really knew what it was—yet. No one had really seen it, but young scientist Blake Wiley figured the monster to weigh at least 20 tons.

Then a second victim. And a third. The mayor wanted it hushed up. But Blake knew that would be suicide. He knew the thing would not stop till it had destroyed everybody within its reach.

There had to be a way to kill it—or to tame it. . . .

THE PRESENCE—a mind-chilling novel of a deadly tomorrow.

THE PRESENCE

Rodgers Clemens

A FAWCETT GOLD MEDAL BOOK

Fawcett Publications, Inc., Greenwich, Connecticut

THE PRESENCE

ISBN 0-449-13890-9

Printed in the United States of America

10   9   8   7   6   5   4   3   2   1

This one is for John and Carol Quinn, and for Cindy, Aggie, Jimmy and Wayne.

The Presence

Part One

THE LAKE

Prologue

It is the midnight of creation. In the soundless, primeval blackness, gasses coalesce into stars. Stars fling out fingers of lacy fire, the fires coalesce, and planets are born. Eons are gone. Planets heat, contract, harden, cool. Some shatter and die, some live.

One lives, and its surface is a cauldron. Heavy elements settle toward the molten core, lighter ones rise and return to the void. There is no atmosphere; the horizon is knife-edge sharp and blacker than death. Light is the pure violence of meteor strikes and volcanic agonies. The planet circles its star a billion times.

The surface cools. A membrane of near-liquid rock forms. An earthquake a second cracks it; a thousand thousand volcanos blast with the force of atomic fission. The new world rumbles and quivers as it drops through the blackness like an egg with no shell. It glows a dull red.

Water trapped in the first cooling now struggles upward through the fissures, flings itself away in the shrieking lava, howls out in superheated steam, riding the backs of mineral crystals. In time, there are two million billion tons of it suspended over the burnt surface.

The planet tilts, core-metals polarize and become magnetic. The equator bulges, the poles flatten. Heat lifts the suspended waters, cold pushes them back down, Coriolis effect flings them around the planet. Hurricanes ten thousand miles wide build ominously.

It rains for seven hundred thousand years.

The waters fall. The planet screams and boils them away again. The waters fall. The planet steams, but no longer boils. The waters lay, and the low places on the planet fill. Waves beat against rock and make sand of it. Rain wears volcanos down to valleys. There are seas and oceans, lakes and rivers.

The atmosphere is nitrogen, methane, dioxides and monoxides of carbon. Traces of other things, but no free oxygen. Heavy ultraviolet bombardment sends nightmare washes of fluorescent red, orange and yellow through the vivid green air. And millennia are gone. . . .

In the achingly clear sea of gasses, elements move at random, their direction changed only by heat and cold, collisions with particles slamming in from space. Gamma rays, beta . . .

Somewhere among the uncounted trillions of atoms, the uncountable collisions, the particle strikes beyond reckoning, two elements touch and hold to each other. An age later, they part again, having affected nothing. An age after this, accident brings another two elements together, and this time they keep their hold. The winds move them for a thousand years. For a thousand more, they cling to a rock. For a thousand more, they fly again at the edge of the blackness. And finally, they come to the sea. . . .

A particle, so minute it will never be measured, comes.

It has traveled at the speed of light for more years than there are grains of sand on the beach of the shallow ocean below it. It is so infinitesimal that it has passed through entire suns without taking notice. It passes now through the sea, and in passing, brushes the melded elements adrift in the womb of the waters. It is deflected so slightly that it will fly for another million years before the deflection can be measured.

But the conjoined elements are changed, and gather others to themselves. Swiftly, in less time than it takes for a mountain range to be born and wear away, the compound proliferates. A layer of soup forms in the oceans. It diversifies, strikes out at other compounds, defends itself. Eventually, parts of the soup begin to specialize and cooperate in definable communities.

In less than a billion years, the soup has learned to walk. . . .

1

The power cruiser rocked on the moonlit lake, not anchored, drifting with the ground swell. Most of her portholes were alight. Music and laughter floated over the water. Figures moved dimly on deck.

A man in a bathing suit appeared at the transom with a bottle of wine in his hand. He squinted over the stern toward the darkness of the diving platform rigged just above the waterline. "Hey, Cheryl! You down there?" He slurred slightly.

There was a splashing a few meters away, and female laughter. "Here I am, Mr. Howland. Out here."

"C'mon in, kid. I'll meet you down on th' platform." He climbed over the transom and down the ladder, holding the wine bottle by the neck. He held the railing for balance, watching appreciatively as the girl swam up and levered herself onto the diving rig with the boneless grace of the very young. He offered the wine. "How's th' water?"

"Full of gunk, but it's really neat swimming at night. I never did that before." She hesitated as he offered her the wine bottle, then took it defiantly. She coughed as the wine went down, turning away from him in her embarrassment.

"Here, Cheryl, siddown." He took her shoulders and half forced her to the platform's deck, then picked up her towel and began drying her back. After a moment he pulled her back against his chest and kissed her behind the ear.

She tensed. "It s-sure was nice of you to invite Dad and me to the party, Mr. Howland."

"Nothin' to it, lover. Your dad's a good employee. One o' m'best." With a light, deft motion, he unhooked the girl's bikini top and slid his hands under her arms to cup her breasts.

She raised her hands to cover his, but did not pull them away. She knew he could feel her nipples stiffening, and the stutter of her heart. "What if somebody comes back here, Mr. Howland? What if Daddy finds us?"

"Not t'worry, lover. I lef' him with that redhead from out west. Th' stewardess." His hands were on her belly.

She made quick little motions of protest as Howland slid the bottom half of her bikini over her hips and down her legs. "M-Mr. Howland, I'm only sixteen. I mean, I know you're Daddy's boss and all that, but . . . "

Howland stopped stroking the girl and glowered toward the shore, half a mile distant. "Damn. Macintosh's let us drif' too close in." He heaved himself upright, muttering, and started for the ladder. "Coas' Guard's got th' whole beach under quarantine f'pollution. If I don' get us further out they'll have a cutter on us—an' probably right at th' wrong time." He handed the girl the wine bottle. "Don' you go 'way, okay? An' hang on to th' rail when we crank up. Don' want you t'fall in an' get chewed up by th' props, do we?"

The girl shook her head, not sure whether she was relieved or disappointed. Mr. Howland was pretty neat, she thought, and a real man. Not like the dumb boys in school. The magazines all said it was best to let a real man teach you.

Shortly, the platform vibrated as the big engines grumbled to life. Cheryl scooted over to the edge of the rig and dangled her feet in the lake, waiting for the massage of turbulence the propellers would kick up. She stared at the glowing skyline of the city, the jewel-string of car lights along the shoreline drive, deliciously aware of her nudity and the prospects of the next hour.

In the burbling water, something soft plopped against her ankle. Instinctively, she jerked her legs back aboard the platform. There was a greasy lump oozing down her shin, a piece of weed embedded limply within it. "Eccch," she said, her face wrinkling with disgust. She brushed gingerly at the lump, and it stuck to her fingers. It looked and felt exactly like mucus.

The engines bellowed to full thrust and the boat lurched ahead, throwing the teenager against the railing. The mucoid lump stretched between her hand and leg. Part of it slapped against her breast and stuck fast. A sharp tingling ran through her flesh where the material touched; almost electric. She grabbed the towel and pushed at the stuff, feeling nauseous. The more she pushed, the harder it resisted. It was like some obscene glue.

Then her eyes widened. The substance was thinning, spreading. It flowed and dripped until it coated her leg from knee to ankle, and her torso from breasts to pubes. As she watched in disbelief, it crept toward her throat.

She pushed herself upright on the pitching deck, small, inarticulate sounds coming from her mouth. The tingling increased, as though there were something acid in the mucus. It was hard to get her breath. She turned toward the ladder, reaching out for it with hands mired in thick, glutinous resistance. "Help me," she whimpered as the boat engines roared to life. "Help me, somebody."

She took one strained step toward the ladder before the thing on her body pulsed, jerking her off-balance. It flowed more swiftly, encasing her torso completely, coming softly around her buttocks like a man's hands. Her body was on fire where it touched. A faint luminescence lit the thing, outlining the girl as though she were a ghost. Tiny lightnings flashed through it.

With a terrible effort, the girl reached out for the ladder. With incredible swiftness the thing flowed up her neck, following the spinal cord, and over her head. "Help!" It came down over her eyes, her nostrils. "Daddy! Daddy!" And over her mouth. She was totally engulfed now—head, body, limbs. As she twisted in horror, the moonlight caught her wide-open eyes, now deep within the horrible gel.

The thing pulsed again; its internal lightnings grew stronger. Slowly, inexorably, it began shrinking in on itself, thickening like a contracting muscle. Tighter, and tighter —and *tighter*.

Howland made his foggy way back toward the fantail, grinning jovially at the couples twining in the muted light of the cabin and deck. Everybody having a good time, yessiree, he said to himself. Especially the sales manager and the stewardess. And ol' Howie was about to have a good time, too. It had almost been worth keeping Court-land on the last three years, just waiting for his daughter to fill out.

Howland leaned over the transom. "Hey, Cheryl! Here comes big daddy!"

The jarring ring of the telephone pierced the early

morning stillness. Blake Wiley burrowed deeper into the
blankets and jammed the pillow over his ears, but it
didn't help. The phone kept ringing. Maybe it would go
away. Maybe it was for someone else.

He cursed and fumbled in the darkness for the receiver.
"Yeah, dammit."

The voice on the other end was sympathetic but not
apologetic. "Blake, this is Saul Nesselroth, down at the
morgue. Can you come down here right away?"

Wiley didn't bother opening his eyes. "No."

"Yes. Something's come up. I need your advice, and I
need it now."

Wiley groped for the lamp and grimaced as the light
came on. He squinted at the clock. "Jesus Christ, Saul.
It's two in the morning."

"I know. I'm sorry."

"If it's alive, hit it with a stick. If it's dead it'll wait
'till morning."

"Now, Dr. Wiley."

Wiley sighed and picked through the litter of whiskey
bottles and overflowing ashtrays on his bedstand, looking
for a salvageable butt. "Is that a tone of command I hear
in your sweet voice, Mr. Coroner, sir?"

"Come on, Blake. Let's do it the easy way, huh?"

Wiley fished a crud-covered butt from the ashtray.
"Okay. Half an hour."

"Thank you."

Wiley hung up and sat with his arms on his knees,
trying to will himself awake. "Sonofabitch." He lit the butt
and stumbled into the bathroom, gagging and coughing.
He took a quick look in the mirror, but the bloodshot,
red-bearded visage glaring back at him proved intimidat-
ing and he avoided further confrontation. He brushed his
teeth and pissed, then went back into the bedroom and
started picking clothes out of the debris on the floor.
"Two o'clock in the fuckin' morning." He was just pulling

on a pair of jeans with a torn knee when the phone rang again. He considered ripping the instrument out of the wall, but answered it instead. "Your nickel."

"Hello, Blake. I hope I didn't wake you." A feminine voice.

Wiley stuck the receiver on his shoulder and poured himself a drink from the half-full bottle on the dresser. "No, but it was a nice try."

"There's no need to bite my head off, Blake."

"Why did you call, Gloria?"

There was a small silence. "Honey, are you alone?"

"No, I've got three girl scouts over here selling me cookies." He eased himself into a worn Marine Corps fatigue shirt. "We're making a movie as soon as the guy with the sheep gets here."

The voice was close to tears. "Just because we're separated—"

"We didn't separate, Gloria. You moved out, remember?"

"Blake, I'm still your wife."

"Yeah, I can't deny that."

"I-I want to come over, Blake. Just for tonight. I'm lonesome."

"Ain't we all."

"Please, honey. Couldn't we just forget all the ugly parts for this one night?"

Wiley was silent while he jammed his feet into a pair of filthy sneakers and found a fresh pack of cigarettes. When he finally spoke, his tone was light, relaxed. "Sure, Gloria. Sure. Come on over."

"Thanks, honey. I'll be there in fifteen minutes."

"Right."

Wiley hung up the phone, put on a rumpled sports coat, and left the apartment, carefully locking the door behind him.

Twenty minutes later he parked his ancient Jaguar in

the morgue's lot, noting that it seemed pretty full for the middle of the night, and went around to the front of the building. A beefy cop met him at the door and demanded to see his identification. "Must be a high-class stiff you got here," he said, showing his driver's license. The cop didn't answer.

Wiley was pointed toward the depths of the building and led by an elderly attendant into the scrub room. "What is this," he asked edgily, "a plague case?" The old man just looked at him and handed him a set of greens.

Wiley scrubbed and allowed himself to be gloved and masked. He was wide awake now, feeling both curiosity and an odd foreboding. The foreboding increased when he was put in the ultraviolet box and decontaminated. He'd been through the routine before, but only in the virulent diseases wards of hospitals. What the hell would he need to be clean for in the morgue?

The light flashed and Wiley obediently elbowed his way through the doors into the autopsy room, feeling a little silly about keeping his hands clean. Inside, he stopped. A group of about a dozen people, all masked and gowned, clustered around a stainless steel autopsy table, concealing it, almost deliberately. One of them turned at his entrance and he recognized the cocker-spaniel eyes of the coroner. Nesselroth walked over briskly and took his arm. "Have you eaten lately, Blake?"

"No."

"Good. Brace yourself and come look at this."

Wiley followed the surgeon toward the table. A butcher job? An acid case? Somebody they'd fished out of the sewer after a couple of weeks?

As the two men approached, the people around the table stepped back. Wiley had the absurd thought that they were a theater curtain, parting for a first-night performance. Unconsciously, he began the detachment rituals that all scientists go through, leaving his senses free to analyze dispassionately.

He stopped two feet from the table. On it was a smear of wet, translucent protoplasm, like a jellyfish out of water. But the smear had long, tangled blond hair, and convoluted bowels lay like a fetus in its depths, and an arm and a leg were dripping off the table. One blue eye faced the ceiling, while the other slobbered slowly around to stare directly at Blake Wiley.

2

A windstorm whips the lake, driving sharp, steep waves before it and breaking their tips into splinters that are flung ahead. It is laced with brief, thin sheets of warm rain that hiss across the surface of the water, etching it like a sandblaster. It has come, this wind, from the south, across the Midwestern farmlands that border the lake. It carries the odors of sunburnt corn, heavy hogs, dirt roads. Here, thirty miles from shore, these reminders of the land are surreal and somehow alarming to the crewmen of the big tug beating its way through the chop.

The captain registers the wind's olfactory information and catalogues it automatically, shuffling it to the back of his mind. He is more concerned with the three big scows his tug is pushing. The forwardmost of them carries deck cargo, and he worries that the green water beginning to

*sweep the bow will unseat it. For the fifth time, he sends
a crewman up the slippery deck to check the lashings.*

*This time his vigilance proves justified. Several pallets
of crated photographic chemicals are shifting slowly back
and forth with the roll and shudder of the deck; the lines
binding them are fraying. The crewman relays this information on the sound-power phone and requests a couple
more warm bodies on the foredeck.*

*Three crewmen swarm around the pallets, lashing, mov-
ing materials, relashing. They shift one pallet at a time,
securing it with block and tackle before cutting the old
lashings, then muscle it toward a more protected position.
The bos'n is an experienced man and times the cutting
and shifting to the roll of the scow, letting the rise of the
deck work for him.*

*A short wave runs beneath the scows, coming in off the
port quarter and angling toward the tug. It lifts the first
scow, and is just dropping it as it lifts the second scow.
The second scow slides down the wave and bumps the
first, moving less than nine inches, for it is securely
lashed in its own right. But the nine inches is enough to
break the rhythm, and the bump transmits as a sharp
lurch. At the bow of the lead scow, the lurch coincides
with another dropping wave, and a pallet snaps free of its
tackle, nearly taking a crewman over the side with it as it
plunges into the water. On the bridge of the tug, the
captain curses roundly, mentally figuring what the missing
pallet's contents will cost him when the broker goes over
the manifest. The seatrain plows steadily onward. . . .*

*Three fathoms down, the water calms. It is, after all,
only a windstorm above. The pallet of chemicals slowly
sinks, turning turtle as the wooden portions fight to return
to the surface. With muffled, sodden thunks, the lashings
part and the cargo separates. The chemicals are in carboys, large jugs, and the carboys are each crated in pine
slatting. They sink into the darker part of the waters. One*

*is caught by a trailing line, hooked by chance to the
rising pallet. Like a gondola beneath a half-filled balloon,
it sinks almost imperceptibly. By nightfall, it is fourteen
fathoms down and three miles closer to shore. . . .*

*There is a presence in the water, a blacker place in the
darkness. It is defined by negatives; no current seems to
be within its boundaries, no sizzle of minute movements,
none of the traffic of whistles, howls and grunts that detail
the lives of the lake's inhabitants. It is as though an utter
sterility hangs there in the cold wetness.*

*And yet, it is not devoid of signs and symbols to show
its being. It has dimension—thickness, and width, and
length, though the extent of these measurements has no
meaning to the animals who hunt each other through the
waters. It has motion beyond the random toss of the lake
that carries it. And it has, were there any capability of its
detection by the fishes, a pulse. A beat. A resonance. It is
this resonance, tuned to a frequency that throbs from the
agonized core of the planet to the bitter edge of the
ionosphere and back, that absorbs the commerce within
its boundaries and leaves it a dead spot in the broadcast
of life around it. Now and again, a wary fish strikes its
boundaries, only to find the boundaries flowing, surrounding, engulfing. . . .*

*The carboy is sixteen fathoms down, drifting southwest-
ward. Beneath it, the presence moves north. A tendril, a
pseudopod, a filigree of substance lifts, brushes, explores.
The carboy is drawn down and surrounded. Within the
presence, dim registrations are going on. Smooth/not-
smooth. Shape/not-familiar/register/store/shape. Food/
not-food.*

*The registrations are not thought. They are accumula-
tions of binary yes/no functions, more idiot than any
computer, less accurate than the urges of plankton toward
the light, as unconscious as the twinning of amoebas.*

But there is a difference. Each bit of experience, each

new piece of input, sticks. The presence, for all its blind mindlessness, learns. . . .

It surrounds the carboy, probing. It notes that the jug doesn't struggle. It senses no life functions diminishing to stillness. And so it squeezes. Hard. At a very high pressure, the carboy's thick glass walls give way. Fifteen gallons of concentrated acetic acid flood out.

The contact is momentary—perhaps the larger part of a second. The presence moves violently away, leaving the acid to disperse in the waters. But where it has been touched, it seethes and smokes, it burns and pains and dies. And even as it withdraws, the parts of itself that it has left behind in screaming ruin are sending last messages of analysis. In less time than the heartbeat of a great whale, every cell in the presence's being has recorded the new information, and has begun to integrate it. . . .

Mayor Spilokos waded ponderously and patiently through the reporters as if he were a genial bear faintly amused by a pack of hounds at his heels. His great, bald head nodded up and down, up and down, and the smile beneath his thick black moustache was wide and filled with perfectly capped teeth. He wore an American flag tie tack and a lapel pin which read *Be Proud You're Greek.*

"Mr. Mayor—your honor—what's the word on the federal funds for the school board? Are we going to get the money or not?"

Spilokos did a parody of the famous Mediterranean shrug that had put him in office. "You'll have to ask the folks down in Washington, son. Or maybe the Russian embassy. They usually know what's going on before the American public does." He grinned broadly at the smattering of laughter and angled toward the door to his suite of offices. A pretty blond woman stepped quickly between him and the door. "Yes, Miss McKittrick," Spilokos said mildly, his annoyance confined to his eyes.

"Mr. Mayor, if you didn't find out anything in Washington, why did you fly back in such a rush? And why are you down here at your office on a Sunday morning?"

Spilokos chuckled. "Well, my dear—"

"McKittrick. *Ms*. McKittrick."

"Yes. Well, Miz McKittrick, let's just say that I love my city too much to be away from it any longer than I have to." He reached around her for the doorknob.

She didn't budge. "You've been on five vacations since February, Mr. Mayor. You extended the one to Bermuda by six extra days."

The smile was still on Spilokos' face, but there was no warmth in it. "Madame, are you suggesting that I am not fulfilling my duties as mayor of this city?"

She shook her head but did not give way, even though the big man's tie tack was only inches from her face. "No, sir, I'm not. I'm just curious as to why you'd be at your office this morning. All of channel five's viewers will be curious, your honor, and I'll have to tell them something." Her own smile was as sweet as it was insincere.

Spilokos got the doorknob and bulled his way around her. "Well, you tell them whatever you see fit, Miz McKittrick, as you usually do. Both the city and I will probably survive."

At the general laughter, he ducked through the door and held up a large hand. "Enough for now, boys. I've got a city to run. I'll talk to you later." He flashed the smile again and shut the door in McKittrick's face.

The smile faded as he walked across the reception room. His secretary was at her desk, still in curlers. She had been with him nine years; she made brisk motions and did not look up.

"Where the hell is Ronald? What's the use of having a press secretary if he's never around to catch the flak?"

"It's Sunday, sir. He's probably in church. I'm not sure he got the word you were coming in, sir."

"Everybody else in town did, dammit. You get hold of him and get him on that pack of vultures out there. All I need right now is some TV snoop finding out the beloved mayor flew in for a heart-to-heart chat with three indicted gangsters—or that two of them are on my payroll."

"Yes, sir." She handed him a large manila envelope as he went by. "The coroner brought this for you. He's been down in the cafeteria for forty-five minutes. He'd like to see you right away."

Spilokos looked at the envelope with distaste. *"Now* what?" He sighed and started for his private office. "Okay, Liz, send him up."

"Yessir."

Spilokos went to the bar next to his files and poured himself a large glass of grapefruit juice, still carrying the envelope. He took both to his desk and sat. After a moment of quiet, he put on a pair of heavy-rimmed spectacles, and took out the envelope's contents. When he came to the photographs, he seemed to freeze in place.

He was still sitting rigid when Saul Nesselroth came in unannounced and dropped into an overstuffed chair. Nesselroth wore the tight-skinned face of a man badly in need of sleep. "I thought you ought to see those, Nikkos."

"I wish I hadn't." His hand shook slightly as he took a long sip of his juice. "No idea what did that to her?"

"None, so far. I've had a team on it since they brought her in last night, but we haven't a clue."

Spilokos pushed his glasses up his forehead. "Team? You mean your people from the morgue?"

"Yes, plus a couple of other doctors and one or two

people from the university; a biochemist and a whiz-kid general sciences man."

"Why did you call in those outsiders?"

Nesselroth frowned. "Those 'outsiders,' Nikkos, are fellow scientists. We're up against a problem of some dimension here, and it's common practice to call in specialists. For all we know, we could be dealing with some transmittable disease. I *am* the city's chief medical officer, and I'm responsible for that sort of thing."

Spilokos nodded. "Of course, Saul. I'm sorry." He stood and went to the big picture window, his hands clasped behind his back. In the distance, the lake appeared leaden in the early morning light. "But since we don't know that it's a disease, or even if it's unnatural—"

"Unnatural! Come on, Nikkos, name me anything that can do that to somebody. Anything at all."

"Or even if it's unnatural," Spilokos continued smoothly, "we'll treat it as an accidental drowning."

The coroner was out of his chair, looking incredulous. "What are you talking about?"

"We'll treat it as routine, and investigate it that way. And we will not, not, *not* make it a public issue." He faced the coroner, looking paternal. "Now, just relax, Saul, and think a minute. What happens if the media gets hold of this thing? Can't you see the headlines now? We'd have a citywide panic on our hands."

Nesselroth blinked, his face calmer but hard. "And what happens if we fish another body out? Or five or ten?"

"Well, then we'd naturally have to do something about it. But unless—*unless*—that occurs, we'll treat this as a drowning." He put an arm around Nesselroth's shoulders and began a practiced series of motions designed to get a visitor out of the office gracefully. "Now, I want you to call off your team, tell 'em to drop it. You can keep your staff on it if you want, but nobody else. And there's to be a complete news blackout. Not a word from anybody to anybody."

Nesselroth balked. "Mr. Mayor, I don't know why you're doing this, but I won't go along with it. I am the chief medical—"

"And I am the mayor, Saul, with complete discretionary power over all the city's civil servants. And I'll use that power if I must. I am not going to risk a panic among a million and a half people just because of an unusual drowning." He opened the door to the outer office and waited politely for Nesselroth to leave.

"Nikkos, at least close the lake."

The mayor shook his head. "That's not necessary. The shore's already closed for pollution, and the Coast Guard can handle the water traffic. I'll put the word on them right now."

Nesselroth held the mayor's gaze a moment, then looked stiffly away. "All right, you're the boss. I owe you. But I'm doing this under protest. I'd like to put an official confidential memo in the files."

"That's your privilege, Saul. Now, you go home and get some sleep. You look as if you could use it."

When Nesselroth had gone, Spilokos thumbed his intercom. "Liz, get me Hurkos on the private line and hold anything else." He waited for the buzzer, then spoke rapidly and intensely in Greek. The name Nesselroth came up several times.

Gloria Wiley marched into the apartment with long, hard-heeled strides, her face registering disgust at the piles of unwashed dishes and moldering meals in the kitchen. "Blake! Are you here?" There was no answer, and she stormed into the living room.

Wiley was sitting cross-legged on the carpet, using the coffee table as a desk. He was surrounded by a litter of papers, books and filled ashtrays, and was writing rapidly on a yellow legal pad. A bottle of Wild Turkey stood on the floor beside him.

Gloria planted her feet and put her hands on her hips. "Blake Wiley, you are a rotten, no-good sonofabitch. Of all the mean, nasty, childish *tricks*." She strode up to the coffee table and glared down at the top of his head. "I sat out there in the hall for an hour and a half last night, waiting for you, you bastard."

Wiley nodded. "Have a drink?"

She gritted her teeth. "Why did you do that to me, Blake?"

"Had a date. Hot stuff."

"You're lying."

"No," he lied.

She threw her handbag on the couch and dropped to her knees across from him. "Some slut?"

"I told you last night; three girl scouts and a sheep. You should have been there, you'd have fit right in."

"Listen, you miserable—"

Wiley handed her a stack of color photographs and went on writing.

She looked at the first two, then put the stack back on the coffee table. "I th-think I'm going to be sick."

Gloria looked at a spot on the wall, trying to control her stomach. She swallowed hard. "What . . . what did that?" she asked, her voice faint and light. "Was she drowned—it was a girl, wasn't it?"

"Yep. Sixteen. Partying on the lake last night and fell in. Fished her out half an hour later looking like that. She wasn't drowned, though. Pass me that calculator. Pretty interesting problem."

"Interesting problem," Gloria parroted incredulously. "Blake, that's a human being in those pictures."

" 'Human being' is redundant. And she's an ex-human now."

Gloria looked at her husband in disbelief. "She's not a bug! Not a laboratory specimen. Whatever awful thing happened to her, she was a *person*."

Wiley put down his pencil carefully and faced her. "Her name was Cheryl Courtland. She went to Central High. Her mother's dead, her father's a sales manager. They live over in Willowdale. She collected Robert Redford pictures. Her father's in County General right now in shock. If she'd been my kid, I'd be in County General myself. But she wasn't, and I'm not, and the only thing I can do for Cheryl Courtland or her father is to find out how she died."

Gloria took a shaky breath. "I'm sorry. It's just . . . those pictures. So . . . "

"Gruesome. Horrible. Ugly. Frightening. But not as bad as seeing the body itself. Or doing an autopsy on it."

Gloria paled and beads of sweat appeared on her upper lip. "I, uh, think I will have that drink."

"Help yourself," he said, bending over the calculator and his yellow pad again.

Gloria looked around vainly for a relatively clean glass, picking one up from the coffee table. "Your girl scouts could have at least washed the dishes," she said, trying to keep it light.

"Kept them too busy."

Gloria's face hardened. "I can almost believe that." When Wiley didn't respond, she peered out of the corner of her eye at the photos again. "Do you have any idea what happened to her?"

"Not a rat's ass. Saul pulled in everybody he could reach, and the general consensus right now is that we could be dealing with anything from a fruitcake mental patient to a voodoo curse." He indicated a large pile of computer readouts. "All we're doing is sifting data, looking for correlations, incongruities, repeating patterns. Plain old scientific method." He lifted a sheet out of the pile.

"Look at this. There was a suggestion of a kind of magnetic alignment of the dipolar protein molecules in the body. Now, what can that mean? What condition or set of conditions could cause that?" He bent over his pad again and started writing, his voice fading to a tuneless whistle.

Gloria set her glass down and stood. "All right, Blake. I forgive you for last night." She collected her purse and ran her hand lightly through Wiley's hair. "I know you're busy with this thing, so I'll leave you alone."

"Right. Thanks."

"I'd . . . I'd still like to see you, Blake."

"Sure."

"Will you call me?"

"Yeah."

"When?"

"Next time Halley's comet comes by."

3

The station manager clasped his hands behind him and followed his ample paunch over to Hannah McKittrick, who had just come storming into the newsroom and was determinedly ransacking the drawers of her desk. "Well, well, the prodigal daughter returneth. To what do we owe the honor of having your keen wit and lust-provoking person here on the premises—finally?"

"Hello, Jim," she said, not looking up. "Is there any money in the slush fund?"

"That is not my department," he answered, pulling a villainous-looking pipe from his vest pocket and firing it up. "My department is insuring that certain overpaid people produce something for my trained ape to mouth at the masses on the six o'clock edition." He disappeared behind a cloud of smoke. "Their failure to do so, Miss

33

McKittrick, jeopardizes my *own* overpaid and comfortable position here at Loonie Tunes."

Hannah tossed film cassettes and filters into her shoulder bag, zipped it shut, and faced her boss. "I think I missed a story this morning, Jim, down at city hall. I want to go after it."

"A laudable ambition. And what kind of story shall I look forward to with bated breath?"

"I don't know."

"Marvelous. Shall I mention that numerous of your fellow defenders of the first amendment have brought me the same news? Or that, curiously enough, they have collectively and individually demanded of me the same freedom to go ferret out this invisible story? While I face the evermore strident ticking of the clock, and the fact that the copy board is barren of news? Should I mention these facts to you?"

She brushed her blond hair off her forehead. "Look, I know you're in a bind, and I know that Larsen and Roskins are both on my story, but—"

" 'My' story, is it?"

"Just give me a little time and some walking money, and I'll bring you back a zinger."

The manager regarded her thoughtfully. "You're aware that mere moments after his return from the tents of the mighty, our beloved mayor started burning up the telephone wires, and that subsequently, that army of Greek goons he keeps under a rock somewhere was all over town buttoning up every source of information in a fifty-mile radius?"

Her eyebrows went up. "No, I wasn't." She looked jubilant. "See, there *is* a story out there. Do I go?"

He pondered, as if not having heard her. "Larsen probably checked out the usual sleazo stringers in the area, so that's covered. And Roskins is too good to miss a quick peek at the phone record. But I wonder if anybody bothered to hit on the newsstand boy in the building?"

"Right! Look, just let me run down and talk to him, Jim."

"You'll be the ruination of me, McKittrick. I shall be forced to return to peddling encyclopedias."

She gave him a huge smile and a peck on the forehead. "You're a love."

He scowled heavily. "Go forth, pride of channel five. But if, perchance, you do not return with at least a Pulitzer-level story, I will feed you through the shredder with my own pudgy little hands. Comprende?"

"Si, amigo. I'll just stop by the cashier on my way out."

"A hundred bucks maximum. This is not a charitable organization."

He watched her appreciatively as she swung off down the newsroom.

The anchorman came up. "You're letting her get away with it again, huh?"

"Of course, m'boy. That is why I am honcho here and you are still taking handsome lessons." He pointed with his pipestem at McKittrick's departing form. "It's the hemline, lad. Whenever she's got a hunch, her hemline goes up. Right now, she's mere centimeters away from a charge of indecent exposure, which means that we're in for a hot story."

The anchorman was still staring at the door through which Hannah had disappeared. "Her hemline, huh? Well, if that's a hunch's worth, I'd sure like to see a late flash."

Hannah signed for a hundred dollars and piled into her Fiat. The station assigned her a car, but its channel five emblem would be more a handicap than a help today. She drove out into the Sunday evening traffic and got on the expressway feeder that circled the city. Maybe that crippled kid who sold candy in the lobby, she thought, would know something that neither Larsen nor Roskins had found out.

She pulled off the ramp and into a McDonald's. A dime got her the boy's home phone, and another got him. Yeah, he'd been working that morning. Lots of tourist traffic, even on a Sunday. Yeah, he'd seen who went in and out. No, he hadn't told fatso Roskins anything. Sure, he could use a twenty—who couldn't?

Hannah was in her car and headed for the morgue. What would the coroner have been doing, meeting with Spilokos? Did that have anything to do with the sudden silence the mayor had ordered? Did it mean there was a body involved? Nobody important had turned up dead last night. Maybe some big-wheel hood?

She cruised by the city morgue, watching out of the corner of her eye. Well, well! A uniformed cop at the door and two Mediterranean-type gorillas lounging outside trying to look inconspicuous. Hannah's hunch began to solidify.

Knowing there was no chance of getting through the door, she drove two blocks, cut over one, and came back behind the place. A twenty-four-hour diner stood catty-corner across from the rear of the morgue. She smiled to herself, parked, and went inside. A boy of twelve or so was behind the counter. It seemed to be her day for kids. She ordered coffee. "Aren't you a little young for this job?"

He grinned. "It's my pop's place. We all work."

"Were you working this morning?"

The grin vanished. "You th' *po*-lice?"

"No, I'm a reporter for channel five."

The boy's grin returned. "Already been a bunch of re-porters in. I told 'em I didn't see nothin' or know nothin'. I didn't even get here 'till most ever'body was gone. I got a paper route."

Hannah cocked her head slightly. "Do you know any of the people who were here?"

"Sure. All them guys that work in th' morgue eat over here. They was there this mornin', and th' doctor hisself. I didn't know none of the others, an' only one o'them stopped in here. Looked like a hippie or something." The boy acquired a dreamy expression. "Sure had a neat car, though. One o'them real old *Ja*-gu-ars." He looked guilty. "I oughtn't say no more. Ever'body supposed t'keep quiet."

Hannah fished a ten out of her bag and laid it casually on the counter. "Just between you and me, huh?"

He eyed the ten. "You won't say nothin'?"

"Reporters always protect their sources."

The boy looked toward the kitchen, then caused the ten to disappear. He leaned over the counter, close to Hannah's ear. "He was a pro-*fess*-or."

"How do you know that?"

" 'Cause th' car had one of them university faculty parkin' stickers on th' windshield, and it was punched f'this year."

Hannah looked pleased. "You're an observant young man. What color was the car?"

"Red, with lots of body putty."

Hannah stood and patted the boy's arm. "Thank you, I believe that will do nicely. You keep your eyes open for me, will you?"

"Yes, ma'am, I'll do that."

Three phone calls later, Hannah had contacted a graduate student who knew the car and its owner, and ten minutes' conversation got an address and a phone number. She started to call the number, then changed her mind and decided to drive by the address—an apartment complex off Lakeshore Avenue. She took her time, letting her mind play with the possibilities. It was already close to six-thirty. If this guy had been up all last night or most of today, would he be asleep now? How would she present herself, just showing up on his doorstep? Would Spilokos have a thug at his door?

The red Jaguar was parked in front of the complex. Hannah eased her car in behind it and went into the foyer. *Wiley, Dr. Blake D.*, was listed as being in 4C. She pressed the call button. There was no answer, not even after three more tries. She pressed 6A. The door buzzed and she let herself into the lobby. The stairs were slow, but maybe the occupant of 6A would be watching the elevator. There was nobody in front of Wiley's door, and no light showed beneath it. A credit card served as key, and she was inside. The place stank of stale smoke, male sweat, and spoiled food. Something dripped in the bathroom. But there were no sounds of breathing. She turned on the light, ready to bolt if anyone showed. The apartment was small and looked just like it smelled.

She picked her way through the mess, mentally cataloguing Blake Wiley. A loner, obviously; he didn't have anyone in to clean. But not always a loner. Bachelors eventually learn to keep their places clean. Some woman had taken care of this guy for a long time. Divorced? Mama's boy? Bottles all over, and dirty glasses. Expensive bottles. Divorced, probably, and recently into hitting the bottle. The old-pro drunks used cheaper stuff. She kicked a pile of clothes with her toe. Well-built, medium-sized guy; size sixteen shirt neck, thirty-four jockey shorts. Picture on the dresser; proud middle-aged couple and grinning boy in a Marine Corps dress outfit. Wiley and parents?

Nothing in the bathroom. Foot powder for athlete's feet, antidandruff shampoo. A professional barber's trimmer. Did he have a beard? Little touch of vanity, there.

Back in the living room, she noticed the coffee table. Why? She went over to it, letting her gears mesh. Ha!

It was clean. There was a pillow on the floor between the table and the sofa, ring marks showed along the right side where wet glasses had been set. But what had been in the middle? What had Wiley been working on, and more importantly, where had he put it? Hannah felt a rising excitement.

"Not bad. Not bad at all."

Hannah whirled, stumbling against the coffee table. "Oh, uh . . . "

Wiley stepped into the apartment and closed the door behind him. He walked to the little kitchen and put down the paper bag he was carrying. "We had a laboratory rat named Herman who could spot the incongruity in a maze in thirty seconds. He even got to where he could pick the relevant incongruity out of a set of three." He pulled a steak and a can of green beans out of the sack and took them to the stove. "You were only in here for a minute and forty seconds."

Hannah pushed a wisp of hair off her forehead and looked quickly toward the door.

"Not a chance. I can still do the hundred in eleven flat."

She smiled in resignation and sat gracefully on the sofa. "We appear to be stuck with each other, then. You *are* Blake Wiley, aren't you?"

"Yeah. And you're Hannah McKittrick, from channel five." At her look of puzzlement, he grinned smugly. "It's on the registration in your car. Scientists are pretty good at investigation, too." He took a bottle of Wild Turkey out of the cabinet and poured two drinks, bringing them over to the sofa. "I saw you punching my button downstairs as I was coming back from the store."

She took the proffered glass but did not drink. "Then you must have a pretty good idea of what I'm doing here?"

"Breaking and entering."

"That, too, I suppose. Dr. Wiley, the coroner was down at city hall this morning, talking with the mayor. Before that, he was at the morgue all night, and so were you. As soon as he left city hall, Mayor Spilokos ordered a large silence laid on."

Wiley took a stiff pull at his drink. "Politicians could use a little silence."

She leaned toward him. "I'd be very grateful if you'd tell me what happened last night. What's going on at the morgue, Dr. Wiley?"

Wiley looked at her speculatively. "Could I trust your discretion?"

"Your name will never be mentioned."

He slid his arm around her shoulders. "Last night," he said, almost whispering, "Spilokos' mistress found out he was making it with a Shetland pony. She committed suicide by leaping off a tenth-floor balcony. She landed on a fireplug, and we've been trying to get the smile off her face ever since."

For a moment, she just stared at him, her face reddening. Then, as he fell back on the sofa roaring with laughter, her look changed to repugnance. "Ho, ho." She stood, clutching her bag with both hands. "I'll just toddle along now. And when I do get the story, I'll be sure to butcher you on several broadcasts."

She started for the door. Wiley lunged off the sofa and dove across the floor to grab her ankle. He looked her up and down lecherously. "Why don't you stay for supper instead?"

She raised an eyebrow. "You're a cocky little monster, aren't you?"

"Maybe I'll get drunk later. You could ransack the place for my deep dark secrets."

Hannah extracted her ankle. "Was it a wife or a girl friend who walked out on you?"

He stiffened, and came off the floor, the cords of his

neck taut. For a moment, Hannah thought he'd hit her. But he relaxed and gave a barking laugh. "You've been in a few gutters, haven't you?"

"I fight dirty, Dr. Wiley." She stepped around him and walked to the door. She watched him, judging. "I like my steak rare. I'll be back in an hour." Then she was gone.

Wiley rubbed his chin, looking thoughtfully after her. Then he went quickly to the phone and dialed Saul Nesselroth.

The Coast Guard patrol craft *George S. Armour* pitched through the waters of the lake, still roiled by the recent windstorm. The Monday morning light was bright enough to etch halos around the crewmen, who stood in postures of kinetic suppression, like coiled springs. Each man was armed. The boat's radar hood swung in tight arcs, as if it were a sonic cobra.

The bos'n stood on the flying bridge with the lookout. He yelled down through the open hatchway of the navigation bridge. "Hey, Sparky, got anything yet?"

"Nope. Radar's clean and so's the sonar."

"Well, keep at the sonar. Boats don't always sink straight down. We'd look pretty stupid getting holed by a submerged wreck, wouldn't we?"

"Yeah, I guess we would."

The bos'n grunted and scanned the water with his glasses. He'd only had time for a single directional fix before the garbled, hysterical radio mayday had been lost in static, and had no idea how far ahead the trouble was. But one thing was certain—the background noises in the mayday, cutting through the cries for help and shrieks of terror, had been gunfire.

The lookout tensed, his binoculars steadied against the pitch of the vessel. "Object in the water, range two hundred yards, bearing three five zero relative."

The bos'n whipped his glasses around. "Port your rudder. Come about ten degrees. Ease your throttle."

The boat slewed to port, steadied, and fell away slightly as the engines throttled down. Two deckhands trotted to the 20mm cannon on the foredeck and looked questioningly up at the bridge.

The bos'n shook his head. "Not yet. Let's see what we've got here first." Unobtrusively, he loosened the catch on his pistol's holster. "What do you make of it, Eddie?"

The lookout shrugged. "Log, maybe. Could be a shit-can some deck ape dropped off a freighter." His tone was casual, but he, too, loosened his holster's catch.

"All stop. Let's not run it under." The bos'n leaned over the railing again and yelled inside. "Sparky, get on the horn and let the shore know we've spotted something. Tell 'em to stand by to send a chopper."

"Aye-aye."

The patrol craft eased up on the floating object, the helmsman juggling wheel and throttles to allow it to pass slowly down the starboard side of the hull.

It was the collapsed and splintered remains of a lifeboat, turned turtle and with its varnished ribs sticking through its hull like bones.

The crewmen caught it with the boathook. One of the boys looked up at the bos'n, his face slightly stricken. "There's somebody down in there, Boats. At least, there's an arm."

The bos'n licked his lips nervously. "Johnson, get the camera out and record this. Lee, keep the hook on it until we get the camera up here, then turn it over and fish the body out."

The radioman stuck his head out of the hatch. "Boats, I think you better come look at this."

"Ah, shit!" The bos'n swung down off the flying bridge and through the hatchway. "Well?"

"Look at the sonar. And listen." He handed the phones over. "Some kind of pulse. It's all over the radar and sonar, and it's jamming the radio."

"Did you get a signal through?"

"No, and I can't get anything inbound, either, 'cept that pulse. I'm damned if . . . "

Both men became aware of it at the same time. The vessel was dead in the water, as still as if on chocks ashore. They looked at each other, then ducked out on deck. "Holy fuck," the radioman said in awe.

For a distance of a hundred meters in every direction, the water was glass smooth, though the lake tossed unabated beyond that limit. The air felt thick and close.

"I don't like this," the bos'n said, his twenty-year-old voice cracking slightly. He pulled his sidearm. "Okay, let's get that body aboard and get the hell out of here."

The two crewmen hung over the side, fishing gingerly with the boathooks. One staggered back, his face pallid. "I c-can't do it, Boats. I never seen a dead person before. It's a-all covered with slime."

The bos'n snarled, thankful for something familiar on which to vent his nervousness. "A dead body is just a piece of meat, Lee. And after nine months' service on this scumbag of a lake, a little sludge won't hurt you."

"Right," Lee said, poking squeamishly with the boathook. "A little sludge won't hurt me."

4

The planet falls through the void. The fierce waves of energy it radiated in its youth are memories now on the faded pages of creation. Its surface has hardened into a wrinkled skin, covered for the larger part with moisture. It is mature now, the planet, and sails with infinite patience toward entropy.

But it still radiates. It reflects energies from its star, and light from the edges of time. Bits of its atmosphere slough off it like a vapor, clogging the blackness with an atom of material per cubic mile.

And it radiates a rare thing in its part of the universe— coherent energies, the creation of the walking soup that inhabits the surface scum. Radio waves, television, intense bursts of patterned electromagnetic shorthand sent, probing the awful distances in hope of companionship. Some simply leaking away, an ever-widening sphere of *leftovers from the walking soup's incessant need to proclaim its continued existence to itself.*

Some energies the planet creates of itself, and not all of these are squandered on the darkness. In its molten heart, the planet pulses to its own, deep beat. The pulse throbs up through the planet and howls into the atmosphere. It rises to the cold night and reflects back. It does this ten times per second. And each pulse passes through the surface scum, and through all that moves and grows and feeds in that scum. In the depths of the building blocks of life, which stack into pansies and polar bears, redfish and redwoods, corn and crocodiles, the pulse touches/ moves/aligns. Aligns.

It is unconscious, this electromagnetic heartbeat. Neither the trees nor the flowers acknowledge it; not the worms that burrow the dark earth or the starfish that creep the floors of the shallow seas. Yet it times them all. Made audible, a rapid tick; made visible, a steady, skittering set of peaks; made tactile, a vibration in the fingertips. Ten times a second, more accurate than the decay of cesium. It is the tuning fork of the planet, the heartbeat of the world, the balance wheel of everything that lives. It gives the steady track. It aligns the ancient forms and the newborn. It beats impartially for the light and graceful, and for the dark, the deep, the monstrous. . . .

Six fathoms down, the presence shifts its molecular structure, becoming more fluid, drifting with the urge of the waters. It is coming, now, to have a dim awareness of classes of difference, and of cause and effect. It now perceives the concept of self, and can differentiate between self and not/self. It now responds to learned stimuli. It knows that certain croaks and whistles, if followed and surrounded, produce feeding; certain variations in light and temperature produce need for more or less energy. It does not know "light" or "dark," nor can it differentiate between the sensations of light and sound beating against its perimeters. It can only judge "sensation" or "no sensation." But it knows which ones to follow to get food.

It is also aware of the generalization that the more heat a thing possesses, the more energy it yields. It now seeks fish and shuns plants. It seeks larger fish and shuns smaller.

And it has recently learned that there are exceptions to the generalization. Though it has no true memory, it can associate, and it has learned to associate propeller beat with the very high emitting things that are like the fish, only different, more powerful, more energy-yielding. It has followed a propeller-beat source, grasped it and pulled it down, shaken and crushed it. And learned that engines cannot be food, even though they have heat and motion.

But there were more of the very high emitting things. . . .

And now, in its response/reaction system, there is an urging toward concentrations of propeller beat, toward the places where they spawn and gather. Each cycle of light and dark now brings the presence closer to that awkward boundary in the not/self, which has neither motion like the waters nor life like the fish, but is impenetrable to the presence's senses. It does not know that the boundary is called "shore," but it does sense, fuzzily, that along that boundary there is a high concentration of emissions, a richness of energy. And it does not know that this richness is composed of engines and wires and a million and a half souls, or that the richness has a name and is called "the city." It doesn't know this. Yet.

Saul Nesselroth stepped over the *Beach Closed* chain sign and made his way laboriously through the dirty sand toward a figure hunched over a scatter of apparatus near the water's edge. He was puffing by the time he arrived, and angry. "What are you doing here, Blake?"

"Taking water samples," he answered, not looking up. "Every five hundred feet for a mile on either side of the spot where Cheryl was killed. You want to hand me that bottle there?"

Nesselroth took off his jacket and mopped perspiration off his face with the sleeve. "That's not what I meant and you know it. We've got orders from the mayor to drop this thing."

"You've got orders. You're a city flunkey, I'm not."

Nesselroth handed Wiley the empty bottle and took a full one from him, stoppering it by reflex and dropping it in a cardboard box with several others. "Look, Blake, we went through this last night. I don't like it any more than you do. I think it's a shame that a politician can step on a scientific investigation."

"It's despicable. It's even more despicable to kowtow to him." Wiley waded out of the water, picked up the box, and began trudging along the shoreline. Nesselroth hurried after him.

"Think what you want. But remember I've got six years invested in this job, and a family to feed. Nikkos could ruin me."

"If you stacked all the doctors, scientists and philosophers who've used that copout end-to-end, they'd reach from here to the moon. I don't have time for that crap."

Nesselroth made a rude noise. "That's quite a romantic image you've got there—intrepid boy wonder, standing off the forces of darkness all alone. But it's no good. Spilokos can shut you down as quickly as me. He's got the power, legally or otherwise. And I've known him long enough to assure you that he won't hesitate to have you removed far from the madding crowd if you push him."

Wiley stopped abruptly, almost plowing into the coroner. "Nikkos Spilokos," he said, speaking carefully and precisely, "can stick his power and his thugs up his

ass. I'm going to find out what killed Cheryl Courtland."
He rounded on Nesselroth. "You can't seriously believe
his horseshit about a panic, can you?"

Nesselroth looked at the sand, then shook his head.
"No."

"Then what's he covering up? Why is he afraid for this
killing to make the news? Instead of being out here
hassling me, why don't you find out what he's hiding? That
way you could put the screws to *him*."

Nesselroth made exasperated sounds. "Blake, you're a
good scientist, even if you are a freebooter. But politically
you're an idiot. You've no idea how much force that man
can wield." He took Blake's box of bottles companion-
ably. "Listen. Why don't you let me talk to Dean Peters,
get you temporarily assigned to my staff? That way you
could come down to the morgue and work on this thing
in peace."

"Uh-uh. That bunch of clowns of yours all have tunnel
vision. They're worse than the cops. Your menagerie says,
'interesting disease,' the cops say, 'mad scientist,' and all
of them have their heads up their asses—which you
know as well as I do."

Nesselroth walked along beside Wiley for awhile, looking glum. "One of these days, you're going to grow up
and stop playing the hero, Blake. You're going to admit
that science is a team effort." He stopped and regarded
the younger man. "I know how you feel. I'm a scientist,
too. But I'm also the chief medical officer of this city, and
that comes first. I want you to come down to the morgue
first thing in the morning. That's where the body is,
remember?"

"I remember. But the body's just the 'effect.' The
'cause' is out here, in the lake. *That's* where the problem
is, and that's where the solution is, and that's where I'm
going to be, period."

"Blake—"

"Dammit, Saul!" He flung a bottle into the sand. "How often does something really new come along? Once a century? Once every two centuries?"

"Maybe that often."

"Well, we've got something new here. You know it and I know it. And I'm not going to let it pass me by. This one's mine, Saul. *Mine!*"

Nesselroth watched Wiley stomp angrily back into the water and jerk at his equipment. He had known the younger man for many years, knew him to be a good and kind and considerate person beneath his egoistic front. But in Blake Wiley's face now was a look as old as the caves and feral as wolves on a winter night. And for just a moment, Saul Nesselroth felt pity for whatever it was, out there, that had become Wiley's quarry.

The gallery was replete with two-hundred-dollar-an-ounce perfume and six-hundred-dollar formal gowns. The men were the sort who were used to having their cigars lit for them. Spotted through the beautiful people were girls in paint-smudged leotards and young men with defiant beards. The artist whose show was opening looked happily dazed.

The Coast Guard ensign's look of discomfort, as he threaded his way through the glitter, could have come from the fact that he was still wearing his workaday khakis. But it didn't.

He navigated between reefs of overcoifed women and shoals of arty dilettantes until he reached a backwater in the festivities, where he found Nikkos Spilokos being held at bay by two ancient women with more money than taste, to judge by their rigging. He signaled discreetly and was rewarded by a grateful look from the mayor. Spilokos indicated an alcove behind a large piece of sculpture and joined the ensign there.

"What can I do for you, son?"

"Sir, Commander Haley felt he should have this hand-delivered." He gave the mayor a folded message and stood unconsciously at parade rest.

Spilokos read the brief note inside, his face professionally calm. "I don't understand this, Ensign. How could you people lose a yacht *and* the cutter sent to rescue it? Was it a collision, do you think?"

"We don't know, sir. As the commander points out, we lost radio contact in some sort of static, and sent a chopper. When it got to the area there was nothing to be seen but some wreckage." The young man shook his head grimly. "I don't think it was a collision. The remains looked as if they'd been crushed. Those boats would have had to have been doing a hundred knots each to splinter like that."

Spilokos gave the boy a sharp look. "Until we know differently, we will officially assume it was a collision, understand?"

The ensign stiffened. "Sir, I am an officer in the Coast Guard. I take my orders from—"

"Yes, of course. Mmmm, look—ask Commander Haley if he has to report this incident to Washington, will you?"

"I know he does. It's regulation."

"Then ask him if he'll do it by courier instead of broadcast."

"Yes, sir. Does this have any connection with the girl who drowned last Saturday night?"

"How do you know about that?" Spilokos demanded.

"I was on duty then. Our cutter brought her in."

The mayor took the ensign's arm in a polite but firm grip. "As far as we know," he said carefully, "there is no connection. No connection at all. But you are aware that Commander Haley ordered a news blackout on that drowning, aren't you?"

"Yes."

"Then why did you mention it to me, son? That was disobeying a direct order, wasn't it?"

"But, I assumed that you . . . Yes, sir, it was."

Spilokos nodded genially, but did not slack his grip. "I have a feeling that Haley is going to issue a similar order concerning this, mmm, collision today. I would therefore strongly advise you—strongly, Ensign—to return to the base with sealed lips, yes?" He let go of the boy's arm and inclined his bald head toward the door. "Politics being the art of compromise, young man, and me being a politician, I'll keep my lips sealed if you do likewise, and neither my plans nor your career will be jeopardized."

The officer looked grateful. "That is a bargain, Mr. Mayor."

"I believe in 'everybody-wins' deals. Now . . . ?"

"I'm on my way."

Spilokos watched until the officer had left, then walked to the back of the gallery and stared unseeingly at a painting on the wall. What was going on out there? He felt a sudden, helpless rage running through him. Goddamn it to hell, he muttered angrily, why couldn't all this have waited! Why did that idiot girl have to get herself killed now? Why did the asshole Coast Guard blow it today? Three more days, that's all he asked. Just give it three more days and he wouldn't care if they did find the creature from the black lagoon out there.

He shook himself into a semblance of relaxation and dove back into the party, angling toward the reception desk where Hurkos stood like a patient shark.

The door opened while Wiley was trying to decide whether to put down the box or keep trying to get the key in the lock with two fingers. Hannah McKittrick stood inside, smiling at him. "Hi. Hard day at the lake, dear?"

Wiley did not smile. "Don't you have a home of your own?"

"Want me to carry that for you? I'd love to see what's in it."

Wiley brushed past her and stopped, surveying his apartment with distaste. It was spotlessly clean. "Did you do this?"

"Oh, no," she said blithely, coming around him and trying to peer into the box. "I just cleaned it up. It was plain that some churl with the manners of a pig has been living here, so I made it all nice for him. Is that my story you're clutching with such determination?"

"Get away from this box or I'll break your arm."

"I love your strong, masculine approach. There's pot roast in the kitchen; shall I pour a trough for you?"

Wiley sat the box on the sofa and dropped beside it. He put his still-wet sneakers pointedly on the polished coffee table. "Hannah, get out of here. I'm beat and I've still got a ton of work to do."

She went to the kitchen and began setting the small table. "Where was it, Blake?"

"What?"

"All the stuff I turned this place upside down trying to find. You're pretty good, you know. Plain bread or toast?"

"Will you just leave?"

"Come and eat. Most of you scientist types aren't really very clever. You hide things under the mattress or in the toilet tank or like that. But I really went over this place and couldn't find a thing. My professional vanity is hurt. Come *eat*."

"Bring it in here."

"You're afraid I'll make a grab for that box."

"Yes."

"You're right." She brought a bowl and toast, and a small glass of red wine. She sat on her knees across the coffee table from him and regarded him seriously. "I know there's a body involved, Blake. I know the lake's involved. I know it has to be something strange or grue-some or important because Spilokos has zipped this town tighter than a eunuch's fly. I know that Nesselroth is desperate about something because he's got everybody from street sweepers to his Aunt Hattie working at not looking desperate. And I know that you are the wild card because everybody else is in medicine, and you're a funky-butt."

"A what?"

"Funky-butt. It's an old musician's term for a guy who can play most anything or any style well enough to get by. You probably like to think of yourself as a Renaissance man, but funky-butt feels better to me."

Wiley spooned some juice over his pot roast. "You're absolutely right, Hannah, about everything. So you don't need me. So go home."

"I do need you, Blake, for two reasons. First, because I need hard facts, and second, because you're going to be the one who figures this thing out."

Wiley stopped with his spoon halfway to his mouth. "What makes you think that?"

"You're cute. The cute guy always figures it out. Don't you read novels or watch movies?"

Wiley sighed and rubbed the back of his neck. "Look, Miss McKittrick—"

"Please. Call me Hannah. After all we've done to each other . . . " she simpered.

Wiley looked at his watch. "I'll give you five minutes to be out of here. After that, I'll kick your rump."

"Promises, promises. I've got a whip and some cream cheese in the car. Wouldn't take a minute to get it."

He regarded her speculatively. "You really want this story, don't you?"

She colored slightly, a little of the humor going out of her face. As if unaware of doing so, she crossed her hands protectively in her lap. "Not that badly."

Wiley laughed without humor and got up. "Okay, enough's enough. I've got work to do. Let's go." He took her under the arm and pulled her upright.

She flowed into his arms and kissed him urgently, almost violently. "Jesus, you're obnoxious," she said breathily, her face in his beard.

"I'm not going to let you see what's in the box."

"I didn't ask."

"I won't go to sleep first, either."

"Will you just shut the fuck up and take me to bed."

"I suspect your motives, lady."

"I'm beginning to suspect your virility."

For a moment, he held her to him, almost protectively. Then he nodded. "Right." He snapped forward at the waist, hoisted her skirt over her hips, flung her bodily over his shoulder, and marched into the bedroom. He stood at the foot of the bed, grabbed the back of her panties, and dumped her off his shoulder. The panties shredded in his hands, and Hannah landed on the unmade bed naked from the waist down.

She had a look somewhere between fright and mockery in her eyes, but the smile on her lips was sincere. "Point made, Blake. Do you want a banana and an old tire to swing on, or shall we be civilized?"

Wiley slid out of his shirt and pants. "Take your choice. You seem to like calling the shots."

"Up to a point," she said softly. She sat up in the bed and unbuttoned her blouse. She wore no bra, and her small breasts showed pale bands of bikini-white, which spoke of much time under a sunlamp or on the beach. Her nipples were surprisingly large. She leaned back on her elbows and appraised Wiley. "I like short, thick men."

"I won't ask in which sense you mean that," he said, slipping into bed beside her.

Once, fiercely, as though in a contest of will and stamina, and once again, in a slow, sweet, teasing rhythm, and then they rested, both sheened with sweat and musk. A cigarette shared, a glass of warm wine brought in from the kitchen, and this time it was making love and not having sex. They explored each other's bodies and reactions, found mutual sensitive places, odd quirks, fine idiosyncrasies. And when it was over, they snored gently in each other's arms.

Five minutes later, Hannah's snores tapered off and she carefully disentangled herself from Blake's limbs. She eased quietly off the bed and tiptoed out into the living room.

Thirty seconds later, Blake stopped snoring, sat up, and slipped into his pants and sneakers. He walked to the living room door and lit a cigarette.

She was bent over the box and jerked upright guiltily, a urine-sample bottle in her hand. "You weren't sleeping," she accused.

"Nope."

She held up the bottle. "Water from the lake, right? Samples from along the shore. When you came in you smelled like dead fish and there was sand all over your pants. What's in the water, Blake?"

"Poison," he said, going back into the bedroom.

She came over to the door. "You're kidding, aren't you?" She almost collided with Wiley as he came back out holding her blouse and shoes in one hand and her skirt in the other.

"I don't know. I haven't checked yet. Why don't you taste it and save me some research?"

"What's out there, Blake? Is it going to kill anybody else? It must be or you people wouldn't all be so uptight, right?"

Wiley plucked the bottle from her fingers and handed her her clothes. "You get a look, not an explanation." He hugged her to his chest and nuzzled her, backing her across the room. "You're very nosey."

"If this is another proposition—so soon—I'll have to give you an 'A' for stamina."

Blake kissed her on the mouth, reached behind her, and opened the apartment door. "Good night, Miss McKittrick."

"Blake! I'm naked! Oh, you sonofabitch! I'll—Blake, wait a minute."

"Get your foot out of the door."

"Promise me the story, Blake."

"You'd best cover your ass. There's a pervert lives down the hall."

"An exclusive. You do owe me, damn it."

"Okay, you get the exclusive. Don't call me, I'll call you." He pushed, but she kept her foot in the door.

"One last thing, lover."

"What?"

"Where *did* you hide the material the other night?"

"Part of it in the toilet tank and part under the mattress."

"You're a nasty man, Blake Wiley."

"Someday I'll introduce you to my wife. You share a couple of opinions." He closed the door and locked it.

In the hallway, Hannah McKittrick climbed hastily into her skirt and blouse, shivering in the cold air of the hallway. Yes, indeed, she thought smugly. Perhaps it *was* time Blake Wiley's wife met Hannah McKittrick. Shouldn't be all that hard to locate the woman, and even less hard to start a little fur flying and a few claws sharpening. She stuck her feet in her shoes and bounced down the stairs to the ground floor.

Back inside the apartment, Wiley replayed the past hour, less interested in motivations than in results. She'd gotten a look at a bottle of polluted water, and he'd gotten her. Seemed like a fair trade to him.

He stood a moment, waiting to see if she were truly gone, then went back to the sofa, unzipped the cushion covers, and extracted his notes and research materials. He spread them out on the coffee table, laying them in neat stacks like a solitaire hand. He lined the sample bottles up along the farther edge of the table, sat on the sofa, and finished the bowl of cold pot roast while he leafed through the papers. Hannah's questions kept running through his head like a tape loop endlessly repeating. What *was* out there? What *did* he have in the damned urine bottles—besides scum-infested water?

He pushed the stacks of paper into disarray, looking for the spectographic analysis of Cheryl Courtland's tissues. He found it and fished in his hip pocket for the spectroanalysis graphs he'd done on the water samples out at the lakefront. One by one, he began matching up the strips against the earlier one of Cheryl's tissue. Would there be anything significant? What the hell was he looking for, anyway?

After the third time through, he gave up. There was nothing in Cheryl's tissue that didn't belong there, nothing in the lake water he didn't know about already, and nothing that matched in any way that made sense. The water from the point nearest the death site was no different from the water a mile away in either direction.

He got up, stretching tiredly, and decided to pack it in for the night. He ran himself a hot bath and stripped, leaving his clothes in a heap in the middle of the bathroom floor. He sat on the edge of the tub, too tired for the moment to lower himself into the water. The tape loop of unanswered questions continued to replay in his head. Absently, he kicked at a lump of mucuslike gunk stuck to his sneaker, wondering how a piece of jellyfish got into a fresh-water lake.

5

"Okay, boy, cast over yonder. Try and get your line out past where the waves are just starting to break. That way, you don't tangle up."

"I can't see where you mean, Pop. It's too dark."

"If it was light enough to see the surf, it'd be light enough for the beach patrol to see us, wouldn't it? Then they'd come run us off this pier and we'd miss th' fishing. Most good fishing's done on th' sly, boy, an' a good fisherman's got to be able to fish by instinct." The man took the boy's head in his hands and aimed it toward a point about ten yards off the beach and a bit to the west of the pier. "Now, listen. Use your ears, 'stead of your eyes. You can hear the waves starting to break almost as good as see 'em. Can you hear 'em?"

"I think so, Pop."

"Then cast where your ears tell you."

There was a whir of fishing line and a tiny plop, nearly lost against the background hiss of the lake. After a time, the boy sucked in his breath. "I think I got something."

"Well, haul it in."

The boy tugged. "I can't. It's really strong. Must be something pretty big."

The man's hands closed on the rod, judging. "You're right." He took the rod from the boy. "Let me give it a try, son."

"Ah, Pop!"

"Easy, boy. I'll just work it close. You can land it yourself." He sounded dubious. "Never felt anything quite like this." He labored silently, pulling the line in by six-inch spurts. Both he and the boy peered futilely at the dark waters below, as if willing enough light to see their prize. The man lurched back from the guardrail, working the reel furiously. "Got it! She's out of the water now. Get the net and grab 'er, son."

The boy scooped the net off the pier and leaned over the guardrail with it.

Something laced with lightning rose crackling to meet him.

The presence has assumed a new role. It no longer prowls the waters in search of food, but has anchored itself in the shallows along the shore. Thick pseudopodia wedge into bottom crevices, surround rocks, clamp to barnacle-encrusted wrecks; tough threads in thousands deploy from the main body to grasp individual aquatic plants; strings of self tie the presence to half-buried cans and automobile tires; ropes of being hold against submerged pilings. The surf rolls and tumbles, the waters charge the shore and retreat, and the presence holds firm and stationary.

It has stretched itself along the shoreline, nearly half

a mile. It lies like a nacreous umbilical cord just beneath the surface, and its shape is not constant.

It has not assumed this configuration by conscious choice, but by circumstance. It has come seeking propeller beat and found instead a sewage outfall. It has spread around this outpouring of nutrients, found that— like an ever-filling balloon—it cannot contain the outflow indefinitely, and it has made of itself a sieve, a membranous surface through which the waters pass and the solids do not.

It has by accident or chance sent feelers in several directions—a tendril of substance here, chasing a vagrant lump of food, a glob on a string there to catch the sinking body of a dying fish. And some of these feelers have stayed in their new location, feeding, and have drawn the parent body along on constantly thickening cords of nutrient and information exchange. And now, the presence feeds continuously, with parts of its being straining nutrition, parts engulfing, parts crushing, and parts actively questing for new sources of food.

There is no gluttony in its actions, for there is nothing finite to fill. It simply grows. And there is no differentiation in food sources besides the yield of energy needed to feed. It makes no distinction between a live fish and a dead one, a soggy box of crackers pulled from the waves and a carpet of algae scraped off the bottom, a bacteria-laden lump strained from the sewage outflow and a boy snatched off the pier. It's all food.

Nor does the presence realize that in its variety of food-gathering techniques it has compressed a billion years of evolutionary divergence into a single night and a single being.

Yet it has done this, nonetheless. Without thought, without prior experience, without precedent, it has not only learned to specialize, but to adapt to the specializa-

tion necessary at a given moment and for a given set of circumstances.

There are other changes going on in the data system that is not a brain, but is still aware. The presence performs a crude sort of analysis on the substances entering its being. It has begun to recognize that all foods break down into smaller units of similar molecular order, and that these units are the same no matter what the source.

None of this is conscious. None of it is labeled. There is no name for the processes or products. There is not even the idea of name. But the presence has learned what is essential in food and survival. It has passed the great predator shark, which knows only to eat and cannot distinguish between food and non-food. The presence does not rationalize. It simply understands. And eats.

Saul Nesselroth looked from one to the other of his assistants, then back to the reports neatly laid out on his desk. "Is this all?"

The two men looked at each other, then at the coroner. "Yes, sir. Six reports from my group, three from John's, and the synopsis."

He shook his head. "I didn't mean it that way, Wes. I meant, is this all you've got to say? 'Death by crushing, with various organic compounds apparently extracted'?"

The assistants exchanged looks again. "Dr. Nesselroth, that's all there is to say. We've autopsied, biopsied, run every test we can think of."

"And all you can do is give me a physical description of the corpse." He leaned his elbows on the reports and steepled his fingers against the bridge of his nose. "Can you recall anything in the annals of science, John, that would react in a way that would produce the body we've got back there?"

"Sorry, I don't have a clue. I don't even have a clue about clues. I can think of nine zillion outlandish methods for applying massive pressure evenly over a whole body, but none that you could do in ten minutes in fifty feet of water. Ditto for ways to deplete a body of specific organic compounds. And I definitely can't name anything that would do both, under *any* circumstances."

Nesselroth leaned back in his chair and locked his hands across his stomach. "Does it occur to you boys that we are going at this thing backwards? That we are trying to make the facts fit the theories instead of the theories fitting the facts?" He did not wait for an answer. "How about we cast aside the conventions, gentlemen, and commit a little scientific heresy. Take the day off, both of you. Go sit under a tree. *Think.*"

"About what, sir? I'm not sure I follow you."

Nesselroth leaned his knuckles on the desk and looked each of them in the eye. "Take the fact of Cheryl Courtland's condition. Take the assumption that something in the lake caused it. And design me the thing that did it."

They were awkwardly quiet for a minute. "You mean," Wes asked carefully, "a, uh, science-fiction monster?"

"You tell me. Maybe so. Maybe a fish we don't know about yet. Maybe a chemical reaction from the garbage out there. Maybe the Martians. I want some intelligent answers. Now, get out."

They left, looking doubtful. Nesselroth had his doubts, too. But he also had Blake Wiley's accusations stinging him, and they stung because he could not refute them. Whatever had killed the girl was not just unknown, it was new. No matter how exotic a fish was, it could still be identified as a fish and catalogued with the other fishes. No matter how unexpected a chemical reaction, it could still be broken down, explained, and fitted into the jigsaw puzzle of chemistry. But this killing: it had no roots. No background, no phylum, no species, no cousins or relatives. And, the coroner fervently hoped, no chance of a repeat performance.

The phone. The phone. The damned phone. Wiley sat up groggily, his hands dangling between his knees. What had he done to deserve this? Getting no answer to fuel his self-pity, he answered the call. "This better be good."

"Blake? You sound awful."

"Gloria, I am going to kill you. If you ever call me again in the middle of the night, I'll—"

"It's nine in the morning. Why aren't you at your office? I called there first."

"Please, Gloria, just let me sleep, huh? I was working half the night."

"No you weren't. I called the office then, too."

"I was working here. Good-bye, wife. Try again this afternoon."

"Your lady friend was here."

Wiley frowned, then sat upright. "McKittrick? You didn't tell her anything, did you?"

"I'd think you'd worry about what she told me." She sounded hurt.

Wiley got up and began pacing the apartment. "What did she want? What did she ask you?"

"Blake, are you in trouble? I think she's a cop. What are you up to that the police want to know about you?"

"She's not a cop, she's a television reporter. Channel five. What did you *tell* her?"

Gloria Wiley sniffed dramatically over the phone. "I told her you were a rotten husband and a man with an ugly sense of humor, and that I'd pull her blond hair out by its black roots if she came near you."

Wiley relaxed slightly. "You didn't mention anything about . . . "

"About what?"

"Never mind. Never mind. She didn't ask about my work?"

"As a matter of fact, she did. And I told her that you

were as big an ass at the university as you were at home. Blake, can I come over?"

"Did you tell her anything about Cheryl Courtland?"

His tone silenced her for a heartbeat. "Well, yes, was that wrong?"

"God damn it to hell! Gloria, you—"

"Don't yell at me! How was I to know; you never tell me what you're doing. Anyway, what's wrong with her knowing about it? Doesn't everybody know?"

"They will soon."

"Blake?"

He slammed the receiver viciously into its cradle, his mind racing. Could he stop her? Should he notify Saul? Maybe he could call the TV station. Maybe he ought to cut her throat—and Gloria's in the bargain. Maybe he ought to call city hall, since it was the mayor's show.

He grunted derisively and started the ritual hunt for his cigarettes. Screw the mayor. He didn't know why Spilokos was keeping the lid on this, and he didn't care. His interest was in having the problem to himself. If McKittrick blew the whistle there'd be a hundred self-made experts jumping down his throat before the broadcast was off the air. And there was a chance, just a chance, that one of them would beat him to Cheryl Courtland's killer.

He gave up on the cigarettes and began stuffing himself into his clothes. Thing to do was find McKittrick. Find her and shut her up. Goddamn reporters to hell.

He trotted into the bathroom and made a quick pass at brushing his hair and teeth, his mind still running at top speed, then grabbed his keys and wallet and headed for the door.

Halfway across the living room he stopped, looking puzzled. Something was trying to get his attention. What? He replayed the past five minutes, from the phone call forward. Cigarettes. Brushing. Bathroom . . .

He moved toward the small, blue-tiled cubicle as if it were booby-trapped, not knowing what had raised his hackles, but trusting the instinct. Ever since 'Nam, he'd had the ability to sense the peripheral danger, the corner-of-the-eye incongruity.

He stood a foot or so away from the doorway and cautiously pushed the door back with his foot. What was he looking for? On the sink, his hairbrush and a dirty glass. On the tub, a used washcloth, the top off the shampoo bottle, a piece of soap. On the floor, his sandy and still-damp clothes, one filthy sneaker up against the side of the toilet, and the more-or-less permanent puddle where a worn washer let the hot water tap leak under the sink.

And halfway between the sneaker and the puddle, a mucoid, sluglike lump oozed with barely perceptible motion toward the puddle.

Wiley felt himself go chill, then flushed. He stepped into the bathroom, telling himself the thing on the floor was a snail, a slug, a whatever, and knowing that it was not. Knowing that there'd never been anything on earth with quite that nacreous translucence, nor with that sinister, almost radioactive glow to it.

He reached out a finger, as if to stroke it, then jerked his hand back. No. Not just yet. He jumped up and ran for the kitchen. He plowed excitedly through the refrigerator, tossing food and mold-coated bowls of glop out on the table. He sorted through the array and selected a chunk of very stale hamburger, a piece of cheese, and a leaf of wilted lettuce. On sudden inspiration, he dove into the dark recesses of the undercounter cabinets and emerged with a frantic, wriggling cockroach. "Yeah science," he gloated, carrying his collection back to the bathroom.

He went to his knees on the floor, humming contentedly, and stuck the cheese, the hamburger and the lettuce in a semicircle in front of the crawling lump. "Okay, beautiful. Let's see what you like for lunch."

The thing bumped into the cheese, quivered, and flowed over it. The lettuce went next, and the hamburger followed. The lump grew opaque, and the coruscations inside it became brighter. "Um-hmm," Wiley said, his face close to the floor. "A balanced diet, an omnivore. The AMA would be proud of you." He opened his left hand, revealing the sleek brown cockroach. "How do you feel about chow on the hoof, amigo? Care for a little fresh cockroach steak?" He took the insect between his thumb and forefinger and poked it experimentally against the nearest end of the lump.

With blinding speed, the mucoid being sprang over the insect and the tips of Wiley's fingers. There was an instantaneous, massive pressure, as if a heavy vise had clamped down on the fingertips. A savage, piercing pain shot through Wiley's hand and up his arm. He felt as if his hand were on fire.

He threw himself backward, screaming at the top of his lungs. Instinctively, he snapped his hand back and forth, trying to fling the thing off. On the fourth or fifth jerk, he succeeded. The lump whipped off his hand, smacked wetly against the wall above the bathtub, and slobbered down to lie on the rim of the tub itself.

Wiley was jammed against the toilet, his eyes bulging and his face white. "Holy mother," he said in an awed voice. He examined his hand. The thumb and finger were swollen, red, the skin roughened and already blistering.

A tiny, minute popping pulled his attention back to the animal on the tub. With a kind of horror, Wiley realized he was listening to the cockroach, still wriggling feebly, being crushed inside the slug.

"My God, my God," Wiley mumbled, holding his wounded hand at the wrist. "Poor Cheryl Courtland." He walked over to the tub, wondering how he'd get the

beast into something safe. Without thinking, he raised his
hurt fingers to his mouth to suck them, as though they
were burnt. He gagged, pushed the hand away, re-
garding it with loathing. Jesus! That close.

He sat on the toilet, thinking hard. "Okay, sport. Okay.
So far it's just you and me. I think I'll keep it that way for
awhile. Long enough to show you who's boss."

6

The station manager watched Hannah hurrying across the employee's cafeteria toward him, knowing from her walk and her face that she had something for him. He rose and bowed slightly as she got to the table. "Greetings, fair-haired Aphrodite of televisionland. I assume from that triumphant look on your face that you either have a story or have finally caught someone sodomizing our weatherman. Will you join me in my gourmet's repast? Chipped beef on toast *à la* Lucrezia Borgia—although we had another name for it in the army."

She dropped into a chair across from him, poured sugar in his coffee, and drank it. "Jim, you *really* aren't going to believe this one."

"As the Queen of Hearts told Alice, I try to believe at least one impossible thing before breakfast each day, or words to that effect. Speak on, my dear—it's about time you justified your salary."

He listened with apparently casual disinterest as she told of bribing her way into Tom Courtland's private hospital room, and of his nearly hysterical account of the death of his daughter. When Hannah gave her second-hand description of the body, the manager quietly put down his plastic fork and laid his napkin over his food. As Hannah snapped off incidents in an excited staccato, he loaded his pipe and fired it up. Finally, he held up a hand to stop the flow. "All right, we know what happened, and we know what's being done about it. But as yet, we don't know what killed her, nor why friend Spilokos wants it kept quiet."

"Well, we'll know *that* much soon enough. I'm going straight over and confront him. I'll have this story on the six o'clock edition, with or without him."

"Wrong on two counts, m'dear." He puffed a contented eruption of smoke into the air. "First, it is not you but I who will go see the mayor, simply because I pull more weight—if you'll pardon the pun."

"But it's my story! Besides, I owe that pompous bastard one and I want to see him squirm."

"Second, I'm not sure this will be on tonight's news."

"Jim!"

"Tut, tut, Hannah. Not to worry. I've lost my hair but not my capacity to think." He reached across the table and patted her hand. "We don't know but what the beloved leader has a valid reason for his silences, do we? And that being so, perhaps there's a better story in *that*, correct? Which being so, I shall take my cheerful and harmless personage into his sanctum and put the screws to him for both of us, devil that I am."

"Mmm. Yeah, that sounds right."

"And you shall gird your loins in whatever it is that you ladies use to render we menfolk helpless and continue

your seduction of this fellow who appears to be superman
and Attila rolled into one. What's his name again?"

"Blake Wiley, and I've had enough of him. He's a
supercilious, egotistical, disgusting—"

"—handsome, exciting, virile young man, who according to you is likely to be the one who shouts 'eureka.'
And since you are so obviously in lust with him—"

"Now, just a minute!"

"—you are the perfect choice to stab him in the back in
the interests of dear old channel five." He got up and
peered down the expanse of his paunch at her. "Remove
the look of venom from thy face, cherie. Regard me as
a father figure. I know what's best. And if you know
what's good for you, you'll get off your butt and get after
Wiley. I'm sure his estranged spouse has lost no time in
letting him know that you were by for tea, yes?"

Spilokos was trying hard to look poised and relaxed
when the station manager was shown into his office, but he
was a little too angular, too taut, to pull it off. He knew
this, and he knew that it showed.

"Ah, Mr. Wintergreen. Good of you to stop in." He
extended his hand, knowing that he had not entirely kept
the dislike out of his voice, and knowing also that the
pudgy man in front of him could read him like a book.
Wintergreen's handshake was cool and firm. The sonofabitch had him, and knew it. "What can I do for you?"

Wintergreen shifted his pipe from one side of his mouth
to the other, smiling blandly. "You could tell me why you
don't want us to break the Cheryl Courtland story."

Spilokos considered playing it dumb, but discarded the
idea almost immediately. He looked regretful. "Ah, yes,
Miss Courtland's . . . unusual demise." He motioned the
newscaster to a chair and sat behind his desk, knowing
that he was taking advantage of the piece of furniture,

letting it make him feel secure in his position. "Mr. Wintergreen, I will be frank with you."

"I think that would be to both our advantages, your honor."

The mayor listened for sarcasm and decided he didn't hear any. He tried to judge the man. "What would buy your station's silence for the next few hours?"

Wintergreen's head tilted to one side. "Are you trying to bribe me, sir? That's a novel position for a mayor—at least when dealing with the media."

"Yes, I'm trying to bribe you, Mr. Wintergreen. But not the way you think. I'm trying to buy you with patriotism." He bounced out of his chair and strode to the picture window, gesturing for Wintergreen to join him. "What do you see out there?"

Wintergreen came over and dutifully stared out the window. "The city. The lake. Smog. There is perhaps something metaphysical I do not discern?"

Spilokos pointed. "Southward. Look at the buildings. Slums from Ninth street to the industrial basin. Eastward. Do you know how many fires we had there this year? How many muggings, robberies, murders?"

"A good number of each. Does this have a bearing on our original topic of conversation, sir?"

Spilokos locked his hands behind him and paced the room. "There's a lot of ways to tell a story. If Cheryl Courtland had drowned, or been shot, or been strangled, what would your station have to say?"

"That she was drowned, shot or strangled, as appropriate."

"But she wasn't. She was killed mysteriously, and her body is not something you see every day. But that's not the way the media would say it, is it?"

Wintergreen thought, then shook his head. "No, sir, I don't think so. We television people would use a bit of restraint, but the tabloids would be certain to get hold of the pictures and print them."

"Exactly." Spilokos went to his desk and picked up a memo pad. "How closely do you follow your own news? Do you keep up with the features section?"

"Not regularly, why?"

"Do you know what is scheduled to occur Thursday morning?" When the station manager indicated he didn't, Spilokos handed him the memo pad. "Two conventions. The National Ornithological Society and the Veterans of American Wars."

Wintergreen's eyebrows rose as the light dawned.

"Right, Mr. Wintergreen. Thirty-five thousand bird nuts and bald-headed veterans, descending on the city for four days. And what happens if, before then, somebody runs a story on Cheryl Courtland? 'Monster in lake turns girl into jello!' Can't you see it now? Thirty-five thousand people, at an average of a hundred bucks a day, for four days. That's a hundred and forty million dollars revenue—down the tubes!"

Wintergreen looked at the big man wonderingly. "Mr. Mayor, do I understand that you are sitting on this potentially lethal problem for the sake of mere money?"

"A hundred and forty million dollars is not 'mere' money. And bear in mind your own word—potential. We've only got one kid dead." He hoped Wintergreen did not know about the Coast Guard fiasco.

"Yes, and whatever killed her is still loose out there. Mayor Spilokos, we're talking about lives being endangered!"

"You're damned right we are." Spilokos pointed out the window again. "How many lives would that money save, Wintergreen? That money represents fifteen more cops for the nightshift. New street lights out by the university. A cardiac emergency unit for County General. Two new fire trucks. Don't tell *me* about lives to be saved!" He gritted his teeth, then willed himself to relax. He brushed absently at his moustache. "I'm sorry. Would you like some coffee, or a drink?"

"No, thank you."

"Look, I'm aware of the risk involved in all this. I've got everybody I can reach working around the clock on it. But I've got to balance all the factors here, and those two conventions are major factors." He sat on the edge of his desk. "I told you I was offering you a bribe, Wintergreen. It's a simple one. If nothing else happens in the lake between now and tomorrow, you give me my silence. I'll give you the exclusive rights on the story."

Wintergreen chewed at his unlit pipe a few moments. "Mr. Mayor, you've got nothing to bargain with. I already have the story, and the constitutional right to broadcast it without hindrance. Furthermore, you are in no position to bargain anyway. You have actively worked to suppress this story, and that fact alone could ruin you if it's made public. Finally, you are asking me to do something that both my morals and my training abjure, which is to be your accomplice in keeping this threat to the public safety quiet." He watched the mayor's eyes. "But I will— provided there are no further occurrences on the lake, and provided you insure this by closing the lake to the public."

"That would have the same effect as broadcasting your story. The conventioneers would stay away in droves."

"That, sir, is your problem. I'm confident you will find a way to make the closure palatable to our hoped-for guests." He put his pipe away, signaling the termination of the conversation. "I have no sympathy for your reasoning, Mr. Spilokos, and very little for you personally. I believe that if this city were being properly managed, we'd *have* all those facilities you have held up as lures for my emotions. I am therefore going to aid your cause to further my own."

"How's that, Mr. Wintergreen?"

"I am going to pray that all turns out well, sir. That the conventions come, that the mystery of Miss Courtland's death is solved tidily, and that the coffers of the city are filled to overflowing. And then, Mr. Spilokos, I am going to hold this story over your head for as long as you are in office. I am going to use it—for the threat will go on forever—to see that you utilize some of those millions of dollars to bring about wonders of civic reform." He allowed himself a tiny, terrible smile. "Do I make myself clear, sir?"

Spilokos watched him calmly for a long heartbeat, then gave way to heavy laughter. He came off the desk and held out his hand. "Wintergreen, you are a prime bastard. You are also a hell of a nice man. I hope you never go into politics."

Wintergreen shook the mayor's hand. "As one manipulator to another, may I say it's been a pleasure to put the boot to you."

"Package for Dr. Wiley." Hannah hoped her beige jumpsuit and the pencil stuck behind her ear would make her look enough like a delivery person to get her past the campus policeman who stood guard at the laboratory building's entrance.

The guard looked briefly at the box under her arm, then at a clipboard on the wall beside his desk. "Where from?"

"Uh, Amalgamated Laboratories."

"You ain't on th' list, lady. What's in th' box?"

"Don't ask me, sport. I just pick 'em up and take 'em where the waybill says. I got a lot of deliveries still to go," she added hopefully.

The guard grumbled. "Never tell me nothin'. How'm I supposed to tell who they want in and who they don't?"

"Hard times. Which way's Wiley?"

"Second door on your right. Sign here."

Hannah scribbled illegibly on the log sheet and went in. Wiley's door was open slightly and she pushed through it unannounced, closing it behind her. The room was filled with chemical apparatus and electronic gear, and the only piece she recognized was the oscilloscope. Wiley was in a far corner, hunched over a microscope and humming tunelessly. A yellow pad lay beside him, covered with notations. At her entrance, he looked up, scowled, and went back to staring into the microscope. She walked over to him. "When did you eat last? I brought you some lunch." She began unwrapping the box.

"When I'm done with all this," he said quietly, "I am going to take you someplace nice and peaceful, and there I am going to stake you out for the ants and piss on you while they kill you."

She stuck a ham sandwich next to his hand. "Did you ever talk to anyone about your repressed sadistic tendencies? But then, they're not all that repressed, are they?"

"Enjoyed your little chat with Gloria, did you?"

"Not much. The light of intelligence in her eyes is really the sun, shining through the back of her head. Why did you marry her?"

He ignored her and indicated the microscope. "Take a look."

She did. "I majored in journalism and back seats, Blake. What am I looking at—besides some horrid little bugs that wiggle around a lot?"

"As far as I can find out," he said, an edge of excitement in his voice, "you are looking at Cheryl Courtland's murderer."

She jerked her face away from the instrument, then checked to make sure Wiley was not joking. *"Those?* What are they, viruses?"

"No. You can't see viruses with a microscope like this one." He reached around the instrument and pulled a

culture dish toward himself. In the dish, something like
thick glue pulsed sluggishly in a bath of lake water. "The
things on the slide are part of this. They're one-celled
animals, and they are very strange indeed."

Her revulsion showed. She would not touch the culture
dish. "And that lump there is a collection of those things
on the slide?"

"In a way, yes. At least, they behave a lot like a
colony or a symbiotic organization. In other ways, they
behave like individuals."

"I don't understand that."

"Neither do I." He tapped the dish, and the thing in it
contracted. "When you have a single-celled animal, you've
got a self-contained creature with limited responses and
functions. It specializes in a generalization of the life
functions. That is, in its one cell, it can capture food,
digest it, expel waste, and reproduce. But all these functions are very primitive.

"Multicellular animals can get more complex because
their cells specialize—muscle cells, nerve cells, brain cells,
like that. You with me?"

"I think so."

"Okay. This critter in the dish responds to all sorts of
stimuli, and in complex ways. It also learns—that's not
impossible, but it's damn rare.

"To be able to do that, it *should* have many different
kinds of cells, right? Each specialized. But it doesn't. It is
nothing more or less than a large clump of the little
one-celled beauties on the slide."

"That doesn't sound possible, if I understand you."

"It's not supposed to be." He pulled the slide and held
it up to the light, as if he could see the individual creatures
in the smear. "Want to hear something worse? Each of
these little buggers—each separate one of them, Hannah
—responds just like a multicellular animal." He waited to
see if that had sunk in, then walked across the room and

flipped the lights off. "I'm going to project the scope on the wall here. Put the slide back under the lens and watch this."

A swarm of ameboid creatures sprang into sharp relief on the wall.

"I'm putting some pulverized bread crumbs on the slide."

On the wall, enormous, jagged lumps suddenly appeared among the creatures. Within seconds, the animals had swarmed over the lumps.

"Good God," Hannah cried. "They're crushing the crumbs!"

"Right. Now, watch what happens when I put a few more animals in." The image on the wall shook, blurred, steadied. A new swarm of creatures appeared.

"Do you see what's happening, Hannah?"

"I-I . . . yes! Yes. The new ones are touching the others, then going for the food. It's like ants or something. They're passing on information. Blake, that's amazing! What can do that?"

The lights came back on. Wiley stood by the switch, looking both thoughtful and a little frightened. "Nothing, Hannah. At least, nothing this earth's seen before."

7

Commander Haley stood braced, as if waiting for the hospital corridor's floor to roll out from under him, or for the fan down the hall to start blowing a gale. With his weathered face and chestful of medals, it was difficult to believe that he was barely into his thirties.

A nurse's aide walked up, smiling sympathetically. "Are you expecting?"

"Mmmph? Sorry, what did you ask?"

"Are you expecting, sir? The maternity ward's over that way."

He glared stiffly from under bushy brows. "I am not married, madame."

She made flustered motions. "Oh, I'm sorry. You looked like an expectant father. They wander around, you know, and we have to steer them back to the waiting room."

Haley's frost melted slightly. "No, I'm waiting for Dr.

Nesselroth, young lady. Thank you." He nodded dismissal, then reddened as he realized that not everything in a uniform was under his command. The aide left anyway, reddening herself but for more romantic reasons.

"Ah, hello, Commander. Sorry to keep you waiting." Nesselroth was still in surgical gown, and the hand he extended was still gloved.

"Not at all, Doctor," Haley said, shaking Nesselroth's hand. "Well, what's the situation?"

"Let's get some coffee. I need it." The coroner led the way through County General, angling for the coffee shop. "When the police brought him in, I was skeptical. Even with what's been going on, a tale about some mass of goo pulling his boy off a pier is a little hard to take."

"But now?"

"Yes, but now. I've heard his story straight, and I've heard it under sedation. I've examined him for drugs or mental aberrants. And I believe him."

"I was afraid of that." Haley took Nesselroth's elbow and halted him. He spoke quietly so that his voice would not carry in the hollowness of the hallway. "Despite the mayor's prohibition, I notified Washington of the loss of our cutter, and that yacht. I did not mention a connection with the Courtland girl. Washington sent up an admiral from Johns Hopkins. He found traces of a kind of slime on some of the wreckage, and concluded that it was organic and had probably been alive at the time of the disaster."

Nesselroth's face showed that the finding was not news to him. "My own team found similar material in the Courtland girl's hair. Badly decomposed, but identifiable as being non-human tissue."

"Um-hmm. And now we have a man whose son was grabbed by a hunk of slime. What does that say to you, Doctor?"

"I'm a medical man, Commander," Nesselroth said cautiously.

"And I'm a sailor. But I'm not an idiot and I don't think you are. There is something alive out there, and it's not 'Jaws.' "

"Yes, there is."

"What are you going to do about it? You are responsible for protecting the people of this city." He said it as a challenge.

"Believe it or not," Nesselroth replied, struggling to modulate his voice, "my authority—by law—does not extend past the waterline of the lake. I can't even condemn a bad catch of fish until it's put up for sale in the city!" He pulled free of the commander's grip, almost defiantly. "Thus far, everything that's happened has happened in the lake."

"But still, there's a moral obligation."

"Yes, but whose? *I'm* under direct orders, Commander, from the chief officer of the city, to keep quiet. *You* aren't. He's 'asked' you to keep this under your hat, but he doesn't have the authority to order you to do so. Isn't that right?"

Haley looked uncomfortable. "Well, yes. But Mayor Spilokos and Admiral Gunther are, ah, very close, and . . . "

"And you're trying to chivvy me into putting my butt in the sling so you don't have to put yours there." Nesselroth's cocker-spaniel eyes were no longer limpid, but hard and disdainful. "What we've got here, Haley, is two men who don't like what they see when they look in the mirror, but don't have enough balls to change the image."

Haley would not meet Nesselroth's eyes for a moment, then he squared himself away. "I can't refute your picture, Nesselroth. But we've got two people definitely dead, plus five more from the cutter and three, possibly four, on that yacht who can't be accounted for and have to be presumed dead. You can't keep that a secret for long, even with orders from God Almighty. It's going to come out, and if it doesn't come from one of us, *both* our butts will be in the sling." He stuck out his hand once more. "Good night, sir. Best of luck."

"Same to you, Commander Haley."

The two men shook hands and parted company, the doctor toward his cup of coffee, the commander toward the door. And each man hoped to the depths of his soul that he had stung the other hard enough to cause a reaction. A public one.

The news of the latest happening at the lakefront was brought to Nikkos Spilokos at the country club by his press secretary. The mayor bagged his clubs and motioned the secretary into the golf cart with him. "What do you think, Ronald?"

"About the death?"

" 'Alleged' death. They haven't found a body yet."

"I don't think they will, either."

"Then you believe the story about a piece of snot grabbing the kid, huh?"

"Yes, sir."

Spilokos twisted the ends of his moustache, then threw up his hands. "Dammit, so do I."

The secretary looked surprised. "Then, you're going to break the news?"

"Hell, no! I'm going to push Nesselroth until he's found some way to kill the thing out there, and I'm going to—*you're* going to—keep stalling the media. Once the conventioneers are here, we'll break the story and play it for laughs. Make a joke out of it. We can set up viewing platforms along the lakeshore and charge them to climb up and look."

"Do you think they'd do that, sir?"

"Sure. Hell, over in Scotland they run tour buses along

Loch Ness ten times a day. People pay six bucks just to look at the water, and not a damn one of them's ever seen the 'monster.' "

Ronald's young face was clouded with the unaccustomed effort of trying to force his views on his employer. "If that would work, sir, why can't we go ahead and do the story now? Seems as if that would pull in other people besides the conventions."

"Wrong psychology, son—drive us over to the clubhouse, will you? Nobody wants to be the *first* kid into the haunted house, but once he's been in, everybody else follows. If either of the conventions cancelled, it'd be all over the news and everybody else would stay away. But with thirty-five thousand outsiders already here, and not being eaten by the snot, we'd get every thrill-seeker in the States." Spilokos hoisted himself out of the cart and retrieved his clubs. "Now, you run on down to the hall and make nice for the bloodsuckers from the media. I'll be over at the morgue."

"Yes, sir." Ronald sat in the cart, gnawing his lip, as Spilokos drove off. Was that Greek bastard really going to pull such a cornball routine? There wasn't a chance in hell that it would work. Unless the old fart could do it on sheer force of personality—and he might at that; he had that ability to mesmerize people into believing the patently ridiculous. Or was Spilokos playing the game on more levels than one?

Ronald swung the golf cart and headed for his own car. What the hell, the mayor's aide thought, it's only the safety of a city.

Hannah looked uncomprehendingly at the culture dish Wiley held out to her. "What's the matter?"

"It's dead." He shook the dish in demonstration. The lump in the water separated into ribbons and globs.

"How did it die?"

"I killed it. Inadvertently. I made it an ocean, and it died in it."

Hannah looked curiously around the laboratory. "An ocean?"

"Yeah, in a flask." He led the way to a workbench containing numerous bottles of minerals and a beaker of greenish water. "See, I was figuring out how this critter could have been born. I remembered Miller's work, back in the fifties." He sat on a stool and began scribbling on his yellow pad, already oblivious to Hannah as anything but an audience. "See, there was a question as to how life got started in the first place. That's harder to imagine than the development of primitive cells into dinosaurs and flowers, right?"

"Ah, right, I suppose."

"So what we had, back at the start of things, was an atmosphere full of attenuated gasses, lots of volcanos, and crystalline rock. Also some oceans. You with me?"

"Oh, sure."

"So this Dr. Miller, he filled a flask with a miniocean composed of the same material as those early waters, and an atmosphere about like that early one, and he threw in a spark." He looked at her. "Lightning, you know."

"Right, lightning."

"Whango! He got amino acids, which are the start of life, the building blocks. Goes from amino acids to protein chains to all the buggers that live—with a little time thrown in. Few hundred million years."

"And you did that here?"

"No. I reasoned that the little fellow there was created the same way, and—"

"Wait a minute, Blake. The atmosphere's different now, and so are the seas. How could life start over again from scratch now?"

"Hell, it probably does it ten times a week, somewhere in the seas. But the primitive acids don't stand any chance

of surviving among the complex creatures out there now."
He was rapidly sketching molecular diagrams. "But about
how it could happen now—the elements are all still
there—ammonia, hydrogen, methane, water vapor. I
figure that just enough of the right combination of elements got shook loose during some lightning strike to
start our friend there on his way. Maybe in the body of a
large dead fish or whale, where it would get some protection from the more savage microorganisms."

He lost himself in his notes for a moment, whistling
between his teeth. Then, abruptly, spoke again. "Question
was, how did our friend get into the fresh water of the
lake, and how did he survive there? Seawater's essential,
you know."

"No, I didn't."

"Sure. The composition of blood and seawater are
damn near the same. Carl Sagan says—and I think he's
right—that animals are just machines that seawater has
built to move itself from place to place. We're really
just walking sacks of seawater."

Hannah looked as if she weren't too pleased with this
view of animal life, especially her part of it. "But you
made a sea for that . . . thing, and it couldn't live in it.
Why?"

He shrugged. "I don't know. Except, he's different. It's
as though he were born in fresh water and somehow
adapted himself to it."

"You mean, like in the lake?"

"Yeah. Probably during one of the storms we've been
having lately. Hell, there's everything from crude oil to
shit in the lake—enough chemical soup to build Frankenstein's monster with."

She peered with visible loathing at the mess in the
culture dish. "Do you have any idea specifically what
killed it?"

"The salt, most likely."

"Ahhh. Then we know how to kill it, and it won't be hard to do. We just dump salt in the lake."

Wiley laughed. "C'm'ere, Hannah." He drew a small beaker of water from one of the taps at the lab sink. "One liter of water, composed of molecules of hydrogen and oxygen. How many molecules?"

"A lot?"

"So many," he said, pouring the liquid down the drain, "that when this liter of water gurgles out into the lake, and eventually into the oceans, you could draw another liter of water anywhere in the world and it would contain *thousands* of the molecules from this same beaker. *Thousands.*"

She considered that. "Impressive, but what are you getting at?"

Wiley pointed with his beard. "Remember that our deceased friend there is a collection of one-celled creatures. There are probably half a million cells in that little piece of him we've got there. Suppose the rest of him is half a mile square?"

"Blake!"

"Okay, let's say he's only ten feet square—although he's not likely to be square. How many molecules? Trillions! Maybe trillions of trillions. And you'd have to kill every one of them, or the remaining few would start replicating again." He walked to the bench and picked up a box of salt. "How much salt do you think it would take to saturate the lake well enough to insure killing all those one-celled critters?"

She made a helpless gesture and shook her head.

"To kill all our little friends," Wiley continued, "we'd have to salinize the lake at least to the consistency of sea water. And that would require a hundred and sixty-six million *tons* of salt per cubic mile of water. Guess how many cubic miles of water the lake contains."

She sat down on a bench, her hands over her ears.

"I don't even want to hear it, Blake. I get the point." She looked depressed. "We can't kill it, huh?"

"I didn't say that. We just can't do it with salt."

She jumped up, angry. "Damn it, stop seesawing my emotions!"

He blinked, then frowned, then looked contrite "Oh, I'm sorry. You're interested in 'killing the monster.' I'm interested in studying a new kind of life. I forget, sometimes."

"Cheryl Courtland's father doesn't, nor the father of that boy your so-called 'friend' killed last night."

"What? I didn't hear about that one. Did anybody see it happen? Did the man get a description? Any idea of the size?"

"Oh, Blake, you're hopeless. Doesn't it mean anything to you that people are dying?"

"Yes. Dying of malnutrition, political abuse, overeating, murder by friends and lovers; dying for ideals and money and frustration." He rattled the culture dish. "You're anthropomorphizing, Hannah. You're getting a hatred worked up, as though this poor little glob of protein were evil. Hell, it's not even got a brain, let alone emotions. It's just doing what everything that lives does—trying to eat and keep alive. Would you feel hatred for a mongoloid idiot who killed someone, not knowing any better?"

"No," she said, controlling her temper. "But I wouldn't let him run loose killing people. And that's what your 'poor little glob' is doing. We don't keep polio viruses for pets, Blake, we exterminate them."

He held up his hands, palms out, in surrender. "Okay, okay. Let's go out and kill Frankenstein. But first let me find a way to do it."

"Have Nesselroth and his people come up with anything?"

"I don't know. I haven't been keeping in contact with them."

"Are you serious? Jesus Christ, Blake, are you still doing the one-man-band act? What kind of a megalomaniac *are* you?"

"I went through this with Saul. That bunch of yo-yos at the morgue won't have anything to contribute, and I'll get more done without them underfoot."

She turned her back on him and strode across the lab to stare moodily out at the campus. "Blake, I understand your desire to have the credit for this . . . discovery. But it's out of place. It's warped your sense of values. This whole thing has warped everybody's sense of values, including mine. But I've come to my senses." She turned to look at him, her posture determined. "I am going down to the morgue to tell the coroner what you've got over here. Then I'm going to the station and let the city know what's going on."

"Spilokos will fit you for a set of concrete sneakers."

"Fuck him." She hoisted her shoulder bag and started for the door.

Wiley beat her to it. "You always seem to be walking out on me."

"Get out of my way, Blake. I've had it with your melodramatics."

"Make you a deal."

"No."

Wiley's arm was across the doorway, and he did not move it. "If I'm going to find a way to stop our friend, I have to get another piece of him to study. How would you like to come along? Wouldn't that make a whopper of a tale to take to channel five?"

She paled slightly. "Blake, you aren't thinking . . . ?"

"Yes, I am. Tonight, I'm going out on the lake."

8

In the great void, a star collapses, perhaps in a matter of moments. Its thermonuclear engine slips over the delicate edge of balance between explosion and implosion, the elements shift their structure, and a giant becomes a dwarf. Size diminishes but mass does not. It becomes a ball only a handful of miles in diameter, and heavy beyond measure. It bends light. It swallows matter, energy, ghosts. It denudes its celestial neighborhood.

In return, for all things must balance, it radiates. It pulses out a ball of energy in waves whose peaks and valleys are micromillimeters long, and they voyage the black emptiness.

One sails unchallenged for a million years, traveling at 186,000 miles per second. Gravity turns it right, somewhere among the sand-grain stars of the M31 galaxy, and it flies for 2.2 million years more. Had it started its

journey a year earlier or later, it would have missed the
entire arm of the Milky Way that contains a certain
insignificant G-class star and its nine planets. A day
earlier or later, it would have missed the star's entire
solar system. An hour and it would have missed the third
planet. A heartbeat, and it would have missed the tiny
window in the planet's atmosphere through which the
wave could be captured.

But it didn't, and it was. The wave of energy struck,
stuck, and slammed to the surface. There, it bounced
high and hit the exosphere. And it bounced back down
again, and up again, and down. Ten times per second,
echoing around the planet as part of a larger wave.
Almost like a heartbeat.

In the lake, the presence feeds peacefully. It has come
to sense a rhythm in the life of the waters. During the
high-energy time, the time of the sunlight, life swarms and
gibbers and explodes. In the time of the low-energy, life
slows, only the predators stalking ceaselessly to fuel their
ever-demanding engines.

The presence has learned that the predators give more
food; that the hunt and attack can be minimized by
feeding on the hunters, rather than the hunted. And thus,
it has become nocturnal. By day it sieves the sewage
outflow; by night it looses its hold and drifts into the
depths. Thus it misses the heat-bearers who come probing
with sonar and radar around the pier, and it is missed in
turn by those who invade the lake like particularly awkward fish who must carry their air in tanks on their backs.
Thus it does not register on the hydrophones dangled
from police and Coast Guard boats running up and down
along the shoreline. For the heat-bearers have weak senses
and fear the night. They are like the preyed-upon instead
of the hunters; they live in the daylight. With the coming
of the darkness, they reel in their artificial ears, switch
off their artificial eyes, gun their artificial legs, and run for

*the docks. Some of the heat-bearers are only a heartbeat
ahead of the presence, though they don't know it. Like
captive energy waves, they thrum toward the pulsing city
to the beat/beat/beat of propellers, while their fragile,
artificial voices cry out, "here we are, here we are," and
the shore answers, "so glad! so glad!"*

It is an odd moment, the pause when twilight somehow
becomes night. There is no legal or scientific definition of
the instant that really pins it down. Nor is there anything
conscious in the five simple senses that can say accurately
that this is twilight and . . . this is night. Yet the moment
is known somewhere in the bones, or the electrons, or the
soul. In every descendant of the ancient caves, there is a
sure and certain knowledge, a fine line. On one side of the
line is soft, lovely, peaceful twilight. On the other—how
did it come so quickly? Hard, fearsome, predatory night.

Jim Wintergreen shuddered, feeling his hackles rise and
the hairs on his arms bristle. He put aside the half-
philosophical, half-melodramatic consideration of night
that had crept into his brain as he stood looking out over
the lake. He wondered briefly if anyone else involved in
The Secret was watching the huge, silent body of water
that looked now like a field of obsidian knives tumbling
in the weak starshine. Was Spilokos brooding at that big
window in his office? Was Saul Nesselroth, that odd little
medical man, sweeping the waters with his troubled eyes?
Did the Coast Guard commander stand at his lighthouse
rail like Ahab, squinting after a freshwater Moby? And
what of Cheryl Courtland's father, or the parents of the
boy on the pier? Wintergreen's mind was suddenly filled
with a phalanx of friends and relatives, acquaintances
and co-workers, all looking out into the cold waters that
had now swallowed yachtsmen, sailors, two children, and
God-only-knew how many others.

But it was not this image, so much, that haunted the

newsman's internal vision. It was when that phantom throng turned slowly, accusingly to stare at him. You knew, their eyes said. You knew and you didn't warn us. You played with our safety, our peace, our lives. And the part that seared most strongly into Jim Wintergreen's soul was the knowledge that they were right, and that he was, in his higher goals and blackmail, no different than Nikkos Spilokos. No different at all.

Wintergreen turned away from the beach and walked back to his car, feeling somehow colder than the night air justified.

Nikkos Spilokos was not staring out his window, nor even in his office. He was in the plush high-roller's poker room of a bordello he owned on the south side. Business boomed in the Greek restaurant out front, and few patrons noticed that not all the gentlemen who went down the corridor to the men's room reappeared, or that others appeared who had not been seen to enter. But the traffic in the corridor was heavy.

In the poker room, Spilokos roved through the cigar smoke like a caged beast. Large men moved out of his way with practiced patience. Three telephones rang discreetly and regularly, and were answered by other large men. "Nesselroth?"

"At the university, boss. Him and those other guys from the icebox."

"All right, get Spiro and Alex over there with them—quietly. Get one of our girls on the school switchboard."

" 'Sbeen done."

"Good. Don't let Saul get anything out to anybody we don't know about. Let him talk to the other brainy types, but no news people. Is anybody covering Courtland?"

"Hurkos sent a guy out there, and we got a man at the Jackson house."

"Jackson?"

"That kid on the pier, his folks."

"Good. What are you doing about the sailors?"

"Every swab that gets off the base tonight gets lucky. We got all the girls from the Sixth street hook shop just waiting to fall in love with them."

A phone was extended to the mayor. "It's the limo service, sir."

Spilokos grabbed the receiver. "Soupy? Listen, the first of the birdwatchers comes in at midnight on Royal's Flight 40. I want you to see that all those dames ride our cars to the hotels, understand. I don't want them to hear or see anything along the way but our boys' smiling faces." He listened sourly. "I don't care how you do it. Give them free rides. Muscle the competition. Screw them in the back seat—I don't care. Just make sure they get registered before they hear any unpleasant news." He listened again. "Don't worry what kind of unpleasant news, just get their names on the registers." He tossed the receiver back to the soldier manning the phone. "See if you can find out what's happening at channel five. I want Wintergreen sewed up so tight he can't fart without my smelling it. And where's that McKittrick broad?"

"She slipped us about eight-thirty, boss. She was with that hippie professor."

"Wiley? What's he up to? I thought Nesselroth had a thumb on him."

"Don't seem so. He's been working on his own. He took some shit over to Nesselroth this afternoon. Louie said they had a hell of an argument. Then he stomped out and went home. McKittrick's been following him around like a bitch in heat, an' they both took off while Louie was in the can at a restaurant."

Spilokos' big head seemed to sink into his shoulders, as if he were a bull readying for a charge. When he spoke, his voice was very low and very calm. "I am going out front to have a bite to eat. When I come back, I want to hear that we have two men in Wiley's hip pocket and another up McKittrick's skirt. Got it? If I do not hear this, I will be unpleasant to be near."

He turned and left the room. There was dead silence as he walked out. Then there was frantic motion.

Fawning waiters appeared at the mayor's table. He ordered feta cheese and olives, and a little wine. He kept his face and posture relaxed, automatically returning the smiles and waves of greeting from the restaurant's patrons. But behind his eyes, his brain was full of lava. Where would it come from? Who would get past his silent wall of invisible men? Would it be Wintergreen, stricken with conscience in spite of his gloating hold over Spilokos' future? Or Nesselroth, working himself up to manhood after years of self-serving abasement? Or maybe Haley, going down nobly with his sunken career? McKittrick in the zealot's righteousness, or more likely in pure malice? Who would stand on the rooftops and cry wolf to the city's million and a half inhabitants?

Or would it be Blake Wiley, the swashbuckler, the egomaniac, the glory hound? Spilokos knew instinctively that he had missed it with Wiley, had underrated the importance of the cocky outsider. Looking back, he could see that the clues had been there, if he'd only caught them. Not so much McKittrick's zeroing in on him at Wintergreen's off-stage direction, aiming her like an arrow at Wiley. Would the long-haired little punk blow the whistle, just to make sure nobody beat him to it?

The cheese and olives arrived. One of the olives rolled on the plate, its pitted interior slewing around as if it were an eye in a horrible, full-color photograph. Spilokos put down his fork.

If only it would all wait! Just let half the conventioneers get on the ground and registered. Just let that money be signed for.

Spilokos concentrated on the money, on the tight web

of kickbacks he'd taken such trouble to set up. The hotels, the cabbies, even the newsstands and shoeshine boys. Of every dollar the tourists dropped in the city, Nikkos Spilokos stood to make eight cents.

He concentrated on the web itself, so nearly broken last Sunday by the media's getting wind of his sneak return from Washington, very nearly learning that he'd come back to meet with his mob underlings.

He concentrated on the tablecloth, the back of his hand, the fork beside the plate. But none of it worked. None of it entirely covered the scraping from the inside of his skull, the noises echoing from the past. Grandpapa Andros, his hard, glittering eyes boring into the goat boy's own. Are you afraid, Nikkos? Afraid of the cliff, here? The blue waters below? Are you afraid of the cave, the dark? The dark, Nikkos?

And Nikkos Spilokos, five years old, knew that there were fears worse than the dark and the water and the cruel caves. Fear of Grandpapa Andros' terrible eyes, his evil, smelly breath, his gnarled, demanding hands.

A shepherd can't fear, Nikkos. Who will guard the goats if the shepherd is afraid, eh? So you will not fear. And to prove it, you will stay here in the cave tonight, here where the rising waters will seal you away. And in the morning, I will be waiting for you, out there, with all praise.

And Nikkos the shepherd was locked away by the thundering sea and the beast-ridden dark while the crabs clicked and scuttled over his naked legs and the seaweed grasped him like dead hands in the night. And he screamed and screamed and screamed.

For a long moment, the past and the future washed like waves through Nikkos Spilokos' brain, leaving him rudderless in time. And even as he fought his way back to control, to the instant, to the table at the restaurant, he knew that he would never completely escape Andros' "lesson." For all the miles and years and Americanization, there was a part of him that was still the boy of the bushes and mountains of Attica. And that part of him was afraid. Deeply, deathly afraid. Of the dark lake, the night waters, and the thing in those waters. It scrabbled across his naked nerves and caressed his fear with dead fingers.

"Blake! Blake, dammit, wait for me!" Hannah ran down the dock toward the power launch quietly chugging in its slip. Wiley stopped loading gear and stood in the boat, waiting.

Hannah puffed up. "Oh, you're a real swine, you are. 'Here, Hannah, run back to the car and get the depth recorder.' That was cute."

Wiley lit a cigarette. "I can't let you come."

"Bullshit. Don't tell me you're going to pull the Sir Galahad routine, protecting the maiden from the dragon."

He nodded. "Something like that. We're not messing with a Walt Disney cartoon, kiddo. Do you want to wind up looking like Cheryl Courtland?" He bent to his loading again. "Better you stay ashore."

"Better you kiss my ass. I've had enough of your chauvinist piggery."

"No chauvinism. Simple logic. Why risk two lives when one will do?"

"Okay, sport, then *you* stay here and *I'll* go get your piece of slug."

He stepped out of the boat. "Fine. All you have to do is calibrate the depth finder, run the recorder, run the sonar, coxswain the boat, keep an eye on the ambient voltometer—you *can* read one, can't you—interpret everything you're watching so that you're sure you've got the beastie and not a school of fish, then—"

"All right. So the whiz kid is essential and I'm not. But I'm going anyway." When he started to protest, she pulled her camera from her shoulder bag. "You can't do all that and take pictures, too, can you?"

They locked eyes and wills for a space, then Wiley backed down. "Get in the boat. But don't try to sue me if you get killed."

"I wouldn't think of it," she said, jumping lightly into the launch. "Where do I sit?"

"In the bow."

"The what?"

"You're going to be a great help, lady. The front of the boat. The pointed end. Jesus H. Christ." He threw the last of the gear aboard disgustedly and started to cast off.

"Blake, how are you going to catch the monster?"

"With brains," he said, tossing the painter into the boat and leaping after it. He stepped over the lashed-down instruments and racks of batteries and took the tiller, easing the boat out of the slip. "Mine and his."

"His? You mean the animal's? Are you trying to tell me that thing thinks?"

"Not exactly. But it learns, and it learns faster than anything I've ever seen or heard of. And I've got an idea that I can use that learning ability to reach him, to talk to him—so to speak." He guided them out of the basin and toward the low breakwater, watching the channel buoy lights. "I had a hint, early on, and it kept nagging me. I couldn't get it out of my head, but I didn't understand its significance until this morning."

"Cone on, Blake, what are you getting at?"

"In the initial autopsies on Cheryl's body, I noticed that the dipolar protein molecules were aligned, sort of entrained. It didn't mean anything at the time, but when I discovered that the individual cells in my piece of our animal were also aligned, I remembered a couple of things I'd read in the journals.

"A few years ago, the National Science Foundation— big hats in the prestige game—held a conference in

Aspen, Colorado. They were gnawing at the interface between biology and electronics. At times, living cells—especially brain cells—act just like solid-state electronic components. They resonate to all the different fields of energy that surround us—that are zapping us right now."

"And?"

"Well, Francis Cole—he's with the Ochsner Medical Foundation down in New Orleans—and E. R. Graf, of Auburn, gave a paper wherein they postulated that organic micromolecules and primitive proteins—like our buddy out there—developed dependency on extra-low-frequency fields in the 10-Hz region." He leaned forward as if to elucidate to a slow student. "That's cycles-per-second. Ten of them.

"So they speculated that these protein molecules could have 'tuned-in' on the Schumann resonance, which is a 10-Hz frequency that bounces back and forth between the earth and the top of the atmosphere, and that they therefore became very efficient and highly-evolved ELF transceivers."

"You mean, kind of 'brain radios'?"

"Exactly."

She considered this as the boat rose and fell on the waves. "That sounds pretty farfetched, Blake."

"Is it, though? The 10-Hz rhythm is built into everything biological. The feeling we call 'peaceful' produces an alpha wave centered at 10-Hz. Tensing a muscle produces 10-Hz microtremors. The frequency is the basic timing mechanism for all living things."

"Then, why don't all the plants and animals have brains?"

Wiley steered a few points to starboard, running for the gap in the breakwater. "The main reason is that individual plants or animals don't produce enough power to broadcast intelligible signals. The human brain only runs on about ten watts. But what if our new animal out here is, say, a hundred feet in diameter—that is, if we rolled him into a ball?"

"Do you think it's that big?"

"Why not? The top of that fishing pier is eleven feet off the water, and the water's seven feet deep there. To throw a pseudopod up that high and grab that boy, he'd have to have enough mass underwater to either anchor himself on the bottom or spread pretty far through the surf. I guess his minimum size and weight—last night, at least—at roughly a hundred feet diameter and twenty to twenty-five tons."

"Twenty tons!"

"Perhaps more. I don't know if his specific density is higher or lower than water's. I didn't think to check that with the chunk I had in the dish, and it's decomposed now.

"But about the brain radio effect . . . At that size, I think he can put out damn near a hundred thousand watts of power. He could broadcast all the way from Los Angeles to Maine."

"Then why don't we hear him—I mean, it?"

"Because, like the other plants and animals, both the transmitter and receiver faculties are tuned to the same little bands, and none of our equipment operates there. For all we know, the California redwoods and the Canadian moss are picking up everything he's saying—if 'saying' is the right word."

Hannah trembled slightly. "That's scary."

"I can put you back on the dock."

"No. No, that's all right. So how are you going to use this supposed brain of his to catch him?"

Wiley smiled in the darkness, noting that she'd begun to use the personal pronoun for the being. "I'm going to run random broadcast patterns in the 10-Hz frequency, and hope that pulls him to me the way a magnet will pull nearby iron to itself by 'broadcasting' magnetism more loudly than the background gravity."

Hannah pulled her coat more tightly around her and turned the collar up to cover her throat. In the stern, Wiley's dim figure was outlined by the phosphorescent wake of the launch. He looked so small, back there, so fragile. She was overwhelmed by the vast gulf between man and the other animals, for Blake Wiley was doing something totally contrary to the laws of nature that governed the rest of the planet's inhabitants. In all of nature, she knew, the immutable law was that the stronger prevailed and the weaker perished. And there sat Blake Wiley, a creature with neither fang nor claw, without poison or camouflage, a creature whose size was puny and whose musculature a joke beside the animals of the wild. And this frail animal, this defenseless primate, was calmly, deliberately, hunting down a deadly predator whose dimensions he did not even know, whose armaments he could only guess, and who possessed—possibly—at least a version of Wiley's only true weapon—his brain.

With this came a sudden sense of the pettiness of all the conflicts going on ashore, of Spilokos' greed and Nesselroth's fears, and Wintergreen's manipulations. She saw with an all-engulfing insight that Blake Wiley was the only one among them who truly comprehended the possibilities, that in a strange way none of the deaths meant anything, none of the fears. She saw with a fiery precision the enormity of the implications. A new form of life. A new form of life! And suddenly, the earth was an alien place, and she a voyager without sure destination. She felt suspended in time and space. Before her, over Blake's shoulders, was the human race, supreme for the moment. Behind, in the suffocating waters, was a giant, born of lightning and chance; leviathan, behemoth, the spawn of stars and death. And as Blake Wiley took the boat through the breakwater and into the swells, quietly switching on the instruments which would sing the giant to him, Hannah McKittrick did not know if she were more awed by the beast in the waters or the man in the boat. For the likes of Spilokos and Nesselroth and Wintergreen, the drama was coming to a close. But for Blake Wiley, and perhaps for the human race, it was just beginning.

Overhead, Royal Airlines Flight 40 banked into its downwind leg and reached out for the earth, its windows crammed with conventioneers whose faces looked, somehow, exactly like those of spectators at a gladiatorial contest.

Part Two

THE CITY

9

Jim Wintergreen's introspective mood had proven stronger than his attempts to dislodge it. It had isolated him from his family at dinner, kept their conversation distant, and their jokes unlaughed at. It had followed him to his den and blurred the pages of the paper, the images on the TV screen. It had gone to bed with him, pushing Thelma to one side, and had risen with him in the early morning stillness. And it had followed him, now, to the airport, gnawing at his heart like an alley dog chewing a drifter's ankle.

He leaned his elbows on the escalator rail and watched the flow of incoming tourists being lifted past him— animated dolls on an assembly line. How many would get pissed enough at the lake's closing to ignore it and go for a little midnight swim? Which of the already soused veterans with their campaign ribbons glued to their caps would lurch down to the yacht harbor to steal a sailboat, just for a little good-ol'-boy fun; something to tell the folks back in Des Moines? Which of the bird watchers from Tennessee or Montana would just have to have a picture of the seagulls circling the fishing piers? Perhaps even the same pier . . .

He shook himself and hopped the down escalator, his hands jammed deep in the pockets of his overcoat. The airport restaurant wasn't open but the snack bar was. And since it was too late for sleep and too early for booze, he'd settle for coffee. Already there were ten or twelve thousand conventioneers in the city. By noon, the figure would double, along with the chances of one of them getting hit by that thing in the lake.

But if the creature minded its manners, and if everybody stayed out of the water, and if nobody talked, Nikkos Spilokos would be in his hip pocket. For the good of the city, yes. For the good of the people.

Suddenly, the station manager knew that he'd made his decision, made it last night or perhaps even as he left Spilokos' office after their confrontation. He knew then that no amount of potential good could justify a single potential death. And with this knowledge, a weight lifted off him. He knew, with a kind of sad joy, that he was, after all, a newsman and a decent human being.

He stood before a line of telephone booths, smiling quietly to himself, then consulted the directory and dialed a number. "Hello? Sorry to wake you, Mr. Jackson. This is James Wintergreen from channel five. I'd like to come over and talk to you about your son's death."

There was a rhythm to the water, a rhythm to the creak and slap of the waves against the hull, and a counterpoint rhythm in the low, steady click of one of Blake's instruments. Hannah fought hard against going to sleep. She wanted to bury her head in the collar of her coat and just drift away. It was cold, and she felt she'd been sitting on the cramped seat forever. "How long have we been here, Blake?"

"I didn't ask you to come." He was hunched over the instruments and spoke as if she were a background annoyance.

"I wish we'd brought a thermos of coffee."

"I did. It's in that satchel beside your foot."

"Don't you ever get tired of thinking of everything? I'll bet you're anal-compulsive."

"Only with girl scouts. I'll take some of that coffee."

"Possession is nine-tenths, friend, and I've got the thermos top—you blew it, smart guy; no cup." She sipped and made a disgusted noise. "No sugar!"

"Thank you," he said holding out his hand for the cup. He drank it empty and passed it back. "There's sugar in the satchel."

"Jesus, what a swine you are."

The eastern horizon was paling. The wind shifted and began to blow shoreward with a cold, steady bite, as though to hasten them back to the safety of the shore. Hannah scanned the waves, consciously aware that she felt safer now that she could see, and aware also that the feeling was illusory. "Blake," she said quietly, "I've got faith in you or I wouldn't be here. But I can't help wondering about something."

"What?"

"Suppose your crazy plan had worked, and—"

"Don't say 'had.' I'm not giving up yet. Maybe he's been out sightseeing all night."

"Suppose it had? What did you plan to do, ask it politely for a two-pound chunk of itself? I mean, here we are in this piss-ass little rowboat—"

"Power launch."

"—waiting for Godzilla and the Blob to come and talk shop. That sounds a lot like standing in front of a herd of horny bull elephants and making noises like a cow in heat. It's not hard to attract their attention, but what do you do when they arrive?"

"Never having been interested in rutting elephants, I don't know. But as to our friend here, I'm going to put salt on his tail."

"Get serious, Blake."

"I am. We can't salinize the lake, but I'd be willing to bet that fifty pounds of iodized salt dumped over the side would discourage him."

"Then how do you get your specimen?"

"Well, I plan to let him throw a punch or two first, then whack off a piece while you add the spices."

Her jaw dropped. "You mean you intend to let that thing climb in the boat with us? You're out of your mind!"

"Not climb in, exactly. I figure he'll just fling a pseudo-pod over the gunwale and pick one of us off. I put the hydrophone up under your end of the boat, so he'll probably come up there."

She gave a strangled little scream and looked frantically over her shoulders, then edged toward the center of the vessel. "Damn you to hell, Wiley."

"Well, if he got me, who'd run the instruments?"

"I've had enough of this. We've been out all night. Just turn this barge around and wind up the rubber band. You can kill yourself if you want to, but not me. I take back everything I've ever said about having faith in you." She stumbled over a pile of equipage and went to her hands and knees in the bottom of the boat. "Do you hear me, Blake?"

The sun cleared the horizon and turned Blake Wiley's face to blood. His red hair and beard became a flaming halo around his head. He sat rigid, his hands gripping the sides of the sonar and his eyes fixed on the screen. "Did you polish the silver, dear," he asked, a quaver in his voice. "I hope so, because we've got company."

The presence has been voyaging. In the increasingly complex set of systems that store, retrieve, correlate, and transmit data, the presence has now an awareness of motion. Previously, it has moved unconsciously, drifting or directed as need dictated, but as unaware of the motion itself as a newborn infant. Its food-seeking has been, until now, an automatic and autonomous reaction; its gradual shift to the shoreline of the lake an impulse toward the source of greater stimuli, the same impulse that has caused it to rise surfaceward in daylight and sink at night.

But through this pattern have run contradictions. On blind impulse alone, on mindless stimulus/response, it would never have become nocturnal. There is something in the data systems now which is capable of survival-oriented value judgments, something that can . . . sense that the energy/value received from nocturnal hunting of the big predators is greater than the energy/value received by the daytime warming of the sun. Something that can discipline the presence to resist the attraction of sunlight, heated waters, and conserve it for the colder night.

And this thing in the data systems can now make value judgments concerning the presence's relation to the not/self, the water. And it has driven the presence, this past night, to go exploring, to seek the limits of the not/self. It has experimented with shape and resistance in relation to speed and progress through the not/self. It has learned that there are more efficient shapes than amorphistic blobs for moving in the waters; has made of itself a galiform body with random finlike protuberances for stabilization, experimenting with motion through the paddle-wave of pseudotails and pseudofins; has made of itself a deltoid sheet and rippled through the not/self as a manta; has learned, in a frighteningly short time, that it can move most quickly as a torpedo, a glutinous cigar pulsing fore-to-aft with timed contractions. It does not know that in its experiments it has become the fastest creature in the waters, the fleetest predator ever to swim the earth, the most efficient food-gathering animal ever formed.

And now the day comes. The presence has gone to a foreign shore and returned, all in a matter of hours. It does not have concepts for "tired" or "depleted," but it senses need for energy, for food, for rest. And it returns, less by instinct than by memory, to that portion of the not/self which has proven so rewarding—the shoreline between the pier and the sewage outfall.

But it does not arrive. As it nears, an extraordinary thing enters its sphere of awareness. A pulse, a beat, a throb, a . . . calling. The presence has not the faculty of artificial memory, of science and writing and the permanent imprinting of learned things. It does not know that the pulse that beats in and around it has been labeled 10 Hz, extra low frequency, or that its being pumps to that electrical frequency. But when that frequency is amplified a million times, and localized, the presence responds. It has no choice, any more than a man touching a high-voltage wire has a choice. And the presence, following an overloading on all the basic stimulus/response levels at once, experiences what in the walking soup would be described as a combination of euphoria, sexual climax, and partial electrocution.

Blindly, willingly, helplessly, it loses its function-dictated torpedo shape and goes amorphous. It moves spastically toward the source of the pleasure.

Wiley whistled softly. "My God. I sure missed the boat on size, didn't I?" He and Hannah were both staring in disbelief at the sonar screen, whose phosphorescent sweep showed a flowing, oozing form nearly three hundred yards across. Each sweep brought the thing a little closer. "Even if he's flat as a pancake, he's got to run a hundred tons. And if we're seeing something really three-dimensional . . ." He fiddled with the frequency broadcaster.

Hannah looked about the boat nervously. "Where's the salt, Blake?" She made no attempt to disguise the fear in her voice.

Wiley thumbed the starter button on the boat's engine. "There ain't any." The engine sputtered but did not catch.

"Please, Blake. This is no time for jokes."

"No joke. Also no salt." He stabbed viciously at the starter. "C'mon, you sonofabitch."

Hannah made abortive motions toward her camera. "B-Blake, why isn't there any salt? What are we going to do? How close is it?"

Wiley was looking a little frightened himself. He kept an eye on the sonarscope, as if fascinated. The blob on the screen now occupied three-fourths of the surface. The waters around the launch suddenly calmed, flattening and turning oily-still. Hannah made small whimpers. Wiley's face was sheened with sweat, and his fingers fumbled as he worked at the outboard.

Ten yards off the bow, something humped and enormous broke the surface, like the back of an obscene translucent whale. A gull overhead screamed terror and fled on beating wings.

Wiley dove for the frequency broadcaster. "Start the engine, Hannah! Keep hitting that starter!" He turned dials with fingers made of rubber, biting his lip until the blood spurted. "Oh, shit, come on, baby!"

The engine coughed to life and the launch leapt toward the disappearing hump. "Turn the bastard, you're heading right into him," Wiley yelled, his voice hysterical. "Turn!"

Hannah leaned on the tiller and the boat slewed to starboard, listing crazily. Water poured over the gunwales. Inches away, something vast and terrible moved just beneath the surface.

Hannah aimed the boat toward the city skyline and held on to the tiller with white knuckles. "Blake, I don't know how to make us go faster!"

He scrambled over her and took control, twisting the throttle until the launch was almost planing. His eyes swung nervously from the sonarscope screen to the boat's wake. After two minutes' headlong flight, he cut the throttle and let the boat coast.

"What are you doing, you maniac? Where is the monster?"

Wiley took a deep breath and fished a cigarette from his shirt pocket. He missed his mouth with it, and missed the cigarette with his lighter. "About three hundred yards back there, see?" He indicated the screen. "And that's where I'm going to keep him." His voice was still shaky, but there was confidence in it now. He made a small adjustment to the frequency broadcaster.

Hannah looked from Wiley to the screen, and then to the broadcaster. "With that?"

"With that."

"How?"

"You like music?"

"Blake, I'm too frazzled for games. Give, huh?"

"Okay. Suppose you are selling a radio with a hundred different stations, all broadcasting different kinds of music, right? And you're out to hook a customer, some guy passing by. So you start broadcasting, hitting all the different stations until you find one that makes his ears perk up. Like, if he's a Mozart freak, you hook him on Mozart."

"Which in this case is the ten-watchamacallit frequency you keep talking about?"

"Which is. So you've got him hooked, only he turns out to be a two hundred pound microcephalic."

"A what?"

"A great big idiot. And he don't know from hi-fi, right, so you have to keep him from slobbering on the set, or tearing it open to see if Mozart is inside."

"I can't imagine a guy like that being fond of Mozart."

"You'd be amazed. Anyway, how do you keep him from crawling over the set itself?" He didn't wait for an answer. "Two ways. You either switch stations—maybe to one of those honk-and-blat third-rate rock bands—or you turn up the volume until it hurts too much." He put a bit more throttle on the launch and made another adjustment to the broadcaster. "I'm using the second method, since for all I know he might like other frequencies too. The trick now is to balance the strength of the 10 Hz and keep him back there, but far enough back there." Wiley's confidence had returned completely, and he wore an expression of smug command. "How's that for smarts?"

Hannah found her own cigarettes and lighter, lit one for herself, and lit Blake's still dangling one for him. She inhaled deeply and leaned back against the side of the boat, her hands clasped around her drawn-up knees. She watched the boat's wake a long time, occasionally peering closely at the waters nearer the boat, or at the sonar screen. When she finally spoke, it was difficult to judge her emotions. "Wiley, we are back to the original question, but I think I know the answer already. Nonetheless, I want to hear it from you."

"Which question," he asked blandly.

"You had no intention of taking a piece of that thing last night. You told me that ridiculous story about the salt to see if I'd swallow it." She flipped her cigarette over the side with more force than necessary. "But the fact remains that you came out here to catch the thing, and that means that you have plans for it. So the question

I asked before still stands: now that you've got it—for the moment—what are you going to do with it?"

Wiley paused to angle the launch to the west, running it diagonally along the now visible shore. "What I'm going to do with our lumpy companion, Miss McKittrick, is take him to a nice warm place where he won't get into any trouble. Right over there, in fact." He pointed. "That's the Trahan shipyard. Can you see that thing that looks like a low red wall?"

"Yes."

"That's the gates to the drydock. If you look close, you can see them opening right now."

"I . . . think I can see that, yes."

"Right. I talked to them last night and rented the dock. I told them to watch for me anytime after midnight last night, and if they saw me coming, open quick!" His laugh now was pure amusement. "The yard foreman thought I was a nut or a practical joker, renting a drydock for a thirty-foot outboard. I can't wait to see his face when he finds out what else I'm bringing."

Hannah looked reluctantly admiring. "It hurts to say it, Blake, but that's brilliant. You're going to bring the thing in there and trap it, just like a gorilla in a cage." Her look changed. "I have to hand it to you, and I do. And I think I have finally gotten the message."

"What are you talking about?"

She gave him a look that was usually reserved for things that lived in dark, damp places. "About you, Blake, and me, and the way you see the world." She turned away from him, watching the drydock gates opening, and spoke over her shoulder. "You could have picked up a telephone any time yesterday and told Saul Nesselroth about your frequency trick. You could have told Spilokos, or the Coast Guard. And there would have been five hundred boats out here hunting the monster. But that would have meant somebody else finding it, wouldn't it? So you sat on it and went through last night's charade. It didn't matter to you that for all the hours you kept quiet, this thing could have been killing people—and maybe was!"

She rounded on him, her eyes filled with tears. "It's all grist for your ego mill, isn't it? The creature, me, people's lives."

"Hannah, listen—"

"What did you bring me along for, Wiley? So you'd have royalties on the book I'd write? So you'd have your own captive biographer right there, a certified witness for Blake Wiley's heroism?"

"Hannah, I swear to you—"

"How much do you plan to charge the suckers to see that poor animal, Blake? Will you set up an amusement park around the drydock?"

"Poor animal! A minute ago it was a monster, killing people. Be fucking consistent, at least."

"I am, Wiley. I've just learned a new definition of the word monster."

She turned away from him purposefully as he eased the launch into the flooded drydock. The waters swelled and rushed out behind them as something of great bulk followed the boat into the concrete enclosure. The rust-bright gates rumbled together and closed with a deep, subaquatic boom.

10

Saul Nesselroth stood with his back to the wall, clutching the briefcase as if it contained his life savings. At the sound of furtive footsteps, he tried to press himself into the bricks. He tensed, feeling asinine at the whole affair, then relaxed slightly as the head that popped around the corner of the wall turned out to be his teaching assistant.

"Okay, Doc, Clara's got the goon distracted. I think we can make the parking lot without being spotted."

Nesselroth nodded and followed the young man around the corner and down the sidewalk, trying not to look conspicuous. Over by the entrance, a pretty coed sat on the steps talking merrily with Spilokos' goon, apparently unaware of the view her short skirt was affording him.

The teaching assistant pointed Nesselroth toward a

green Datsun and handed him a set of keys. "Brakes pull to the right."

"Thanks, Phil. Uh, I appreciate this."

"Don't worry. I'll remind you about it when it's time to defend my dissertation." He patted the coroner on the back. "Better scoot. If I don't go bail Clara out she's liable to get laid right there on the steps."

Nesselroth got in and drove off, not breathing freely until he was away from the campus and into the traffic. He kept one hand on the briefcase all the way to the park.

Haley and Wintergreen were waiting for him by the carousel. Each carried a briefcase. Wintergreen smiled politely. "Ah, the last conspirator arriveth. What do you call a gathering of this kind, gentlemen? A coven? A pod? A sneak? Yes, that's about right; a sneak of conspirators. Did you bring yours?"

Nesselroth affirmed that he had, and they retired to a bench. Each man opened his case and extracted type-written papers. "Shall we be democratic and vote on who goes first, or shall we let the greater guilt prevail?" Wintergreen's smile was rueful. "In which case, I might as well lead the parade." He passed copies to Haley and Nesselroth. "To save time, what you're holding are sworn statements from the Courtland and Jackson fathers, plus my own position statement, and, of course, admission of complicity." He puffed out a breath, as though in relief. "The final paper is my resignation from channel five."

Haley sat stiffly with his hands flat on his papers. "I didn't make copies. I've got testimony from my officers and men, and reports my board of inquiry made after the Courtland death and after we lost the *Armour*." He looked at his gnarled hands. "In my case," he said heavily, "I don't think a resignation will be allowed."

"Come, now," Wintergreen said gently. "Surely after your years of service . . . ?"

"The Guard is the smallest service, Mr. Wintergreen.

Also the oldest, the proudest, and the most scandal-free. I will be made an example of."

They sat uncomfortable for a minute, then Nesselroth cleared his throat. "I've, uh, got the formal protest I wrote to the mayor. It's probably no good, since I didn't actually send it. I've also got the medical reports on both deaths and a little testimony from my colleagues and employees at the morgue. I couldn't get much out of them," he said apologetically. "They're civil servants, you know. Afraid of reprisals."

The three men spent some time looking at the papers, as if unwilling to make the first move. In the end, it was Haley who slammed his briefcase shut and stood, taking command. "Let's get on with it," he snapped.

They took the Coast Guard station wagon, leaving the other two cars in the lot, and drove downtown. As they arrived at channel five, Nesselroth spoke. "Mr. Wintergreen, are you sure you can get us on the air?"

"It's my shop, m'boy—at least for the next few minutes."

They walked to the elevator that would take them from the basement garage up to the studios and crowded in, each clutching his briefcase before him like a fig leaf. As the car lurched upward, Nesselroth spoke again, thoughtfully. "There's two good things coming out of this—three, really. First, we get Spilokos, and that makes me feel good."

"Second," Wintergreen added with a little pride, "we get to look in the mirror tomorrow morning and like the man we see."

"Yes. And third, we now stand a chance of protecting the city from that thing in the lake."

When the elevator door opened, Hannah McKittrick stood in front of it.

"My word, child," Wintergreen said. "You look as if

you've spent the night in a locker room with the Green Bay Packers."

Her bloodshot eyes drooped and her smile was wan. "I've been on the lake with Blake Wiley. He's captured the monster, Jim. It's locked up in the Trahan shipyard drydock. I told you I'd bring in a zinger."

And then she fainted.

The council chamber was a turmoil of amplified voices and agitated figures. People waved their arms and shouted into their microphones. A councilwoman shook her fist at a black councilman, who made a rude gesture and yelled back at her.

On the podium, Nikkos Spilokos sat wearily, his chin on his fist, and looked over the brawl. He glanced at his watch, his look changing to relief, and pounded his gavel until the room quieted. "Aside from having seen better performances on the monkey island at the zoo, and heard better arguments there I might add, I will point out to the honorable legislators that it is two-thirty. Meeting is adjourned."

"Mr. Mayor, I demand to be heard!"

"The chair does not recognize the distinguished member from the eighth ward."

"I protest!"

"The chair recognizes your protest, Mr. Hurter, and advises you to keep your mouth shut. Meeting is *adjourned*." Spilokos stomped off the podium and into the private office behind it, slamming the door pointedly. Hurkos was waiting.

Spilokos frowned. "I thought you were at the morgue."

Hurkos shook his head. "Wiley got the thing in the lake."

The mayor's eyebrows, moustache and glasses all rode up his face. "Well, I'll be damned. The little shit pulled

it off, did he?" The component parts settled back into
place and the mayor rubbed his bald head vigorously,
smiling. "That's the best news I've heard since last Saturday night. Did he kill it?"

"He's got it penned in a drydock."

Spilokos eased himself into an overstuffed swivel chair
and began to spin idly. He shook his head, snorting. "I'll
be damned. Penned it up, eh?" Spilokos thought rapidly,
running through the alternatives. He could make capital
out of this. Turn the little fucker into a hero—which is
what the kid wanted in the first place. Ham it up. Key to
the city and all that. And a lot of spillover gravy for
Nicky-boy. Maybe even capitalize on the monster itself.
Now that it wasn't a threat, he could play up the scientific
angle. Get one of the boys to translate the scientific
doubletalk into language he could use. Shouldn't be that
much trouble to make it look as if he'd spearheaded
this thing. Hell, he might even get an honorary degree
out of the deal!

A shadow passed through Spilokos' mind as he tried to
envision the creature itself. He felt a momentary shame
at his weakness back in the restaurant. "What's the thing
look like, Hurkos? Did you see it yourself?"

"No. Nobody has. It's big, though. Fills the drydock
from what I hear."

It took a moment for the reality of that to filter through.
Fills the drydock? *Fills* it! Spilokos did not know much
about drydocks, but he knew they held ships, and he knew
how big ships were. "Madonna! That would make it the
biggest thing that ever lived."

"Yeah. That's what they're saying."

Spilokos bounced out of the chair. "They who?"

Hurkos shrugged. "The drydock guys, Wiley, McKittrick. Nobody's keeping it a secret."

Spilokos' mind went into high gear. "Hurk, we've got

to keep a lid on this a little longer. The, ah, the town's not safe yet. As long as that thing's alive, there's danger. Panic, if nothing else." He clenched his fists. Danger all right. He'd have to put the arm on Nesselroth and all the rest of them, have to help them get their stories straight.

"Excuse me, your honor," the door was open and the council recorder stuck his head in, "but I think you'd better come and see what's on channel five."

The presence is in ecstasy, though it does not know that term. Above, the launch has been hauled out of the water, but the hydrophone it had carried is still under the surface. A steady pulse thrums out of the phone and permeates the presence's being. Electrical energies generate in batteries, flash through transformers, condensers, transistors; run down wires; vibrate metal tympani; race through water; strike flesh; resonate; align/align/align . . .

The presence's data retrieval systems do not retrieve. The old communicators, which are like neural synapses but not exactly, fail to communicate. The input systems no longer feel the gradations of heat and light and pressure, no longer sense the food/not-food status of the environment. The survival systems in their submolecular pathways stagger drunkenly, unaware that there is too little water, too little oxygen, too little room. The presence has no concept of "prison" and so does not feel confinement. It has no concept of the ratios of not/self to self which are necessary to supply its vastness with the fuels of life. It does not feel hunger or thirst or depletion. It feels only a primeval gratification, an atomic lust eternally satisfied, eternally renewed.

Yet, the drydock is too small. The waters too confined. The huge doors of the dock are proof against all but a minute trickle of water: they are meant to be. No food passes through those gates. No fresh water, and with it, fresh oxygen.

With every pulse, the presence consumes the air of a thousand elephants. With every pulse, it burns the energy of a hundred whales.

With every pulse, in a bliss perhaps never before known on the planet, the presence is dying.

11

The head nurse had the physique and personality of a bulldog. She informed Wintergreen that County General was not accustomed to making exceptions, especially those involving patients who were suffering severe exhaustion. Wintergreen assured her of his good intent, his saintly motive, and his spotless character, none of which impressed her, and was eventually allowed five minutes. Miss McKittrick, he was informed, could be found in 503.

Wintergreen took himself to the fifth floor and let himself into the room soundlessly. Hannah smiled wanly without opening her eyes. "Hi, Jim."

"Ah, Madame Hannah—knows all, sees all, even with her eyelids closed. You've obviously missed your calling, pride of the airwaves. Are you perchance the seventh daughter of a seventh daughter?"

"I have a nose."

"Gad," the manager said, clearing off the hospital-green dresser and placing a bulky machine on it. "We'll have to get a new sponsor for the quiz show. I've been using the wrong deodorant again."

"It's your pipe. That thing stinks up your clothes." She pushed herself upright in the bed with some effort. Her face was pale and drawn. "What's that?"

"Surely a couple of days' absence from our beloved sweatshop has not caused you to forget the lovely hours spent staring enthralled at this little jewel?"

"No, I know it's the videotape player. What I meant was, why did you bring it here?"

He bent with some difficulty and plugged the player into a wall outlet. "Well, *ma cherie,* I thought you might appreciate seeing the results of your determination to break your own story. I have spared no expense to see that none of the wires we held you up with were visible to the viewing public."

"I seem to remember that it was you and Commander Haley who held me up."

"More a case of Nesselroth's smelling salts. Ready?"

"I'm not sure. I think I know how I must have looked."

"Lights! Camera! Pulitzer nomination!" He hit the switch.

"Oh, lord," Hannah said as the tape began to roll. *"That* bad?"

On the small screen, she looked fifty years old. She swayed and a hand came onscreen to steady her. Her hair hung in limp strings around her face, and there was a smudge of oil on her chin. But her voice was clear as it came through the tiny speaker.

"Good afternoon. This is Hannah McKittrick reporting. I have just come from the Trahan drydock on Willoughby Road on the west side of the city. In that drydock is a creature which Dr. Blake Wiley, a general sciences expert from the university, captured with sonic transmissions approximately three miles out in the lake." On the screen, she wavered again, then caught herself.

"According to Dr. Wiley, this creature, a flexible mass consisting of billions of one-celled animals, is an entirely new form of life on earth." Her bloodshot eyes looked out of the screen calmly. "I have seen this creature myself, and can tell you that it doesn't look like anything I've ever seen or heard of before.

"There is speculation that the creature is responsible for two deaths and the disappearance of a Coast Guard vessel and a yacht, earlier in the week. But city officials . . . "—she looked off-screen for a moment— " . . . were not aware of the creature's existence until Dr. Wiley found and captured it." She consulted a notepad held in fingers that trembled with fatigue. "The creature is estimated by Wiley to be as large as ten whales, and to weigh nearly four hundred tons. This makes it the largest animal ever to live on the earth."

Wintergreen snapped the player off and turned to face her. He was smiling, but his face was serious. "Hannah, my dear, I want to thank you on behalf of Haley and Nesselroth as well as myself. You know what we were about to do, don't you?"

Her own smile was shy and a little embarrassed. "I'm a reporter. I don't like to speculate."

"Mm-hmm. And you didn't know anything about a certain mayor's impeding an investigation, or about a certain coroner's doing the same thing? Or about your cute and lovable old employer going along with it for fear of his own hide?"

"Not as fact. Just my unconfirmed thoughts and Wiley's assertions—rumor, you know." She reached out for him and took his hand. "What's that old saw about sleeping dogs, Jim? It's over now. Blake's got the thing, and there's no point in ruining three decent men—although it would have been fun to burn Spilokos. Anyway, if you'd quit I might have gotten a boss I couldn't con."

Wintergreen looked indignant. "Madame, do you mean to say that I am a slack employer?"

"You're an old fraud, and I love you dearly."

"You bring a tear to my worn and rheumy old eye." He pulled his hand free softly. "I owe you, Hannah. My career, for openers. I won't forget that."

As they shared a quiet moment, Wintergreen wondered briefly if their relationship would ever be quite as lighthearted as it had been. He hid behind his pipe-stuffing ritual. "Speaking of our führer, Spilokos didn't waste any time capitalizing on your broadcast. He was at the station five minutes after the ambulance took you off, and he already had a spiel about the scientific wonder our brave Dr. Wiley had captured."

"That figures."

"He's pumping the boy as the hero of the hour, and himself as the patron saint of science. That ought t'make Dean Peters roll over in his mortarboard. Spilokos has shortchanged the university for as long as he's been in power."

Hannah shifted her pillows, trying to find a comfortable position. "What's he planning on doing with the animal?"

"That I don't know. I think Wiley's locking horns with him about it. All he's done so far is quarantine the drydock, which is intelligent. What he's concerned with right now, I think, is seeing that he stays in the catbird seat. There's already five hundred scientists and government boys loping into the city like Hell's Angels at a free beer festival."

"How are the people reacting?"

" 'Bout like you'd expect. Hordes of them clogging up the area around the drydock. The commissioner called in the National Guard to keep them out."

"How about the conventions?"

Wintergreen sneered. "Worse than lemmings. The vets are taking it like a giant party and are all out there saying, 'when *I* was at Iwo Jima, boy, I coulda took that thing with one hand.' "

"That's just what we need. I hope the guard's got a good wall up."

"The commissioner thinks it'll be okay."

Feeling suddenly weak, Hannah lay back and closed her eyes again. "Well, I did my part. Wiley's got his glory, the monster's under control, and everybody lived happily ever after. I think I'll go back to sleep, Jim. Would you wake me next month?"

Wintergreen smiled around his pipestem. "Sure. A.M. or P.M.?"

But Hannah McKittrick was already asleep.

He quietly unplugged the video player and left, closing the door behind him as if it were made of eggshell.

It was almost eight o'clock before Spilokos got to the drydock. It looked like a fortress by then. Portable towers had been set up along the shipyard's fence, and floodlights mounted atop them. Edgy national guardsmen with their rifles at the ready manned the towers, and patroled both the inside and outside of the fence. City police in riot helmets and state troopers in Smokey-the-Bear hats patroled between the guardsmen.

Outside the fence, the scene reminded Spilokos of a cross between Mardi Gras and a refugee camp. At least fifty thousand people and nearly as many cars filled Willoughby Road for a mile on either side of the shipyard and spilled over several acres of the weedy mudflat across from the yard itself. Entrepreneurs, hawking everything from beer to balloons, filtered through the mob, and firecrackers were going off with regularity. Spilokos, watching through the tinted windows of his official limousine, gauged the crowd's temper at somewhere between exuberance and belligerence. Every now and then as the car inched its way through the press, a fist was shaken at it or a beer can bounced off it.

At the gates, a harassed police detective checked the car's occupants visually and motioned them through the cordon of armed men who were screening out the would-be gate-crashers and publicity hounds.

Once inside, the crowd thinned and became more orderly, but it was a crowd nonetheless. Newsmen and camera trucks wove through the half-built tugboat hulls and huge yard cranes. Policemen argued with scientists, who argued with officials, who argued with persons of no particular persuasion, who argued with the night-shift yardworkers, who had all come to work anyway just to be in on the fun.

There was a hastily erected barbed wire fence around the drydock itself, and another layer of armed men behind the fence. Spilokos could see Wiley's red-bearded face among the knot of people standing on the lip of the dock.

A police lieutenant opened the door for him when the limousine stopped. " 'Evening, sir. Have any trouble getting through?"

Spilokos shook his head as he got out. "They're getting restless out there, though." He went through the one-man-wide gap in the inner fence, motioning his entourage to stay behind. He caught Wiley's eye and beckoned him over.

As Wiley came around the end of the dock, Spilokos became aware of an almost overpowering stench. It reminded him of a herd of diseased goats that had been killed and left on the hillside when he was a child back in Greece.

Wiley grinned as he came up. "Should've brought noseplugs, your honor."

The two men sized each other up as they shook hands. Spilokos was surprised at Wiley's muscularity. He'd pictured the scientist as being pale and stooped, with thick glasses. His grip, the mayor noted, was challengingly firm.

Wiley was not surprised at the mayor. In person, he looked exactly as he did on television: big, well-groomed, hard.

"You're, ah, not what I expected, Dr. Wiley."

"I'm not what I expected, either. I was going to be a baseball player." Wiley lifted his right leg and pointed his foot sharply. A small but audible snap accompanied the motion. "One of our little brown brothers changed my plans for me in 'Nam. Plastic ankle, souvenir of Uncle Ho." He gestured toward the drydock. "Want to see him?"

Spilokos shook his head again, a small shiver running up his spine. "Not just yet. There are a couple of things I'd like to discuss first."

Wiley looked around, then hopped on a capstan. "Step into my office." He watched the mayor expectantly.

Spilokos sat down on a nearby bollard, trying to preserve his sense of dignity. Couldn't let the little bastard get a psychological jump on him. "Dr. Wiley," he began, keeping his tone neutral, "I'd like to thank you for your efforts in capturing this menace to the citizens of the city."

"You're welcome. What do you want?"

Spilokos clamped his jaw and his temper. "You're rather direct, aren't you."

"Only when someone's putting the bite on me." His grin was almost malicious.

Spilokos smoothed his moustache. "The, ah, real question here, Doctor, is not what I want, but what you want."

"What makes you think I want anything out of this?"

"Don't be coy, Wiley." There was menace in Spilokos' tone, though he did not raise his voice. "You've grandstanded this affair from the first. You've refused to cooperate with the appointed authorities, you've withheld research information, you may even be responsible for the deaths of several people."

"Crap."

Spilokos refused the bait. "If push came to shove, you could be prosecuted and probably imprisoned for your conduct, and you know it."

Wiley laughed. "You're whistling in the wind, Spilokos. I was—and am—an independent investigator. I was asked to help out, not 'ordered.' Nobody paid me, nobody signed me up for anything, and nobody even asked for my research." He leaned his palms on the capstan and leered down at Spilokos, looking vaguely like a red-headed vulture. "Save your bluff and make your point. We both know that if anybody's ass is in the sling, it's yours. If the truth ever comes out, they'll tar and feather you."

Spilokos stood, feeling happier now that he could look down on Wiley. "All right. We'll keep up the little charade. You be the knight in shining armor and I'll be the proud papa. But don't think you'll come out clean if the shit hits the fan." He paced back and forth in front of the capstan. "Let's try it again. What do you want out of this, now that you've got your name in the history books and all that? Why did you refuse to let my men take charge of that animal?"

"First off, because you've no right to do so. It's mine. Mine personally, just as if it were a fish I'd caught out there."

"Your 'fish' has killed people, and that gives me the right to take it into city custody or to dispose of it. Don't quote me the law, Wiley; I'm an attorney."

"Second," Wiley continued, "none of your bozos are qualified to deal with him—nor are any of that herd of lambs who've been squirting in from all the universities.

I'm the only man in the world who really knows what we've got here, and how to deal with it."

Spilokos stopped, his eyes narrowing. "Do I understand, Doctor, that you're trying to keep the scientific community away, too?"

"Not trying, Mr. Mayor: am."

"Ahhh." Spilokos put a great deal of meaning into the soft exclamation. "I'm beginning to understand why you have caused such an uproar." He walked around Wiley as if inspecting an insect. "I underestimated you, Doctor. I thought you were a simple egomaniac. Now I see that you're a *complex* egomaniac." He planted himself in front of Wiley. "You're going to try and blackmail the entire scientific world, aren't you? You're going to sit out here with that homicidal slug and study it while your compatriots eat their livers out, aren't you?"

"That's relatively accurate."

Spilokos's bald head gleamed in the glare of the spotlights. He was hunched, now, in his bull stance. "You can't do it," he said flatly. "They won't let you, and neither will I. They'll get court orders—I'll give 'em to them. They'll storm the fence—and I'll let them."

"I've hired the drydock, Spilokos. It's private property."

The mayor grinned wolfishly. "You're counting on public opinion, aren't you? The bad guys overrunning the brave servant of science. But it won't work that way. I can commandeer your animal there, friend, by declaring it a public menace. That's the law, and it can be backed by a similar declaration from the state or the feds." He relaxed and crossed his arms over his barrel chest. "Sorry to punch holes in your dreams, Wiley, but that's how it is."

Wiley slid off the capstan and looked up at Spilokos. "You try that and I'll let the public know about your part in the past week."

Spilokos stared unflinchingly at the scientist. "Go ahead."

Wiley blinked. "What?"

"I said, go ahead. That thing over there is dangerous. It's killed people and could kill more if it got loose again. I am going to destroy it."

Wiley studied the mayor. Did he mean it? Would he do it? If so, why? Could it be that he was actually concerned for the safety of the city?

Wiley cleared his throat. He would have to take a step away from his inflexible position. "Mr. Mayor, it won't be necessary for you to kill him. He's dying right now. Can't you smell it?"

Spilokos was thrown off-balance. He had not expected Wiley to make a stab at a compromise. "Is that what it is?" He was stalling for time.

"Yes. There's not enough oxygen or food, and he's dying from the outside in. Come look." He walked toward the edge of the dock.

Spilokos moved woodenly after him, unable to keep his eyes off the rim of the dock, trying desperately to hide his emotions.

Wiley stopped and stood looking into the dock. "Ever see anything like that?"

The mayor came up and willed himself to look down. The water was gray and greasy. About a foot beneath the surface, something bloated and sick throbbed and oozed, causing waves to lap back and forth and splash up on the lip of the dock. Spilokos backed away in horror.

"I figure he's got another ten to fourteen hours," Wiley said, coming up to him. "Then he'll be so much rotten meat. We'll keep him here for another day, then dump in a few truckloads of salt just to make sure. After that, we can open the gates and flush him out in the lake."

Spilokos controlled his stomach. "T-that's fine," he said

weakly. "What keeps it from jumping out of the water at us like it did to the Jackson boy? For that matter, why doesn't it just crawl over the gates back into the lake."

"See that cable leading into the water? That's the hydrophone I pulled him in with. I'm still broadcasting. I've got him stoned out. He's like a junkie in heroin heaven right now. Doesn't know or feel anything except his high."

"I see." Spilokos mopped his forehead. "Okay, Wiley, play it your way. Just make damn sure the fucker's dead by tomorrow night." He held out a hand. "Truce?"

"Truce." Wiley shook his hand. "Now, I'll get back to my tests."

"Right. And I think I'll get back to my office. Don't think I can face supper tonight."

Wiley watched the mayor climb back in his car and depart. He then signaled to one of the men he'd hired that afternoon. "How about getting everybody out of here. Move them all back beyond that building over there, will you?"

He walked back to the side of the dock while his man was clearing the people out. How you feeling, he thought. Do you know you're dying? Can you feel it all slipping away? Or are you lost in the electronic dope I've given you? But don't worry, babe. Over there in my car I've got a five-gallon tank of nice fresh water with some nice dead fish in it. And I've got a forty-foot pole. And as soon as all these yo-yos are out of the way, I'll poke that pole into you, down into the center where you're still vital and alive and fighting. And I'll pull out a hunk, a few million of those weird cells of yours. And I'll put them in the tank and take them home, yes, indeed. Then I'll let the clucks have their field day with all this stinking decay here. Let them shake their fists at you and count coup on your poor dead body and feel like big brave men. But you'll live, sweetheart, you and your strange brain-that's-not-a-brain. And maybe you and me can have a talk one of these days, yessiree.

"Sir, the area's cleared."

Wiley gave the man a friendly pat. "Good. Now, let's douse these lights. They just speed up the decaying process and it stinks bad enough as it is."

"You can say that again!"

"It stinks bad enough as it is."

12

Spilokos was sitting at a poker table in the high stakes room of his restaurant. It was a good way to unwind but relaxation still eluded him. He motioned for a telephone to be brought to him. "Be with you in a minute, boys," he said, dialing with short stabs of his thick finger. A man set a bourbon and water beside his elbow.

"Hello, Sasha? Nikkos. You got anybody free at the moment? My boys are all tied up. . . . Yeah, I want a tail put on Blake Wiley. . . . Okay, so he's just a kid; this shouldn't be difficult. You have him go out there to the shipyard and see Tom. Tom'll point Wiley out and you have your kid make like flypaper. I want to know where Wiley is every second from now till dawn. Give the kid one of those walkie-talkies you boosted from the cops and give Tom the other one. He's got a phone patch to me. Got all that? Good." He hung up the phone and tossed off his drink.

"Gentlemen, we've got a busy few hours ahead of us. Spiggy, how many soldiers you got?"

"Eighteen, maybe twenty."

"I want them at the drydock by eleven-thirty. That's the shift change out there, and your boys are going to be yardworkers tonight. You stop the incoming workers and send your boys in instead, right?"

"Right. And?"

"And Willie's troops will be out there in the tourist crowd making a lot of racket, enough to pull the cops and Guard."

He stood and pointed to a squat man. "Santos is going to come through the gates with five dump trucks full of salt."

Santos looked startled. "Where'm I gonna get salt this time of night, boss?"

"Try road maintenance. They've got it stockpiled."

"Right."

"Okay, Spiggy. We get the salt in. At twelve-thirty-five, you drop those dumpers right on that slimy bastard in the drydock."

"Trucks and all?"

"Trucks and all. Santos will dump the other trucks at the same time." The big Greek wore a look of pure malice. "We'll fry that sucker to a crisp, once and for all."

Spiggy looked uncomfortable. "Ah, boss, ain't that a little hasty? I mean, all them science guys an' like that? There's liable to be some squawkin'."

"Let 'em. I'd rather deal with that than with a monster threatening all of us, wouldn't you?"

Spiggy licked his lips. "I guess so, boss. But my Regina, y'know, she's been going t'college. An', uh, she talks about scientific values . . . . " He stumbled into silence, then shrugged helplessly. "It just don't seem right."

The mayor walked over and put a hand on his shoulder. "You remember back home, Spiggy, when your grandfather was dying? You remember how all the doctors just shook their heads? What did science do for Grandpa Zorba, huh?"

Spiggy hung his head.

"Now, let's get moving. We don't have all that much time."

The mayor turned his face to the back of the room as the men filed out and allowed himself a small, grim smile. His confidence was coming back. Oh, the scientists would yell all right. There'd be denouncements in the papers and on the TV. They'd call him a Neanderthal, a traitor to knowledge. The bleeding hearts and pissed-off scientists would foam at the mouth internationally.

And he'd let them. He'd welcome it. Because Nikkos Spilokos would become a name known to everybody in the world. The man who destroyed the monster.

Spilokos poured himself another drink and raised it to the bar mirror in a toast. Here's to you, Blake Wiley, you smug little shit. If you want to muscle in on the deep-water action, you'd better learn about the sharks.

The water sloshed in the tank as Wiley threw the Jag around a corner and into an alley. He doused the lights and sat watching his rearview mirror.

The blue sedan that had tailed him from the drydock flashed across the alley entrance and was gone. Wiley waited three minutes before backing out.

"Well, ol' buddy, it looks like we shook him. What d'you think of that?" He looked to the tank jammed between the passenger seat and the door. "Just you and me, huh?"

The football-sized lump of translucent matter undulated through the water in pursuit of a piece of fish and did not answer.

"Now, don't go getting any ideas about turning Papa Blake into lunch," Wiley admonished, backing the car into the street and gunning it forward. "Papa's got a nasty surprise for you if you try." He made a melodramatic face in the direction of the tank. "That's not sand around the rim of the tank, ol' buddy, it's salt. You'd best get used to salt, 'cause that's what papa's going to use for his behavior mod program. Fish when you press the right button, salt when you press the wrong one. Nothing personal, you understand?" Wiley drove in a stair-step series of one-block zigzags, aiming diagonally across the city toward one of the older, well-kept suburbs. "You and me are going to be a two-man university. I'm going to teach and you're going to learn. You and that nutty brain of yours. We're going to plug it into a computer and play around with it, little friend, 'cause I have a hunch that you're not only new but different. I got a hunch that you might have a thing or two to teach us bipeds about learning and thinking. And if my hunch is right, hoo-boy!"

He wheeled the car down a quiet residential street, checking house numbers by the dim light of the street lamps. "See all those bloodhounds back there, friend? All those suckers who want a piece of the action? They'll have my place covered, and the school covered, and damn near every place else covered. But they won't think of looking for us here."

He turned into a driveway, humming contentedly.

The young trooper looked dubiously at the sergeant. "What do you think?"

The older man shrugged. "With drunks, who knows? 'Specially with this many."

Even this late at night, there were several thousand

sightseers, conventioneers, and general hell-raisers milling around outside the drydock. The television crews were there with their trucks and lights, and the whole thing had acquired an air of spontaneous partying. But the gaiety had an ugly edge to it, an undercurrent of potential violence that was making the state troopers and city police patroling the crowd nervous. "I don't like it, Sarge," the young trooper muttered, clutching his pistol's grip spasmodically. "It's too much like a fraternity beer-bust, only these guys are all overage. They're acting like we promised them a show and didn't deliver."

"That's the television people's fault. We'd have had these clowns dispersed if the TV guys hadn't come in and started filming. Point a camera at a drunk and he's got to show off." The sergeant fingered his own weapon. He wasn't worried about the crowd itself as much as the effect a riot here would have on the rest of the city. He'd seen city-wide riots before, and didn't want to be in the middle of one again. Even with the monster under control, the city was on the edge of flipping out. Nobody was used to having so many guns and uniforms showing on the streets. They were scared, ready to bolt. Or burn.

Somewhere in the crowd, someone set off a string of firecrackers. The young trooper gave a short, high shriek, dropped to his knee, and leveled his pistol at the crowd.

"No!" The sergeant dove for the trooper. The pistol exploded.

On the fringe of the amorphous mass of drunken conventioneers, a fat man staggered backward, clutching the widening red stain on his arm. "They shot me! F'Chrissakes, they shot me!"

A low, ugly murmur spread through the crowd.

A captain of state troopers barked orders and dove for his bullhorn. Lights and guns swung on the crowd.

The murmur began to swell. A rock came sailing out of the crowd to smash against the windshield of a police

cruiser. A heavy, bass voice yelled from deep in the mass
of men. "They're protectin' th' monster. Let's get 'em,
boys! Let's kill th' monster!"

With a sound like a gravel avalanche, the thousands
began shuffling cautiously forward, picking up rocks and
sticks as they came. The police and troopers gave way
slowly, grimly.

A side gate opened and five dump trucks with head-
lights off rolled into the shipyard. Men only dimly visible
in the shadows, trotted alongside them.

Near the drydock, a gaunt, ten-story assembly began
to move, its enormous single arm swinging.

Outside the shipyard, a cry punctuated the noise. It
took on rhythm and became a chant. "The monster! Kill
the monster! Kill the monster!" Slowly, relentlessly, the
mob surged toward the fence.

The men who were accompanying the dump trucks
scurried purposefully around the drydock. One stood,
listening. He waved an arm at two other figures. "I think
th' rubes're bustin' down th' fence out there. Get ever'body
inside here. Move it!" The figures hastened inside the
second fence. The dump trucks rolled up, hesitated, and
plowed over the barbed wire. "All right," the first figure
commanded, "get that fuckin' crane over here. You guys,
get outta them trucks. Chico, get the other three trucks
down along the sides of the dock and get ready to dump."

The police fell back against the shipyard fence and at
command began to fire rubber dum-dums and tear gas
into the crowd. A newscaster atop a TV truck, who had
been gleefully detailing the scene, caught a dum-dum
just under the chin and fell backward off the truck. He
was dead before the onrushing mob trampled him into
mush.

Drunken tourists, frenzied and brandishing whatever
they could pick up, rolled over the policemen and smashed

down the shipyard fence by sheer weight. They stormed toward the drydock.

The big yard crane lumbered forward, its huge wheels smashing aside the litter that lay across its rails. A packing crate slat snapped under the wheels. A yardworker's hardhat was flattened. A cable was sliced through. . . .

And in the depths of the drydock, the hydrophone suddenly went silent. There was a pause, and then the greasy water heaved, as if the gargantuan creature lying within had come awake. . . .

The mob poured around the assembly building, raising a great, bloodthirsty howl as it spotted the drydock.

"Lift them trucks! Lift them trucks!" Spilokos' man looked from the dock to the salt dumpers to the crowd and swore savagely. "No time." He cupped his hands and yelled. "Chico, dump 'em! Now!"

One of the trucks scheduled for lifting stood near the man in command. He sprinted to it and gunned it to life, intending to try and get its cargo into the drydock. He yanked the wheel and threw it in gear.

The yard crane smashed into the truck, teetered, then began to fall, slewing crazily off its rails.

The mob tore through the inner fence.

The dumpers upended and threw tons of salt into the drydock.

The falling crane struck a nest of high-voltage lines, turning the night into a glare of welder's sparks.

Hell rose out of the drydock.

Pushed by those behind, hundreds of people fell screaming into the water and were absorbed. In the actinic stutter of the broken power lines, shapes like moving mountains rose, reached out, fell, absorbed. Gouts of mucoid matter the size of houses flung into the night, hit the severed wires, and fried with the stink of an open grave.

People staggered, shrieking, pieces of pulsing, throbbing

matter clinging to their flesh. Sixty tons of pseudopod whipped through the air like a scythe and reaped a hundred souls into the churning water. The crane came down like final judgment on a press of humanity so dense it splashed like a red wave.

And in the terrorlight of the electric carnage, the dry-dock emptied, a vastness rising to flow over the rust-covered gates. Chunks of rotting, stinking slime as big as whales sloughed away and fell on the dock. And a glistening, naked something, enormous still, with lightnings pulsing angrily through it, dropped like the afterbirth of a nightmare into the cold black water of the lake. And freedom.

13

In the depths of the lake, as in the depths of the great void between the stars, life is sparse, heat is absent, light but a ghost. In the depths of the lake, there is weight. Molecule stacked on molecule for three kilometers, each adding its infinitesimal burden to those below until the accretion caves in a three-inch-thick plate of armor steel.

But it does not crush the presence, hanging without motion in the utter blackness, an ovoid detectable only through the faint phosphorescence of its internal energies. The presence has made of itself a gossamer, a lace of molecule-thick chains proof against the pressure, which sieves through its apparent solidity and is strained for the oxygen and energies it possesses, almost as a sponge sieves life; automatically, unconsciously, instinctively.

But there has always been something more than instinct in the workings of the presence, and now that *something has increased in complexity. Perhaps even in basic nature . . .*

Now there is an association on levels more complex than can be made by plants or fishes. Now there is in the presence's innermost being a . . . memory, a conscious or continuing set of data that constitutes an "awareness."

Awareness of ecstasy pounding through the self at 10-Hz per second, obliterating even the need for energy. Awareness of a kind of non-being, a negation, a . . . death.

And an awareness of an awakening. Cold, sharp, terrible. Awakening to suffocation, to depletion, to the self diminished. The horrible knowledge of confinement and of a self gone unresponsive. Of tons of corrosive, painful, death-bearing chemical poured onto the self.

Awareness/memory/searing-into-the-being/ . . . Memory of sudden thrusting for sheer survival, of heaving up out of the stagnant water, sloughing off the putrefaction of the dying parts of the self, striking out at the heat-bearers in a blind, primaeval urge to live, struggling toward the life-giving waters of the lake.

And now, in the profound gloom of the deep waters, the presence's strange molecules and stranger subatomic flows shape themselves into new patterns. Stimulus/ response breeds a third concept: judgment.

It is not a thinking, not a weighing of values and relativities. If thus-and-so prevails, 'therefore . . . It is simpler than this, more direct, more efficient. Thus is so. Thus threatens.

Therefore . . .

The molecular structure shifts, the presence rises. At ten meters depth, it takes the torpedo shape of motion-efficiency and begins to drive for the shore and the city. It does not know the concept of revenge, but it now knows the concept of "threat." And that which threatens must be destroyed.

Spilokos slitted his eyes against the rotor blast, but did not turn away as his aides did when stinging dust rose off the tarmac.

Around him, the airport had taken on the look of a military base. There were more army craft scattered around the field than jetliners, more soldiers than civilians, more jeeps than baggage tractors. Still, the big Delta and National and TWA jets were getting off with monotonous regularity, each bearing a load of scared conventioneers and city citizens. Well, screw them! He'd gotten a third of their money, anyway, and that was a sizable pile. Even flying out, they left taxable airfare behind. Silently, the mayor cursed the news media for making a mountain out of a molehill, cursed his men for blowing the job last night. And most of all, he cursed the governor, whose early-morning phone call had made it clear that the man now landing in the big Sikorski banana copter had complete authority over Nikkos Spilokos.

The chopper touched down, bounced lightly, and settled on its landing gear. The hatch opened immediately and a tall, trim man in crisp fatigues and paratrooper's jump boots leapt to the tarmac. He walked briskly toward Spilokos, disdaining to bend down under the whirling rotors.

Spilokos stood, awaiting the man. He extended a hand and an insincere smile. "General Tobin. Good to have you here. I'm Nick Spilokos."

Tobin shook his hand hurriedly and glanced around the field. His aide, a young major, was now out of the chopper and running to catch up to him. "Nice to meet you. I'll want those two hangars over there cleared of civilian aircraft. Inform the tower that army personnel will take over traffic control in thirty minutes. Civil defense is sending a crew to city hall to man your switchboards. Please keep a line open to my headquarters at all times. Let's go." He motioned to his aide and strode briskly off toward a waiting jeep.

For a moment, Spilokos was unable to move. He clenched his fists and trotted after the general. Tobin and the young officer were already in the jeep when Spilokos got there. "General, I think there are a couple of things we need to get straight."

Tobin spread a map of the city across his knees and studied it. "Such as?"

The mayor glanced at the sergeant behind the jeep's wheel. "Perhaps if you'd step over here . . . "

Tobin looked at Spilokos noncommittally. "I can hear you from here, Mr. Spilokos."

The mayor fought down his anger. "General, there are certain, eh, jurisdictional problems which might best be talked over before you, mmm, get involved here."

Tobin folded the map. "No, there aren't. This city is under martial law. I am the ranking military authority. I am in charge—of everything. Is there anything else you'd like to discuss?"

Spilokos' shoulders bunched. A vein in his forehead pulsed angrily. "General, I am aware that you are in charge. But the people of this city are civilians. They are not used to military discipline, nor are they used to taking orders from men in uniform. They *are* accustomed to following the suggestions of their mayor. In the interests of avoiding any further confusion among them, and of preventing a panic, I strongly suggest, General, that you take these facts into consideration before you start throwing your weight around."

Tobin sat with his hands folded neatly in his lap, watching Spilokos with unblinking eyes. "Very well, Mayor Spilokos, I'll consider those facts. I'll also consider the six hundred casualties you caused last night—"

"Now, just a goddamn minute!"

"—and the several you caused earlier in the week. I will consider the fact that there has already been a near riot in this city, that you've done next to nothing to alleviate or deal with a potentially explosive situation, and the fact that as far as I can ascertain, your sole concern has been and continues to be your own 'image.'" Tobin grabbed the map and tapped Spilokos' chest with it. "Now, *you* do some considering. Consider that the governor of this state is already founding an investigative panel which will at least impeach you and most likely bring criminal charges against you. Consider that your actions henceforth will have a serious bearing on the outcome of the investigation." His face was filled with repugnance. "I've no time for your strutting, Mr. Spilokos. Do I make myself clear?"

The mayor took a shaky breath and dropped his eyes. "Yes, you do."

"Fine. Now, please have—" He consulted a list. "Doctors Nesselroth and Wiley at the National Guard Armory in one hour."

"Dr. Nesselroth will be there, but I can't get Wiley for you."

"Why?"

"Well, he seems to have, er, disappeared."

Tobin eyed Spilokos a long time, then turned to the major. "Lennie, have the MPs find Wiley."

"Yes, sir."

"All right, let's go. Good-bye, Mr. Spilokos. I'll keep you informed with instructions and hourly reports."

As the jeep drove off, Spilokos resisted a momentary urge to salute, and a longer one to give the general the finger.

Hannah got gingerly out of the car, feeling as if she were made of glass and cotton candy. "Thanks, Jim. I appreciate the lift."

"Nothing to it, m'love. Are you sure you're okay? I can have one of the sloths from the station come babysit you."

"No, I'll be fine. I'm just a little weak yet."

"Right-o. You put your pulchritudinous young rump in a horizontal position for awhile, huh? And not to worry about work. I'll cover for you to the boss."

"You *are* the boss, boss."

"Never mind. I'll cover anyway." Wintergreen gave her a friendly wink and drove off, leaving behind a small cloud of pipe smoke.

Hannah made her way up the driveway and was nearly at her door when she noticed a dribble of oil coming from beneath the garage door. She went over and rubbed at the grimy window until she could see inside. Wiley's Jaguar sat there. "Oh, shit," she said tiredly.

She let herself in the unlocked front door. There were dirty dishes and an empty Wild Turkey bottle on top of the television.

The kitchen was a mess of unwashed, discarded instruments, and half-eaten sandwiches. The refrigerator door stood open several inches, leaking water. An aquarium sat on the kitchen table, filled with what looked like dark blue ink. Wiley was bent over it, poking wires into the murk and whistling tunelessly.

Hannah dropped her bag on the floor and leaned on the doorframe. "One of your ancestors had to be a goat. Or a pig."

Wiley started, then looked up, a mixture of relief and apprehension on his face. "What are you doing here?"

"I live here. It's my house."

"No, I mean what are you doing out of the hospital? I called three times to check on you. They said you'd be laid up for a couple of days."

"From you, that's positive tenderness. Are you getting soft in your old age?"

"Was that a sexual question?" He grinned.

She sighed. "So much for my romantic illusions."

"Okay," he said quietly, not looking at her. "So I missed you. I worried."

Hannah brushed at her hair, trying to hide the quick little smile of pleasure. She put her snide face back on, knowing that a tender moment with Blake Wiley could be destroyed by admitting its existence. "What are you doing here, Blake—besides turning my house into a junkyard?"

"Furthering the interests of science, naturally. That's what I'm all about."

She sat carefully in a kitchen chair. "Have you been here all the time?"

"All what time? I spent my early life in Dayton, then we lived in California for awhile. After that, I was in Vietnam."

"Blake, dammit! The whole city's looking for you."

"Today der city, tomorrow der vorld. Price of fame, Hannah."

She shook her head. "How can you be so damn flip after what happened last night?"

He stopped playing with the wires and cocked his head. "After *what* happened last night?"

"You don't know? Haven't you been watching the news—no, you wouldn't, would you?"

"Sometimes, but not now."

She told him about the attempt to kill the creature, and about the death and destruction.

He listened intently until she was done, then whistled softly. "Came right out of the dock, huh? I wonder if he did it with contractions or by gripping and pulling? He doesn't have true muscles, you know."

She made vague, exasperated motions with her hands. "It doesn't mean anything to you that all those people died? Or that the monster is loose in the lake again? It doesn't reach you at all, does it?"

Wiley shrugged. "Yeah, it does. But it doesn't matter."

"Six hundred people dead doesn't matter?"

"It's their own faults, Hannah. They had no business in the shipyard. They were there like mindless juvenile delinquents, looking to hurt something that couldn't fight back."

"It fought back well enough to kill them!"

"You're anthropomorphizing again. Did he go out lusting after them? Did he jump out of the drydock and chase them through the city? Hell, no, he didn't! They came to *him,* Hannah, to kill him."

She looked contrite. "I suppose that's so. Still . . . "

"Still, hell! I put him in that nice safe drydock where he couldn't menace anybody. I personally arranged his death —I murdered him, just to protect those bozos. He was half dead when I left the shipyard, and if those fuckers had left him alone, he'd be history now. But they couldn't do it, could they?" He was pacing angrily around the kitchen, waving his arms and shaking his fists. "Oh, no! They had to prove how tough they were, had to show everybody how brave they could be. Like a bunch of savages running up to kick a fallen elephant." He stopped and sneered. "No, sweets, I don't feel sorry for them. They deserved what they got." He threw himself into a chair and glared out the window. "Stupid bastards."

Hannah got up, feeling dizzy and a little trapped, and closed the refrigerator door, ignoring the odor of spoiled food that huffed out as she did so. She began aimlessly to make tidying motions around the kitchen. "Blake, no matter what you feel, you've still got to face the fact that the animal kills people and it's loose again. You've got to get out there and help capture it."

"Uh-uh. They don't need me. Saul's got the frequency

information; from what you say, the army's got the city under control, and the government's got the ships and planes to find him with. I'd just be in the way."

Hannah put a dishpan in the sink and began running soapy water. "You're just going to sit here on your duff, then?"

"I'm going to continue my research."

Her eyes widened. She looked at the aquarium on the table. "Blake, you haven't . . ."

"Yes, I have."

She backed against the sink, looking ill. "Get that thing out of here," she said, her voice intense and trembling. "Get it *out* of here!"

Wiley shook his head. "Not till tonight. Relax, he can't hurt you. I've got him under complete control." He bounced out of his chair and went to the tank. "I've dyed the water, see, to simulate night or extreme depth. I've found out that he prefers to hunt nocturnally, which explains why we didn't net him earlier. He was out in the deep water. He doesn't seem to mind pressure—I had him in your pressure cooker for a while this morning."

"Ugh!" She inched away from the cooking utensil, which sat on the drainboard.

"The thing is, he learns so damned fast. I did a reward-punishment thing with him using fish and frequencies. It took him exactly two tries to figure out the reward response. Two! It takes a dolphin seven tries, a chimp five, an octopus ten. Sometimes I even think he's smarter than us." He jiggled a wire dangling in the tank. "I'm getting him used to having wires stuck in him. I think he knows already that the wire is just a conductor for the punishment or reward. He's not fighting it anymore, or trying to eat it. He breaks his food down chemically, secreting something that builds into a kind of gastric acid a lot like the sharks use. But he does it with every individual cell. He's got no specialized glands or anything to make the juice with."

Hannah crossed to the table, keeping a distance from the tank itself. "Blake, please. Whatever you want to do with this thing here, you've *got* to get out there and help the rest of us."

Wiley went on as though he had not heard her. "Tonight I'm taking him downstate to the Primate Studies Center. They've got equipment there for doing interspecies communication—remember Washoe, the chimp they taught to communicate with symbols and sign language?"

"Goddamn, Wiley! It's not bad enough the thing kills people, now you want to teach it to recite poetry. Don't you see what you're *doing?* If you teach that thing to think, you're just giving it another weapon to use against us."

Wiley put his hands on her shoulders and sat her down in the chair he'd been using. "Yes, I see. But you don't." He squatted on his heels in front of her and rubbed her knees affectionately. "Hannah, you're missing the key idea."

"I'm sure you'll enlighten me," she said sarcastically.

"I'll try." He indicated the window. "Out there we've got my buddy's big brother. He's trying to survive, just like the rest of us, right? And he learns, right? What's he learned so far?"

She shook her head. "I don't know. You're the expert."

"He's learned that humans are out to get him, that's what. He's learned that we're the enemy—it's our own fault, but that doesn't matter now." He got up and went to the tank, tapping on its side with his knuckles. "What matters now is this little fellow. And you know why? Because I'm here to teach him and learn about him." He came back to her, his face serious. "And because that animal in the lake learns, the only chance we've got is to out-think him. I've got to teach this little guy all I can, and learn all I can from him, just so we can stay a step ahead of his big brother."

Hannah McKittrick studied Wiley's eyes. "I see your reasoning, Blake. I even agree with it. I just wish to hell I could believe it will do some good."

14

Flanked by two majors and a city councilman, General Tobin stalked across the basketball court, oblivious to the damage his jump boots were doing to the fine maple flooring. He had taken one look at the antiquated National Guard armory and moved his command to Lakeshore High School. The gymnasium now had a ring of switchboards, map stands, desks and first-aid stations around its walls. An anonymous student had chalked *Godzilla 600, Army 0* on the scoreboard behind the stands.

Tobin marched to the big doors, where Saul Nesselroth and two assistants stood waiting. "You're the coroner?"

"Yes, sir. Saul Nesselroth. Sorry I'm late; I thought you people were over at the armory."

"We were. Thank you for coming." He gestured toward his desk and started for it. "I read your report on the way up from Fort Dunham. I get the impression that you disagree with Dr. Wiley's conclusions."

"Well, not exactly, General. It's more that I don't really know what his conclusions are. All he told me was that we've got a multicellular aggregation of single-celled animals—"

"Which you agree with?"

"Yes. And that they have some unique properties—which I also agree with."

"But you do not think the animal possesses the capacity for thought?"

"No, not as we define the term." Nesselroth made a deprecating gesture. "Blake Wiley's a fine scientist, sir, but he's . . . somewhat romantic. He tends to, mmm, overstate the case."

"So I gather." Tobin scanned a report an officer handed him, okayed it and handed it back. "My concern, Dr. Nesselroth, is to find the animal and render it harmless. What I want from you is your opinion on whether we should try for a capture or a kill, and on the best method of carrying out either option. I am a soldier and therefore expert in the execution of orders. I would like you to advise me."

Nesselroth was taken aback and showed it. "I'm not sure I understand you, General."

"This is a scientific problem, Doctor. You are the scientist, not me. You tell me how to catch the animal or kill it, and I will do so."

The coroner felt a happiness swelling in his breast. Finally, he would have a chance to redeem himself. A wave of gratitude went through him. "General, I'll get you your answer, as soon as I can."

"Thank you, Doctor. I'm counting on you." A lieutenant appeared at Tobin's elbow and Tobin spoke without looking at him. "Lieutenant, please arrange for the coroner to have a desk in the building and an open line to our field units."

"Yes, sir." The officer guided Nesselroth off across the basketball court.

The general picked up a telephone that had been winking at him for a short while. "Hello? Yes, Commissioner, thank you for returning my call." Tobin leaned back in his chair and closed his eyes. "Sir, I have a favor to ask of you. I'm a military man, an outsider. This thing we have here is, as I see it, basically a police matter. And I know when to turn to the experts. I'd like your opinion on how best to kill or capture this animal. . . . Yes, that's right; you feed me ideas and I'll execute them."

The planet rounds its star, covering a nearly exact minute of arc each time it completes a rotation on its axis. Energies fall upon it, energies radiate from it, energies pulse and stutter around it.

It is mostly water, this planet. Water with an astounding abundance of elemental particles suspended in it. In a single cubic mile, the waters bear four billion tons of oxygen, five hundred million tons of hydrogen, ninety million tons of nitrogen, fifty million tons of sodium, six million tons of magnesium, four million tons of sulphur. Every element the planet owns is borne in the rolling waters.

There are places, say the thinkers among the walking soup, where the elements and the energies cannot be told apart, places where motion becomes matter becomes energy becomes form. And none can say precisely how one becomes the other, or how each reacts.

On a body of water small by the planet's standards, large by others, energies grid the surface and cone the depths. Artificial birds cross the lake in regular patterns, bouncing energies off the surface, seeking, seeking. Artificial fish glide the surface and swim the depths, bouncing sonic questions through the blackness, seeking, seeking. Each bears a lure, a sirensong devoid of scale or harmonic, carrying only a monotonal 10-Hz rhythm, drumming a single message: come, come, come.

The presence skirts the fringes of the questing energies. It keeps to the low places, it conforms to the bottom topography, it moves only in the empty spaces between the sonic probes. It camouflages its existence with a cloak of stealth and a cloud of cunning.

The presence resists the lure. Alone among animals save for the dreaming apes that hunt him, the presence can sense the danger behind the offered bait. It is a remarkable achievement of intelligence. Even the walking soup will go to destruction knowingly if the lure is strong enough. The soup will pump euphoria into its veins, perfectly aware that the euphoria carries death with it.

But the presence? No. Alone, fanatic, singleminded, it resists the temptation to ecstasy, to surrender, to dissolution. It blankets itself against the calls of the hydrophone borne overhead by a destroyer; it slides away from the kiss of a submarine's hydrophone; it ignores the seductive whisper of a C-103 gulling a hundred feet over the water.

Pausing only to snatch a school of fish or mow an aquatic lawn of kelp, it moves steadily, purposefully toward the city.

"That about wraps it up for this edition, ladies and gentlemen. We'd like to remind you that channel five will continue its on-the-spot coverage of the lake drama with bulletins and interviews. Now, before we return to our regularly scheduled programming, here is station manager James Wintergreen with a special editorial message." The anchorman gave the camera his left profile and held the pose until the light winked out. Wintergreen, facing camera three, straightened his tie and cleared his throat.

"Good afternoon. It is not every day that a city becomes the focus of world-wide attention, especially under such extraordinary circumstances. Because of that attention and these circumstances, channel five would like to take a moment to review exactly what is happening here and to make a request of the citizens of the city."

Wintergreen stepped to a map which showed the city and the lake. "Right now we are hosting close to fifty thousand visitors, eight thousand military personnel, hundreds of scientists, and one rather unique and uninvited guest, the animal in the lake.

"I want to emphasize, as General Tobin did earlier, that the animal *is* in the lake, not the city. I will also emphasize that the entire lakefront area for a hundred miles on either side of the city is being patroled."

Wintergreen swept the city portion of the map with his chubby finger. "Most of us are unused to the sight of tanks and soldiers in our streets, and are annoyed or frightened by the inconveniences this causes. But it is good to remember that the military, along with our friends and neighbors who serve in the city's police and fire departments, are here to protect us."

Wintergreen faced the camera squarely. "With the entire world watching, and the situation here as unusual as it is, channel five believes that it behooves all of us to act calmly, graciously, and responsibly. We ask that each of you go about your business, that you treat our visitors and the military with cooperation and respect, and that you do your best to contribute to a smooth conclusion to the operations now underway." He allowed himself a sincere smile. "Thank you."

Wintergreen held his smile until the engineer cut the camera, then left the studio and went into the newsroom. Roskins was sitting at Hannah McKittrick's desk, using her typewriter. "Haven't found her yet?" Wintergreen asked.

"Nope. But you find Wiley, you'll find her. He was at her house last night."

The manager lifted an eyebrow. "And how do you arrive at that observation?"

Roskins chewed his unlit cigar, still typing. "Her driveway's full of Castrol. She drives a Fiat. He drives an old Jag—and conscientious Jaguar owners use Castrol. Fiats don't."

"Indeed? I think you missed your calling, Pat." Wintergreen fired his pipe and offered the lighter to Roskins. "Have your brilliant powers of deduction given you a clue to their current whereabouts?"

"Would I be here?"

"Astute, m'boy. Astute."

Roskins yanked the sheet out of the typewriter and added it to a sloppy stack nearby. "What d'you think, Jim? Is the city going to flip out?"

Wintergreen thought about it. "Depends. Tobin's managed to get more of the officials behind him—except Spilokos, naturally. But there's already been some looting. And we've got a religious fanatic preaching the end of the world—lot of people listening to him unfortunately."

The reporter gathered his papers and got up. "I don't think that's what we've got to worry about. I think the problem's plain human nature."

"How's that?"

"There's a 'monster' out there, Jim. Something we can't define. We could handle a giant shark, or a plague of crabs or something. But we're all the product of what's been done to us. Years of horror movies and childhood nightmares have their effect."

"Granted."

Roskins shook his head. "I can't help remembering that underneath their uniforms and brass buttons, the cops and the soldiers are people, too." He gave his boss a

sober, level look. "And I wonder if it will be a soldier who
reacts when he sees the animal, or a frightened kid? If
you were standing on the shore with a rifle and a uniform,
and a thing out of your nightmares jumped out of the
water at you, do you think there'd be enough starch in
your khakis to keep you standing there?"

Wintergreen sucked on his pipe, thoughtfully. "I'm
afraid that starch wouldn't be the only substance in my
khakis."

Roskins ground his cigar into an ashtray. "Somehow, I
can't convince myself that all those boys out there are
going to protect me when it gets down to nitty-gritty time."

"You believe it will come to that? That the animal will
attack us? It doesn't work that way in nature, Pat. Given
the choice, any animal will run away if it can. The first
thing the animal did at the drydock was get back into the
lake as quickly as possible."

"Yeah, and the first thing we did was go after it. We're
not going to give it a chance to run, Jim. We're going to
hunt it down and back it into a corner. And I don't think
we'll get a second chance if we blow it the first time. Wiley
says that thing's not like other animals. He says it thinks."

"Nesselroth doesn't agree with him."

"Good for Nesselroth. But if Wiley's right, who takes
the weight?"

Wintergreen could not answer him.

"Pressure?"

"Two-point-six."

"Outflow?"

"Four thousand per. Make that four and a quarter."

"Right. Okay, stand by to shunt."

"Standing by."

"Shunt." Both men threw their switches. Beneath them,

the building trembled as steel shutters rose and fell. "Green here."

"Gree—no, hold that. I got a non-function."

"Main or outflow?"

"Both. Looks like we got a jammed gate."

The foreman swore and reached for a telephone. "This is pumping station nine. We've got a jammed gate on the east side sewage feeder. Request permission to shut down and clear it." He listened, then chuckled. "Gotcha." He hung up the phone and smirked at his companion. "The military mind ain't changed since I was in. They want to send a squad over with one of those microphone things, just in case we've got that blob down there."

The technician did not return the foreman's grin. "Hey, this ain't no laughing matter, man. That fucker *could* be down there for all we know."

"Sure, an' the moon could be made out of green cheese. C'mon, let's clear that gate."

"You're not gonna wait for th' army?"

"I had enough waitin' for them in Korea. Get your spanner."

They went down a spiral steel ladder to the pumping station's lower deck. The foreman undid the lugs on a hatch in the floor. "Okay, if King Kong jumps out, you hit him with the wrench." Laughing, he lifted the hatch.

A blue-green glow showed for just a moment, illuminating the foreman's round face. Then a thick bulge of mottled being smashed up out of the hatchway, ripping the heavy steel hatch off its hinges and flinging it clanging down the steel deck. The foreman's scream was sliced in half as the animal slapped itself wetly over his face and arms. It began oozing back down the hatchway, dragging the kicking foreman with it.

The technician stood as if rooted, unaware that he was howling in turn. His eyes were wide and popped, and his neck muscles were as rigid as a catatonic's. But as the foreman's torso began to slide down the hatchway, the technician found himself lunging forward and grabbing desperately at the man's legs. "Help me," he screamed. "Somebody come/help me! Oh, Christ, it's taking Sam away!"

He was sliding across the deck toward the hole, being dragged down along with the foreman. Tendrils of lightning-shot flesh were creeping out of the main mass and feeling their way back toward the technician. He looked around wildly and spotted the steel cable and winch, used to raise and lower heavy equipment into the pumps. He let go of the foreman's twitching legs and grabbed the cable. A quick turn around the lower body, scooting the cable up under the thighs; a snap of the pelican hook: a punch of the starter button. Oh my God, would it cut him in two? Would it strangle him? Would it make any difference?

The cable grew taut. The technician grabbed a dogging wrench and beat frenziedly at the gelid mass imprisoning the foreman, not noticing that the beating had no effect. The foreman's legs stopped twitching.

The cable slackened. The foreman's body fell limp against the rim of the hatchway. As if losing interest, the creature engulfing the foreman sloughed away and dropped into the blackness of the sewage feeder with a sickening, slurred thump.

The technician staggered over and grabbed the foreman by the ankles. "It's okay, Sam. I gotcha. I gotcha. You're gonna be all right." He was crying, but did not know it. "Come on, now, Sam. C'mon."

The body slid out of the hole, face down. The technician took it by the shoulders and turned it over. Then he sat down on the floor and screamed and screamed and screamed. The foreman's face and chest were gone. In their place were huge, gaping, raw holes, with brains and lungs and shreds of fiber sogging wetly out onto the floor, and pound-sized lumps of mucus still moving, still feeding noisily in the hollow cavities. The foreman's heart, slewing out around a rib, had not yet stopped pumping.

15

Hannah came out of sleep feeling drugged. She rolled over, wincing as her numb legs pinpricked to life. Wiley had thrown her coat over her, she noted.

She got off the couch. The lab's lounge was dark and empty. A light shone from down the hallway outside, and she padded in her bare feet toward it. Elsewhere in the Primate Center, monkeys howled and an ape thundered. The whole building smelled like a zoo.

Wiley sat at a keyboard, surrounded by notepads and the remains of a case of beer. He looked up as she entered the room and gave her a distracted grin.

"Don't you think you should get some sleep?" she asked. "It's nearly midnight."

Wiley shook his head. "Not now. Amazing things are happening." He typed rapidly, then waited with an air of expectancy. In the aquarium, sitting on a workbench nearby, the mucoid lump quivered. Wiley's keyboard began clacking away of its own accord.

"Blake, what's that thing doing? Surely it's not talking to you?"

"Not yet, but I don't think that's far off." He scanned the readout sheet critically. "You know anything about the learning process, Hannah?"

"Not much."

"Well, there are stages a mind goes through on the way to true intelligence. A chicken can't learn to run a simple maze, though it can learn to peck a specific lever to get corn. A rat can run the maze, but can't figure out short-cuts. And a chimp can figure out what a maze is, and what it's for, and can go on to build itself a door." He looked to see if she was following him. "So I've been running the baby there up through the scales, so to speak. And he's already gotten to the point of symbols and abstract concepts. I've taught him the difference between declarative and query. I can say, 'this is food,' or '*is* this food,' and he can say 'yes' or 'no.' That's the first step toward actual communication." Wiley looked as proud as a new father. "With the help of the computer, I'll have him talking by tomorrow night."

Hannah came over and studied the readout, not looking happy. "And then what, Blake? What are going to talk about, you and the monster? Are you going to say, 'now that I've taught you to think, tell me how to kill you'?"

"No. Would you tell someone how to kill *you?*" Wiley pulled at a stale beer and stretched hugely. "I keep telling you, Hannah, that he's not got the kind of mind we have. It's not even a mind; just an intelligence. He'll be like a computer. He can only work with the data I give him, and I'm not about to bring up the question of his demise. Did you know that children have no concept of death until they're taught it or see it? Even then, they don't really personalize the idea of their own death. A kid simply can't conceive of himself as dead." He scooted his chair over to the tank and looked at the creature in it with something close to fondness. "I'm not going to put any negative thoughts in his head, lover. I'm just going to let him jump through a few hoops for me."

"Then what's the purpose of this whole charade, Blake? Why bother training an idiot? We've got enough of those as it is—present company not excepted."

Wiley got up and took her hand. "Let's go get something to eat." As he steered her out of the laboratory and switched off the lights, he patted her rump familiarly. "There are a lot of kinds of idiot, kiddo. Computers are one, and where would we be without them? Maybe our friend in the tank will prove equally useful."

In the darkened laboratory, the only sounds were the quiet humming of the computer and the soft bubble of the aquarium's aerator. A green light set beside the tank caused the creature in the water to glow with a jade pearlescence. It pulsed, moving restlessly from one end of the tank to the other, plastering itself against the glass like a slug. The wires trailing from its body scraped along the top of the tank. The creature seemed to draw in on itself, becoming first ovoid, then globular. It became opaque, the internal lightnings growing murky with effort.

Across the room, the keyboard carriage tinged and returned, throwing the bottom of the readout sheet clear of the platen. The sheet fluttered to the table behind the keyboard. The keys began to clack in a repeating rhythm, their inked impressions lost on the black, hard-rubber surface of the platen. A single word, repeated over and over and over.

ME ME ME ME ME ME ME ME ME ME ME ME ME ME ME ME ME

Nikkos Spilokos pushed his way past the protesting

corporal and strode across the gymnasium toward Tobin, who, with several officers and civilians, was bent over a large map of the city that had been spread over two ping-pong tables. The general saw him coming and straightened up, waiting calmly.

Spilokos stopped at the edge of the tables and gave Tobin a flinty look. "I hope you realize what you've done."

"I have quarantined this city."

"You have guaranteed a goddamn panic, that's what you've done. I've already gotten reports of people trying to shoot their way past your roadblocks. I understand that your lockstep types even shot down a private plane!"

"No, sir. We turned it back." Tobin's voice was calm, controlled. "We are not preventing people from leaving, Mr. Mayor, just from carrying unexamined water with them."

Spilokos nodded his large head. "Oh, yes. Examined water. General, just how long do you think two million people can last in a city living on bottled water? Nothing to cook or wash with. No fire protection. They can't even flush their crappers."

A colonel stepped up. "Sir, we are right now setting up high-voltage generators at every reservoir, incoming pipeline and pumping station in the city. By twenty-two hundred hours tonight, we'll be able to fry the animal if it tries to get out of the sewers. In the meantime, we're flying water in and bringing it in by train and tank truck."

Spilokos leaned across the ping-pong tables and rapped a point on the map. "Did you know, General, that we've got a warehouse burning over here? What are we supposed to do about it, piss on it?"

Tobin clasped his hands behind him and exuded patience. "The corps of engineers is leveling a firebreak around that block. We can afford the loss of one warehouse."

"And what if it's a hospital that catches fire next? Or an old-folks' home? Are you going to plow them under, too?"

"Mayor Spilokos, your concern for the citizenry is admirable. It would be more admirable if you could find something more positive to do than harass us."

"I will find something to do, Tobin, never you mind. And until you show a little more care about the people of this city, I'll continue to protest your actions in every legal fashion."

"I'm sure you will, sir. Now, if you'll excuse us. . . . "

Spilokos turned and marched toward the door. As he reached it, he was struck by a thought. He corralled a passing officer. "Son, are there any sections of the sewer that've already been inspected?"

"Yes, sir. The area under the Arts Center."

"And you're sure that area's safe?"

"Yes, sir. Why?"

Spilokos patted the officer on the back. "You're doing a good job. We appreciate it."

"Thank you, sir."

Spilokos went to his car and leaned in the window. "Hurkos, get hold of Ronald. Tell him to have the news people in front of the Arts Center in fifteen minutes. We're going to take a personal hand in the search."

The coroner's fingers moved in millimetric precision, guiding a probe whose visible end was a pencil-sized shaft of stainless steel and whose invisible end was a scalpel-edged wire fifty times narrower than a human hair. With his left hand, Nesselroth made equally minute adjustments to a knob on the microscope's specimen table, causing it to shift a hundred-thousandth of an inch. Through the twin eyepieces, the probe looked like a log, and the table shift was a dizzying lurch. But between log and lurch, the single-celled animal dodging stubbornly through the water droplet was chivvied, finally, up against the edge of the water and trapped.

"Inserting probe," Nesselroth said, speaking for the benefit of the recorder humming at his side and the three assistants at their instruments. "I've pierced the membrane. Give me one trillionth of a volt, please." He watched closely as the voltage was trickled through the probe. "Normal reaction thus far—wait a minute." He adjusted the eyepieces. "Ah, the mitochondrions seem to be attacking the probe, as if they were absorbing the electricity."

"Doc, that's crazy. A mitochondrion produces energy from food bits. It doesn't *eat* energy."

"This one does, and so do the rest of them in this cell." Nesselroth frowned into the microscope. "No, that's wrong. There seem to be two kinds of mitochondrions here. Some are reacting normally and some are absorbing energy." He whistled. "That's scary." He moved the probe delicately. "Okay, let's go further in. The endoplastic reticulum has a very heavy coating of ribosomes, indicating that the animal not only makes an excessive amount of protein but is prepared to ship it out to other cells."

"Do you see any Golgi bodies, Doc?"

"No, but that doesn't mean the cell can't ship. It's got a number of things I can't identify and any one of them could be protein carriers. Further in, now; give me a little more juice."

The technician obligingly stepped up the miniscule current.

"Entering the nucleus—whoops! The animal doesn't like that. The nucleus is slipping around inside the cell. I didn't think they could be that elastic or mobile."

"What does the nucleolus look like, Doc?"

"There are two of them, both about the same size. They look normal but occupy a larger part of the nucleus than you'd expect. The chromatin has a sort of network of filaments running through it. They are either luminescent or are electrically charged. You can actually see a glow."

"Didn't Mr. Jackson say the animal 'had lightning flashing in it' when it took his boy off the pier?"

"Yes. I wonder if we're looking at the creature's nervous system. Maybe that's what made Wiley believe the thing can think. If it's got an extensive inter- and intracellular communications system—these filaments—it could give a good imitation of thought just by the complexity of its responses."

"Then, you're—"

"Hold it! We've got a reproduction going. Also an alarm reaction. It's put out a rim of trichocysts—they look like spears. Now the nucleus is dissolving."

"Both nucleoli?"

"Both of them. Here it comes, here it comes . . . now! Two cells. Nucleus reforming. Cytoplasmic membranes defining. Gimme a jolt; maybe this is the stage where we can kill it."

"How strong?"

"Just give me electricity, dammit."

Nesselroth appeared to be trying to crawl down inside the eyepieces. His whole body tensed and contorted. Then he groaned and slumped back, rubbing his eyes. "So much for that good idea." He regarded his assistants with a look of defeat in his soft eyes. "Whammo. It just ate the juice up."

One of the technicians looked from his watch to a graph recorder. "Jeez. It took less than twenty seconds to divide."

"That's not what bothers me," Nesselroth stated. "I'm worried about the fact that division is taking place every seventy minutes. No wonder the thing got to be the size of a crude-oil storage tank in less than a week. If it were left to run free it would fill the lake in a month and a half." He carefully took the slide from beneath the microscope and held it over a lit Bunsen burner until the water droplet had boiled away. "How many more specimens do we have?"

"Half an ice cube's worth, Doc. Maybe six, seven thousand."

"Okay, make sure the freezer's locked tight and let's take a break. I'll spring for the coffee."

"You're all heart, boss, all heart."

Nesselroth led the technicians out of the room, save for the last one who stayed to lock the freezer. The man checked the lock carefully, turned out the lights, and started out. He stopped, thinking sourly of the taste of coffee made with ozone-filled, electrocuted water from the tank the army had brought them. Then he unlocked the refrigerator again and fished through it. Somewhere behind the bottles of formaldehyde and stacks of culture dishes there should be half a carton of orange juice—if that goddamn Whorton hadn't drunk it as usual.

The juice was there and he extracted the carton. Feeling slightly guilty, he relocked the freezer with extra care. Then, holding the carton in front of him and smiling the wicked smile of a man indulging in forbidden delights, he chugged it.

His only thought before the suffocation panic hit was how did it get in the juice. . . .

16

In the city on the lake, the first acids of panic are beginning to eat at the foundations. There are not yet real riots, but here and there people are picking up clubs, smashing windows. There are not yet holocausts, but here and there a building is fired, a truck is overturned. There are not yet the frenzies, the brutalities, but here and there a girl is trapped in a dark place, an old man is beaten into senselessness. There is not yet a general greed, but here and there a group of people will suddenly congregate around a store, their eyes darting from one shiny thing to another, their hands opening and closing like mechanical jaws.

It is a mood, a stink, an awkwardness, for this is a city that has never before known uniforms and guns and tanks in its streets. This is a city whose country has always exported the violence, has never imported it. Housewives find it hard to shop in stores filled with armed men. Businessmen drive to work tensed, as machine-gun snouts idly and randomly track their cars down the streets. Children grumble at the dusk curfew, then grow silent at their parents' fear. And no one takes a bath, or drinks coffee, or turns on a tap unless there is someone else standing nearby. . . .

In the city on the lake, the men in uniform plot graphs and snap orders and finger their weapons, and they are as afraid as the citizens. They fear the mood of the city. They fear the look in their neighbors' eyes. And they fear the shadowed thing that lurks . . . where? Beneath their feet? In the lake? Inside the sewer grating two feet away?

In the city on the lake, there is a vibration. It is slower than the 10-Hz frequency that pulses the planet; a jungle-deep throb, unheard but felt in every shivering spine. And at each beat, it shakes mortar from between the bricks of order. It is only a matter of time before the edifice crumples in a cloud of chaos.

In the dark arteries beneath the city, in the bowels and lungs and veins that pump to keep the city alive, the presence moves unhampered by imagination, unfettered by fear, unburdened by pride or panic. It oozes in the dank cisterns, slops from level to level of the sewage pipes, undulates up the drains, strains through the filters, eats its way through the waste traps.

In its time beneath the city, it has learned every ancient pipe, every new drain, every mossy reservoir. It has learned the dozens of outflow pipes by which it can get back to the lake, and the thousands of water pipes by which it can get out into the suburbs, and the millions of faucets by which it can lift itself into the strange boxes that hold the airbeings.

And it has learned that the airbeings, the threateners, the killers, are trying to trap it in the sewers. Each outlet *to the lake, each major pipe or drain into the city, each pumping station now sings with the shrill voice of high voltage.*

And the presence has learned that the song dims with distance, that high voltage becomes low voltage becomes almost no voltage as it disperses through the waters. And within the curious, double-nucleolus cells of its communal being, the presence has learned to create mitochondrions that feed on the voltage. Feed and grow hungrier, more tolerant of the charge, more adaptable.

The presence does not consciously realize that this knowledge is a weapon. It knows only that when the time comes, it can escape; that the weapon the airbeings have chosen to use against it is harmless. Nor does it make the logical step toward the knowledge that with electricity for food it need no longer hunt crudely as other animals do, for it is not a creature of logic.

It simply waits, the presence, knowing somehow that the killers will come to it, and that it will annihilate them.

"Okay, would you mind getting a set of lights over there?" Ronald played tug-o'-war with the news crews, trying to get the cameras set up to show his boss off to best advantage. When he was satisfied that he'd gotten everything in the best compromise, he signaled Hurkos, who signaled a man at the end of the block.

Spilokos' limousine came around the corner and parked beside the open manhole. The mayor stepped out, dressed in a set of overalls and a hardhat. On cue, two soldiers in full battle gear flanked him and all three proceeded to the manhole looking suitably grim. Ronald pointed to a newsman and gave the go sign. The reporter and his cameraman stepped up and went through their motions, following the mayor as he disappeared down the manhole, leading a disproportionately large contingent of armed bodyguards and National Guardsmen. Two of the soldiers carried a large cable through which, presumably, the juice would flow to electrocute the monster.

Spilokos descended the ladder cautiously. He knew it was perfectly safe but his stomach lurched. A trickle of sweat seeped down his backbone. As he stepped onto the narrow brick walkway that ran beside the sewer drain, he was struck by how much the place smelled like the caves of his boyhood mountains back in Greece. He'd expected the pungent acridity of raw sewage, but the air was clean, almost sweet.

"Be careful of the water, Mr. Mayor. In case the voltage lines slip in."

"Right." They were all watching him. Spilokos drew himself up fully, seeming to fill the tunnel with his presence. "All right, gentlemen. The party's over. We're here, so let's do something useful." He waved his arm in the classic "follow me" gesture.

In single file, Spilokos leading, soldiers in the middle, and a nervous cameraman at the rear, they passed into a blackness relieved only by flashlights. Soon, only the muffled susurrus of their footsteps disturbed the silence beneath the manhole.

A few heartbeats later, there was a sloshing sound in the water from the opposite direction. A ripple moved through the water, passed beneath the sunlit manhole, and disappeared after Spilokos' search party.

The entourage came to a branching in the tunnels. "Engineer," Spilokos shouted.

A woman worked her way up the file of soldiers. "Yes, sir?"

"Where are we? Where do these branches lead?"

"We're under, mmm, Vine and Monaghan Streets. The left branch goes to some smaller feeders under Bloominthal's department store, and the right one dead-ends about a block away."

"A dead-end tunnel that size?"

"It used to serve pumping station eight, but the freeway foundations cut through it. We rerouted the drains in—"

A scream of terror came from the back of the file. Without conscious thought, everyone started running. Spilokos, his knees weak but his jaw squared, tried to stem the flow. "Stand fast, goddamn you!" But someone bowled into him. He slipped, staggered, and fell into the sewage. A blind, overwhelming panic gripped him. As if far away, he heard himself screaming for help. He clawed with bloody fingertips at the scummy side of the sewage channel, his every nerve tensed for the touch of something terrible and fatal.

He grabbed a passing leg and used it to hoist himself upward. The leg's owner beat at his face with a rifle butt, howling terror, but Spilokos did not feel it. With a final heave, he rolled out of the filthy water, not caring that he'd shoved the other person in. He scrabbled like a crab on his hands and knees, trying to get as far away from the water as possible. In the total blackness, he felt everything closing in on him. He stood and ran, his hands held before him like a sightless man. He ran until he slammed into a solid concrete wall and fell back in the trickle of water which coated the curved floor. Upright again by instinct, he felt the walls frantically, knowing with a sick fear that he'd run up the dead-end tunnel.

With his breath coming in great, painful gasps, he put his back to the wall and stared wide-eyed into the unfathomable dark. Gradually, the cries of terror from the main tunnel died out and silence shrieked in his ears.

Then, ever so softly, he heard a slithering, a wet, slobbering something. It was coming up the tunnel.

Tobin was out of the jeep before it stopped moving, and down the manhole before either his aides or the newsmen could reach him. Fifty feet underground, he stepped into the floodlit main junction of the city's water system and started snapping orders. "Get some fans going and get some air in this place. Corporal, stop waving that rifle around before you shoot somebody." A reporter jumped off the ladder and Tobin pointed to him. "Get that man out of here."

"But, General," the newsman protested.

"No media. Get topside."

Collaring a captain who was running past, Tobin barked, "What news on Spilokos?"

"Nothing yet, sir. We're still trying to get into that part of the tunnel. We've got the thing slowed down with a combination of salt and frequency, but it's still coming on. We're afraid that it'll split into several lumps if we let it get close to an opening in the system."

"What makes you think it hasn't already done so, Captain? I want every faucet and every toilet in a fifteen-block radius watched, and every underground pipe."

"Yes, sir."

"Hayes! Anderson! Get six flamethrowers down here pronto. See if the city's got anything that'll make large quantities of CO_2, any kind of dry-ice generators. If so, get them down here."

"Isn't that contradictory, General?"

"Yes, if you're only planning one kind of attack. But I'm not. However weird this animal is, it's still an animal, made of flesh. And flesh will burn, or freeze. One way or the other, we'll get it. Now, move!"

The officers trotted off and Tobin stomped over to three city engineers who were cowering near the wall. "How do you people get around down here? Do you have boats or something?"

One of the men stuttered negatively, and another spoke. "Crawlers, General. Carts with electric motors."

"Get me half a dozen of them and bring them here." He rounded on his adjutant. "Lennie, as soon as the crawlers and the flamethrowers get here, take three crews and one of the city men and get 'round behind that section of tunnel Spilokos is in. I'll take the other three and come in from this side."

"Sir, do you really think the mayor's still alive in there?"

Tobin looked at the major. "We will proceed on that assumption." He swung on the room. "Everybody not essential, clear the area." Turning to a technician standing nearby he added, "That means you, buddy."

The civilian shook his head. "Got a phone call for you, General."

"No phone calls. Have the command post take it."

"It's the White House."

Tobin stood as if wishing he'd already left, then took the telephone. "General Tobin here." He listened with his head down and a noncommittal look on his face. Finally, he said a crisp "yes, sir," and handed the portable phone back to the civilian.

"Lennie, it's your show. I've got to go brief the President." He looked sour. "His sense of timing sure could use some work."

The general went to the ladder and climbed energetically. At the surface, he snapped last-minute orders, jumped in his jeep, and was gone. At the airport, an officer met him with the news that Blake Wiley had been located at the Primate Center. "Good. I'll be back by nineteen hundred hours. Have him at the command post."

"He refuses to come, sir."

"Oh, he does, huh? Well you give him a message for me, okay?"

"Yes, sir."

"You tell him that Ed Tobin will personally come down there and break his arms and legs for him, *after* I kick in all his teeth. You tell him those exact words, Captain."

17

"He said that?"

"His exact words, Dr. Wiley." The captain looked patient. "General Tobin has the legal right to order you to the city, or to have you arrested if you refuse. Please, let's do this the easy way."

Wiley growled and walked petulantly around the laboratory, ignoring the two burly MPs standing by the door. He glanced speculatively at Hannah McKittrick, then turned back to the captain. "Look, another twenty-four hours here and I'll have the animal figured out. I'm more useful here than up there. Can't you understand that?"

"You'll have to take that up with General Tobin, Doctor." The captain consulted his watch. "Now, I can't hold the helicopter any longer. Please, let's go."

Wiley threw up his hands. "All right, all right. I guess

I'll have to play your damn game." He indicated Hannah. "Give me a minute to talk to my assistant and I'll be right with you."

The captain agreed and led his men out of the lab.

Wiley took Hannah by the arm and spoke quietly. "Stay here and watch him. I don't trust those guys. Don't let anybody near him until I get back. You don't have to do anything, the computer'll feed him and keep him quiet. Just see that nobody gets close to him. Got that?"

"Blake, I don't want any part of that animal."

"Hannah, just be cool. Do it for me, okay?" He watched her intently until she nodded a reluctant affirmation, then he kissed her and left.

She stood in the cluttered room, wishing she'd been firmer, wishing she was back in the city being the reporter she was supposed to be, wishing she'd never heard of Blake Wiley or the beast in the lake. What was it about that loathsome redhead that made her give in to him?

"Excuse me, Miss McKittrick." The captain stood in the laboratory doorway with a small package under his arm.

Hannah looked at the captain, then at the package he carried. "Yes?"

The captain looked uncomfortable. "I believe Dr. Wiley wants to speak with you, Ma'am. Outside."

Hannah's emotions seesawed. It would be so easy to walk out. It would all be over, and they'd all be safe, and she wouldn't have to do anything but believe the captain's lie. She shook her head. "I don't believe that, Captain."

He looked relieved. "I don't do it very well, do I?" He looked to the aquarium, then placed the bag he carried on a table and began opening it. "I guess you can stay and watch if you want to. There's nothing in my orders against it."

"You're going to kill the animal." It was a flat statement.

"Yes. That's my orders."

"Even knowing it thinks and feels?"

He regarded her with his head tilted to one side, quizzically. "I thought you were all for destroying the beast."

"I-I don't know. I'm just all against murdering something helpless."

The military man's look changed to exasperation. "Ma'am, I won't argue this with you. It's not a moral question. And even if it was, I'd follow orders."

"You'd kill it even knowing it has feelings?"

"Even if it were an orphan in a wheelchair," he avowed. And suiting the action to the words, he ripped the top off the ten-pound sack of salt and moved purposefully toward the aquarium.

"No, damn it!" Hannah flung herself on him, grabbing his arms.

They grappled, with the soldier trying to maintain a gentlemanly disdain of her attack. "Miss McKittrick, I'll have you—"

They crashed into the aquarium table as Hannah put an unladylike knee between the captain's legs. The table went over with a loud crash. Suddenly, they were both on the floor in a slosh of briny water, and a pulsing lump of matter was sliding through the wet toward them. They both screamed and tried to scramble away. The captain yelled for assistance, but the helicopter bearing Blake Wiley was taking off outside, its noise drowning out anything short of an explosion.

Hannah skidded on her hands and knees through the water, fetching up against a cabinet with a stunning jolt.

The captain, clawing desperately, got his hands on the bag of salt just as the animal clamped onto his shoe. He brought it over his head, his teeth clenched and his eyes bugged wide in fear, and down on the animal with all his weight. The bag split, filling the air with a bitter cloud of salt. An inches-thick crust of salt coated the animal, which spasmed so hard it leapt completely clear of the floor, then fell back, writhing violently.

The captain scrabbled clear, never taking his eyes off the agonized animal. He scooped Hannah's still-dazed form off the floor. "You all right?"

She shook her head. "No, I feel like mugged." She held on to the captain's arm for support, and watched with pity and disgust as the animal on the floor went through its death throes. "You feel proud of yourself, Captain?"

"Not much, no." He stood her up and took her hands off his arm. "But I did what I'm paid to do, Miss McKittrick, and that's what I came to do." He gave her a sardonic salute. "Now, if you'll excuse me, the last copter's waiting."

She nodded, still watching the animal. "Yes, you get back to your medals. I'll stay here as I said I would."

The captain turned without a word and marched out. Moments later, the second copter rose and flew away north.

Hannah walked unsteadily to the lump on the floor. It was still quivering feebly. In a very few minutes, it would be dead. . . .

Commander Haley leaned his elbows on the railing of the cutter's bridge and stared gloomily at the city a quarter mile away. The falling sun painted the concrete cliffs of the office buildings a lurid red, the effect heightened by the pall of greasy black smoke rising steadily from several points. Even at this distance, the constant clang of fire alarms could be heard.

"Sir!" The bridge com had a look of excitement on his face. "The shore reports that the monster's coming down the number three outflow pipe." He looked confused, his hand pressing his earphone more tightly against his ear.

"Wait one. . . . It's coming down pipe seven. . . . Sir, it's coming down *both* pipes."

Haley swung to the wheelhouse. "Port fifteen degrees, all ahead flank." He squinted toward the shoreline. "Looks like Tobin was right after all."

"Sir?"

"The animal's a collection of millions of smaller ones. There's no real reason for it to stay in a lump."

"You mean it's split in half?"

"If we're lucky. It could as easily split into a hundred pieces—or a thousand." He grabbed the intercom. "General quarters, all hands. General quarters."

The cutter drove for the shore, her guns trained on the outflow pipe. On a two-mile front, other cutters and several helicopters were converging on each of the pipes. When Haley's vessel was five hundred yards offshore there was a boiling in the water around the outflow pipe. Electric flashes rose bubbling from the water. "It's coming out," the commander yelled. "Open fire! Let's not give the beast sea room."

The quad forties began a jackhammer pounding. Tracers spat from the barrels and slammed into the mouth of the sewage pipe.

"Sonar, can you track?"

"It's coming out like toothpaste, sir. Moving west along the shoreline."

"Helmsman, bring us broadside. Take us in."

"Sir, there's less than two fathoms. We may ground."

"Run us in! We'll beach the bastard if we have to. Get the hydrophone in the water. Full volume at 10-Hz. Swanson, get the salt bags on the depth-charge launcher."

"It's done, sir."

"When sonar gets a fifty-yard range, launch." Haley strained up on his toes, struggling to gauge the reach of the monster.

Sixty yards away the water foamed. A huge, slimy mass

broke surface. The forty millimeter guns pounded it, blowing half-ton blobs of matter far and wide but having no effect. As if enraged, the animal swung and torpedoed for the cutter.

"Salt!" Haley commanded. The launcher thumped and five hundred-pound burlap bags of salt arched through the air and landed on the animal.

"It's going to ram us, sir!"

"Hard about, helm." Haley drew his sidearm and shot futilely into the mass.

The creature flowed around the cutter, stopping it dead in the water. Sailors ran from one gunwale to the other, trying to find an escape route. A bos'n stood on the bow, calmly and methodically lobbing hand grenades down on the animal. He was still doing so when it rose over the rail and engulfed him. As it slobbered across the deck and up the front of the bridge, Haley found himself wondering dispassionately how many thousands of one-celled animals he could destroy before he sank into the lightning-riddled interior. It looked, he thought, a little like strawberry jam. But strawberry jam did not cut off your breath, or squeeze you until your heart burst with a sound you could actually hear. Very curious. Very . . .

Tobin was briefly annoyed that he was still in battle gear, but suppressed the feeling. Maybe his appearance would impress the President with the seriousness of the situation. He stood in the marble anteroom, waiting to be summoned into the Oval Office. How many people had cooled their heels here? Or sweated through their expensive pants on the expensive chairs, wondering if Number One would buy their idea or plea or plan? For a moment, Tobin hated all civilians.

The big white doors swung silently open and the President's secretary beckoned.

Tobin marched in erectly. The President was sitting with

his sneakered feet on the polished oak desk. He was wearing an expensive business suit for a change, instead of the blue-jeans he preferred. The famous smile was gone, though, and the President was nearly buried beneath piles of reports and photographs, which he was scanning with disciplined speed. "Please sit down, General Tobin," he said courteously.

"Thank you, Mr. President." Tobin sat stiffly on a hard chair beside the desk. The Oval Office was smaller than he'd imagined it to be.

"Edward, isn't it, General?"

"Yes, sir."

"What do people call you?"

"Ed, sir."

The President flashed the famous smile. Tobin noted that it was genuine. "General Walsh says you're known as 'Iron Balls' in the Pentagon."

Tobin flushed in embarrassment, then laughed, knowing that the President was trying to put him at ease and wondering why. "I understand that's correct, Mr. President."

"You should hear what the Joint Chiefs call me— behind my back, of course."

"Yes, sir. I know."

The President stood and stretched tiredly. "Ed, you're a man capable of taking the long view. Is that true?"

"In what way, sir?"

"Do you remember Coventry, during the Second War? Rather, do you remember Churchill's connection with the city?"

Tobin edged forward on his chair, frowning deeply. "Yes," he said cautiously.

"Churchill knew the Germans were going to bomb Coventry. But he could not warn the people because the Germans would then know that their code had been broken. So he let them bomb the city, killing thousands."

The President was looking into his wastebasket, as if he'd lost something there, or as if wishing to avoid looking at Tobin. "Churchill did not know whether owning the secret of the German code would shorten the war. He didn't even know if it would save any lives. But he thought or hoped so, and he risked it. He allowed thousands of people to die, in the hope that he could save many thousands more."

"Sir, I'm not sure I like where you're headed."

The President leaned on the sill of his picture window and smiled genially at Tobin. "Neither do I, Ed, but I've got to go there anyway. You can't stop the animal, can you?"

"Sir, given sufficient manpower and sufficient time, I can stop anything. Fire will stop it. Maybe cold. We know it doesn't like salt. . . . " Tobin stopped and returned his commander-in-chief's gaze. "No, sir. We can't. It's too mobile, it lives in the water, and it can get into places we can't."

"And how long do you think it will be before some part of the animal slips through your defenses? Perhaps gets into a river system? How long before it eludes the Coast Guard and escapes into the lake again? There are thirty million people living on the shores of the lake."

Tobin shook his head, unconsciously kneading his hands into fists. "Maybe twenty hours, maybe less."

"That is my estimate, General. Just before you came, I had a report that it has segmented itself and part of it sallied into the lake and attacked our ships there. The district commander was killed."

"Haley?"

"Yes. His cutter and a low-flying helicopter were destroyed about twenty minutes ago. For the moment, they're holding it at bay with a net of salt and acid, but both materials disperse rapidly and the supply cannot be replenished quickly enough."

Tobin stood and drew a deep breath. "Then . . . ?"

The President said the grim words. "You have until tomorrow morning, General Tobin. If the animal is not destroyed by nine-thirty, the Air Force will drop a nuclear device on the city and the nearby area of the lake."

Part Three

THE STARS

18

The chopper came in from the southeast, keeping above the heavy smoke that now blanketed a good portion of the county. The pilot leaned toward Tobin and indicated the ground. "Perimeter was finished an hour ago, sir," he said, yelling over the *thup/thup/thup* of the engine. "Seems to be holding."

Tobin nodded but did not speak. The perimeter he'd ordered before he left—a fifty-yard-wide barrenness, bulldozed through everything in its path—had stemmed the flow of escaping cars, whose occupants might have inadvertently spread the monster to other areas. Now all cars had to be thoroughly inspected at one of fifteen checkpoints.

"Put you down at the command post, sir?"

"Yes. Then stand by to ferry personnel out if needed."

The pilot looked speculatively at Tobin. "Is it true, sir? They're going to bomb?"

"If you spread that rumor, Lieutenant, I will have you busted to private."

"Yes, sir," the pilot answered crisply. So it *was* true!

The chopper landed and Tobin hopped out, automatically putting on his calm, disciplined command face. The truth would get around very quickly, and he'd need all the charisma he could muster to keep his people in line. Damn that beast to hell.

He squared up and marched into the gymnasium. "Corporal, get me the adjutant."

"I'm here, General," the major declared, appearing at Tobin's side. He was in shirt sleeves with his tie loosened.

"Lennie, what's the status on Spilokos?"

"Unknown. We got through to the dead-end tunnel by frying off a big chunk of the animal, but Spilokos wasn't there. We don't know if he got out somehow, or got killed. There were no remains in the part of the animal we got. By the way, the thing seems to be developing a tolerance for electricity. If you don't jolt it quick and heavy, it seems to thrive on the juice."

"That's what Nesselroth predicted. Keep a team looking for the mayor and anybody else down there. Did Wiley get up here yet?"

"Captain Herzog brought him in. He's over there, fuming."

"The one with the beard?"

"Yes, sir, the redhead."

"Send him over as soon as I finish talking to Herzog. And you stick around, too."

Tobin went into his office, where he was joined by Captain Herzog. They spoke quietly for a few moments, with the general nodding satisfaction, then Herzog saluted and left. Wiley came in like a boxer answering the bell. Tobin was ready for him. He put on a disarming smile and extended his hand. "Dr. Wiley! Thank God you're here; we really need you."

"The hell you do," Wiley said, ignoring Tobin's hand. "You know as well as I do that I should be down at the Primate Center. You know the line I'm following, and you know it's the only thing that will work. I demand that you let me go back to my research."

Tobin retrieved his hand without appearing to notice Wiley's rudeness. "Let me ask you a question, Doctor. You are augmenting the animal's intelligence, is that right?"

"No, it's not. I'm educating him, trying to find out how his intelligence functions. I've been running him through the programs the center uses to determine animal intelligence, then training him to use his mental faculties."

Tobin nodded, managing to look tired and domineering at the same time. "That's commendable, Doctor. 'Know the enemy' is an axiom of military command. But I can't help wondering *why* you are learning the animal's thinking processes. The beast we've got here doesn't think —not the way your trained specimen does. It responds like any other dumb animal, or at best like a clever idiot. Is that essentially correct?"

Wiley's look was suspicious, but he agreed. "Essentially."

"Then what you're doing is studying how to win philosophic arguments with a moron, isn't it?"

Wiley's fists bunched. "That's cute, General. The entire city is being threatened and you're playing debate-team semantic games. No wonder we lost Vietnam."

Tobin reddened in turn, but showed no other sign of annoyance. "I am happy to see that you've noticed the plight of the city, Dr. Wiley." He stepped around the scientist and gestured across the gymnasium. "Over there, in the locker room, you'll find a notebook which Dr.

Nesselroth left for you. Please get it and go down to the morgue."

"Listen, Tobin, you're not going to sidestep the issue."

Tobin held up an admonitory hand. "Wiley, I appreciate what you were doing downstate. I even agree that it's the correct approach—from the scientific viewpoint. But the crux of the matter *right now* is the city." He came up to the scientist and looked down at him almost pleadingly. "Your specimen's safe downstate. Let's kill the animal here before it kills all of us. Please, Doctor, get down to the morgue and help Nesselroth."

Wiley stood there, feeling frustrated but unable to do anything about it. He realized he'd been snookered, and realized also that Tobin was right, at least from his own point of view. He cleared his throat. "Okay, General. I'll go get in the way at the morgue. You got the shotgun. But don't think this is the end of it."

Tobin had already turned away and was back at his papers. "Let's just try to keep it from being the end of the city, Doctor." He looked up and smiled quickly. "I don't particularly care what you think of me, Wiley, and I assure you I don't think much of you. But you whip this animal for me and I'll kiss your coattail on Main Street."

"I'll whip it. And I'll find something else for you to kiss."

"I'm sure you will." He shuffled his papers until Wiley had disappeared across the gymnasium, then crumpled a set of notes into a hard ball and flung it into a corner. "Overbearing little creep," he spat. He took a deep breath, shook himself, and consulted his watch. Ten o'clock. Eleven hours to do it or . . . die.

"You wanted me, Chief?"

"Oh, yes, Lennie. Come in. What's the status of the perimeter?"

"We're holding. We've got the checkpoints set up and are funneling through about ten thousand people an hour."

"Any trouble?"

"Mostly from people with fish. They don't like to see their pets electrocuted. But we did find a hunk of the beast in one guy's thermos bottle."

"Did you trace it back?"

"Yes, sir. West side. We quarantined the whole block and fried all the water lines."

Tobin nodded abstractedly. "Lennie, pull every man we've got out of the city and put them on the perimeter. Open up as many checkpoints as we have electric generators. Get the people out."

The major's face was professionally blank. "How long have we got, Ed?"

Tobin looked, for the first time, defeated. "Until nine-thirty tomorrow morning."

"Then . . . ?"

"Yes."

The major shuddered. "We can't get them all out. We can't even get most of them out. There'll be a half million people left. And when I pull the troops to put them on the perimeter, the city will go crazy. Mobs will be trying to get out in a massive panic."

"Yes."

The major looked at his shoes, then saluted slowly. "Very well, sir."

"Lennie, I want every media person still in the city conscripted and brought here. We've got to keep word of the bomb from getting out."

"Yes, sir."

"Okay, let's get on with it."

Tobin walked slowly out into the gymnasium, an island in the swirl of soldiers and civilians who were going busily about their tasks as if this were another exercise. The full weight of five hundred thousand lives that would be obliterated soon if he couldn't stop the beast settled on him. The terrible ticking of the clock pressed in.

There was a kind of relief in knowing that if worst came to worst and the bomb brought its all-consuming fire, Ed Tobin would go to the darkness with it, and not have to face the history books as the man who failed to win the greatest battle of all time.

"We urge you again," Wintergreen said, facing the camera, "to remain calm, to follow the instructions of the military and civil defense personnel, and above all to do nothing which might contribute to the present emergency. Please remain in your homes until it is time for the evacuation of your area."

"That's it, Jim."

Wintergreen's eyebrows lifted questioningly. "Power's still on, isn't it?"

"Not at the transmitter. Guess all the juice is going to fight the monster. We're off the air, boss."

Wintergreen sighed and got up.

"I think we'd better get while we can," the cameraman said. "For all we know, the monster will be coming up the sink."

Wintergreen fished a full bottle of liquor from his desk drawer, uncapped it, and sat down. "You go, m'boy. I believe I'll just sit here a while."

"Don't be a hero, Jim. It's stupid."

"No heroics intended. I'm fifty-three, fat, and have fallen arches. No monster would want me."

"Boss . . . "

"Scram, lad. That's an order from numero uno."

The cameraman shook his head, then turned and sped out the rear exit.

Wintergreen raised the bottle, as he listened to the shrieks of the mob outside. My God, he mused, you'd think the world was coming to an end.

Somewhere in the building, a telephone rang.

Wintergreen weighed the possibilities. A short? An aural

illusion? The phones had gone dead an hour earlier. The newsman's instinct won out and he went to look for the operable instrument. He went down to the first floor where a huge pile of desks, UPI readers and filing cabinets was jammed against the big front doors.

The phone was a field unit normally carried by one of the reporters. Wintergreen picked it up. "Horatio at the bridge," he answered lightly. "Ten o'clock and all's hell."

The voice on the other end was patching through from a sister station in Virginia. A rumor had been heard from a helicopter pilot.

"What sort of rumor, m'lad? Famine in China? Scandal in the upper echelons? Fear and loathing in Miami?"

Wintergreen paled as he listened. He shook his head. "No, I hadn't heard that. Can you get through to Tobin? I appear to be out of commission here."

No, the caller couldn't. Media people were being rounded up all over the country and sat on. "That sounds like it's true, then, doesn't it?"

"Yes, it does."

"What are you going to do, Jim?"

Wintergreen took a slow, thoughtful swallow from his bottle and replaced the receiver without answering. He went back upstairs and found a tape recorder. He took another quick pull at the bottle and thumbed the recorder on. "Good evening, ladies and gentlemen. This is James Wintergreen, live and untarnished, bringing you the end of the world—mine, at least—"

The personnel carrier ground to a halt on the sidewalk in front of the morgue. Its bay opened and Wiley hopped out. He went inside, past two policemen and another soldier guarding the door. "Nesselroth?"

"Down that way, buddy. Watch yourself, though; that fuckin' monster's loose in the autopsy room."

"You serious?"

"Killed one o'them doctors."

"Thanks, I'll be careful." Serves them right, the idiots. Wouldn't listen to *him*, no. But best be calm. Saul was the last chance, the last hope. If he couldn't convince him . . .

Nesselroth looked haggard and guilty when Wiley found him. He was sitting on a packing crate in the hallway outside the autopsy room, holding an untouched cup of cold coffee and watching the fire-blackened autopsy room door as if expecting it to leap for his throat momentarily. Several other technicians and soldiers were there.

Wiley came up, looked the situation over, and sat beside the doctor. "Who'd it get?"

"Delaney. Choked him, we think, got right down in his own esophagus." Nesselroth made small, twitchy motions, like a man on the edge of breaking into fragments. "It was in the orange juice, Blake, in a refrigerator. I can't figure how it got there."

"One cell, Saul, on somebody's hand or glove. That's all it takes." Wiley felt a cold, deliberate elation building inside him. "I was right," he said bluntly.

Saul nodded. "Yes. I just couldn't believe it. It learns so *fast*. Grows so fast. It's like a nightmare."

Wiley studied the door. "It tried to come out?"

"No. After we took Delaney's body out, we went back to kill it. When we opened the door it was as big as a king-size mattress and was coming across the floor at us. One of the soldiers jumped at it with a flamethrower and shut the door behind him. We . . . we heard him for some time. Then there was fire. Then the automatic sprinklers went on."

"Giving the animal more water."

"Yes. When the water started seeping under the door, we burned it." He turned feverish eyes on the scientist. "How are we going to stop it, Blake? What can we do?"

Wiley took his elbow, kneading it. "Help me get back to the Primate Center, Saul. You come, too. Let that asshole Tobin strut around and play hero. Let's get down there where my specimen is."

Nesselroth shook his head sadly.

"Saul, it's the *only* way, the only chance we've got. If we leave this wild animal wild, it will cause its own destruction and ours, too. We've *got* to train my specimen, teach it, and get it up here to teach its big brother."

"Wiley—"

"Don't be a fool, Saul. We can program my specimen's education, teach it what we want it to know. We can convince it that it must be docile, captive. It *is* an idiot right now, but if we don't give it the input we *want* it to have, pretty soon it'll be smart enough to get its own. And then we're really up the creek, maybe for good."

Nesselroth's look of guilt deepened. "I'm sorry, Blake, but it isn't possible. Tobin had your specimen killed, right after you left."

Wiley sat very still for a while. "No," he said, his voice strained and carefully quiet. "That can't be. I left Hannah in charge of him, and she wouldn't let them murder him."

Nesselroth stared into his cold coffee. "She did, Blake. Tobin didn't want his name connected with it, just in case we win."

After a long while, Wiley stood up, not really focusing on anything. "Well, he doesn't have to worry about that contingency now. We've already lost."

19

Hannah staggered out of the ditch and stared back down the highway, where her Fiat was already disappearing, seven people inside it, and another five or six piled on the hood and top. It was being driven half off the road because the press of fleeing refugees was too solid to drive through.

She brushed at her hair—now sticky with blood from the cut on her scalp—and directed a half-hearted malediction at the people who'd taken her car, then turned and trudged against the stream of escapees, her face reddened by the glow of the burning city ahead. She clutched her shoulder bag with a fierce determination.

There was an *ooogah-ooogah* behind her, causing her to jump. She turned with a sinking feeling. A motorcycle eased up, its extended front end sliding suggestively between her legs. A small man with a ring in his ear and hooded eyes regarded her laconically. "Wrong," he said. "The exit's back that way, lady." He had a bayonet stuck through his belt and a submachine gun slung over his shoulder.

"N-no," Hannah pleaded, backing away. "Please. There're lots of girls. I've got to get back into the city."

The man laughed and gunned up beside her. "Figured that. Couldn't get through the crowd in time to stop the bozos from takin' your car, so I thought I'd give you a lift." As her face changed, he grinned. "Yeah, lady, I'm th' good guys. Get on."

Hannah climbed on the bike behind him, feeling a mixture of relief and apprehension. "You're, uh, going to the city, too?"

"Been in and out six times since noon, bringin' out kids that ain't got anybody t'watch out for 'em."

"That's very . . . decent of you."

He shrugged, gunning the bike down into the ditch and out into a field. "Yeah, maybe. Who knows; they might be mine."

He rode with great speed and greater expertise, weaving though the night and crowds and wrecks until the perimeter strip came in sight. Hannah leaned forward and yelled in his ear. "Will they let you in with this gun?"

"They ain't lookin' this way, lady. Hold on."

Hannah was slammed back against the sissy bar as the front end came off the ground. The night blurred, the engine screamed, and the motorcycle bent into the ditch and leapt out the other side. She had an instant's vision of white, upturned faces and mouths opened in surprise, and realized that they were sailing right over the checkpoint, diagonally. Then the machine hit with a jar that compressed her spine and snapped her teeth together, and they were off through flame-lit back streets at seventy miles an hour. As if far off, she heard the biker singing at the top of his voice.

He asked her where to and she told him channel five. Twice, groups of ugly people blocked the streets, but took a look at the black motorcycle and its rider and parted to let them pass. When they reached the empty station, he stopped and sat with the engine idling. "You sure you want off here, lady? Looks like the party's over."

She climbed awkwardly off the bike. "Yes. Yes, thank you. I'll make it okay."

He gave her his hand. "Name's Conglon. If we're all here next week, I'll come say hello."

She shook his hand warmly. "Yes, please do that. And thank you again."

He reached down and pulled a pistol from his boot. "Here. Little piece of insurance."

"I don't know how to use one of those."

He put it in her hand. "You know that, and I know it, but maybe the guy who comes after you don't." He winked, gunned the bike, and was gone up the dark street.

Hannah turned away slowly, and entered the station building. Jim would have left her a note, or directions, or something. At least, she hoped so.

But a thorough check of the building proved her wrong. With Wintergreen gone, she was at a loss. How would she get to Wiley? She wished she'd asked the biker to take her to Tobin. Not that he'd help her, but at least she'd be safe there while she tried to get through to Wiley.

There was a stealthy noise in the darkness. She froze in terror. Then, remembering the pistol, she crawled behind a desk and stuck it over the top, shakily. "All right, t-that's far enough!"

The noise stopped. A slurred male voice called. "Y'wouldn't really shoot, would ya? Pretty little piece like you, heh?" A large, dim form stood across the room and lumbered toward her. "C'mon, baby. Let's you an' me—"

She closed her eyes and fired into the air twice. There

was a curse, audible through the ringing in her ears, and the form stumbled off through the building at a shambling run.

Hannah got up from behind the desk, feeling herself somewhere between tears and savage elation. Then she saw the hand protruding from behind the desk that had hidden the would-be assailant. The hand belonged to James Wintergreen, she saw as she came up. But it wasn't *her* Wintergreen. Not this one, for this one had an enormous red patch on its chest, and eyes that stared sightlessly at the ceiling. Hannah found herself sitting on the floor, crying and cradling the already-cold head against her lap.

It was some time before she saw the tape recorder, its microphone still clutched in Wintergreen's hand and the machine still humming. Even in her sorrow, the news hawk in her made her thumb the tape to rewind and then to replay. Her tears dried as she listened to Wintergreen's slightly drunken, slightly hysterical recording. Her face became a mask of disbelief and horror. "They *wouldn't*," she whispered. "Not the bomb!" But she knew they would, and in less than ten hours, too.

Drawing Wintergreen's stained jacket tenderly over his head and vowing a silent retribution, she took the tape recorder and pistol and made her way back to the street. Several buildings were burning luridly, and three blocks away a group of people scuttled furtively between buildings, but at the moment it didn't look too dangerous. If she could just get to a police or army unit . . .

A car rounded the corner a block away and came cautiously down the street toward Hannah. Hannah weighed the odds, then stepped in front of the auto with her pistol extended. "Stop!"

The car swerved around her, drove several feet, then screeched to a halt and backed up. Gloria Wiley stuck her head out the driver's window. "Well, well. Taken up mugging, deary?"

Hannah let the pistol dangle foolishly. "What are *you* doing here?"

"I'm on my way out of town, like everybody else with good sense. This is the most direct route between the house and the checkpoint." She looked Hannah up and down with mock concern. "Been spending a lot of time on your back, darling?"

Hannah's smile was icy. "I'm beginning to understand why Blake traded you in on a newer model."

"Listen, you bitch—"

"You listen," Hannah said, opening the car's back door and getting in. "We're going to drive around until we find an escort to wherever Blake is."

"Like hell! *You're* getting out of this car before I spoil all the work the plastic surgeons did on that skijump you're using for a nose."

"Sticks and stones will break my bones, but this pistol will blow your head off, Mrs. Wiley. Now, start driving."

Wiley paced the halls of the morgue, his face a sufficient deterrent to conversation. He stopped now and then to kick at the floor or to pound his fist against the wall.

"That's a pretty good imitation of a temper tantrum," Nesselroth said, coming up with a wilted sandwich. "Here, eat."

Wiley took the sandwich but did not eat it. "I wish I'd listened to you, Saul. I wish you'd listened to me. I wish we'd paid more attention to Tobin's moves. He knew you were locked out of your own lab, didn't he? He sent me here, knowing he'd killed my specimen, just to neutralize both of us."

"It looks that way."

Wiley beat his head against his palms. "Damn. We've been a pair of prime asses. Me so busy touting myself I couldn't see anything past my nose, and you so busy organizing you couldn't even see that far. And Tobin . . . . " He growled and tossed his sandwich in a wastebasket.

Nesselroth watched the younger man. "Well, now that we've flogged ourselves, why don't we take another crack at the beastie?"

Wiley looked tempted, then rueful. "It's no good, Saul. It'd take days to retrain a specimen, and by that time our buddy in the sewer will be in control. We'll be goners."

"We're goners already," came another voice.

"Gloria," Wiley exclaimed in disgust. "I should have known you'd show up. Somehow you always do, like a vulture. How did you get here anyway?"

"I was forced by your charming lady friend and her charming little pistol. And I've had enough of—"

"Hannah? She's here?" Wiley peered over his wife's shoulders, brushed past her, and trotted down the corridor toward the front of the building.

Gloria's face contorted. She took a step down the corridor. "That's right, run after her, you bastard. You deserve each other."

Saul put a hand on her shoulder. "Mrs. Wiley, what were you saying about our already being goners?"

Wiley found Hannah sprawled on a bench, the pistol still hanging from her fingers like an afterthought and her shoulder bag propped beneath her as if it were a pillow. She smiled weakly as Wiley came up and squatted in front of her. "Just gave out, Blake. Couldn't make the last few yards. Guess I'll never make halfback."

Wiley shook his head, stroking her knee. "That's okay." He worked at flashing her a reasonable facsimile of a calm expression. "I, ah, know they killed my specimen."

She giggled, an incongruous sound coming from her

tired face. "In English, you're saying 'why'd you let them do it?' "

"I know you did all you could."

"Too bad it failed, though."

"Goddammit, Hannah! I'm trying to be reasonable. I'm giving you the benefit of the doubt. I am acting adult about it in *spite* of the fact that you let the bastards murder the last chance we had. So get off my back, huh."

Hannah pushed herself upright on the bench, laying the pistol down with a grimace of dislike. She fished in her shoulder bag and brought out a small, white jar. "Do you think the animal could eat cold cream?"

Wiley's eyebrows went up and his jaw went down. "Hannah, did you . . . ?"

"I don't know if it was still alive when I got it and scraped the salt off, and I don't know if it's alive now. But there's a piece the size of a birth control pill there in the jar."

Wiley grabbed the jar, bouncing up on his toes. "That's it! There's still a chance. We . . . " He frowned and looked at Hannah closely. "How did you save this piece? How did you get it in the jar?"

She looked at the floor and shuddered. "On my finger," she said quietly. She held up a raw, blistered forefinger.

Wiley stood stock still for some time, then drew a long breath. "I think that's the bravest thing I've ever seen or heard of. And when this is all over, I'm going to apologize to you for a lot of things."

"It's all over now, Blake."

"No it's not," he said, becoming enthusiastic again. "In fact, if I can get to a couple of things fast enough. . . . " He was off down the corridor, clutching the jar and looking somehow as if he were scribbling on a nonexistent pad. Hannah was, for the moment, already forgotten.

He was almost running as he came into the hall. He bowled past Gloria, ignoring her hot outburst, and waved the jar at Nesselroth. "Saul, where can we get a computer? The university?"

"No good. The power's off in that part of the city."

"Mmmm. How 'bout County General? Don't they have one of those little Sperry Rands over there? I know they've got their own power."

"Yes, but—"

"Good. They'll have a computer tech, too. Let's get packed up here and go commandeer that computer. Hannah saved a piece of my specimen, and we just might be able to pick up where I left off this morning." He was pacing, once more arrogantly in command. " 'Course, we'll need another and larger chunk. Maybe we can sucker him under the autopsy room door again? Freeze whatever he sticks under the door, and break off a couple of pounds." Wiley became aware that no one was moving or talking. He stopped and faced them. "What is it?"

Gloria sniffed in his direction. "Your heroics are too late this time, big shot."

Wiley looked from her to the aides to Nesselroth. "Saul?"

The coroner wiped his glasses. "Wintergreen's dead, Blake. Hannah found a tape recorder with the body. It appears that the President is going to drop an atomic bomb on us at nine-thirty tomorrow morning unless we stop the beast."

Wiley deflated, but looked determined. "All right," he said quietly. "We'd better get on it then."

20

"Okay, give it a shove," the soldier said. "And watch out; that mother's fast."

Wiley nodded. "Yeah, I know. Boy, do I know." Wiley was on his knees about four feet from the autopsy room door, holding two broomsticks wired together. A piece of bacon was lashed to the forward end of the construction. "Here we go," Wiley said. He pushed the bacon under the bottom edge of the door. The two soldiers with the liquid oxygen bottles were braced against the wall on either side of the door, their eyes on the crack beneath. Everyone else was farther down the corridor.

Wiley poked and jiggled with the broomsticks. "I don't think—wait. I've got a nibble. At least he's still alive in there." He hunched over the broomstick and began easing it out. "Now don't let too much of him show before you—"

The broomsticks were yanked from his hands with blistering speed. Caught off balance, Wiley fell forward against the door. Someone shouted in fear, and one of the men with the lox pressed his nozzle, spraying Wiley's shoulder and his own legs with numbing liquid. In the cloud of condensation filling the corridor, everyone scrambled away from the door, certain that death would come oozing from under it. But nothing happened. As Wiley and the soldier were massaged back to functionality, Nesselroth grimaced at the door. "Do you really have to have a bigger piece, Blake? It doesn't look like he's going to come out."

"Yes, I do. I need at least two pounds to give me a large enough cell count. You can't make a flea into Einstein—or a flea-sized brain into a reasoning brain." He went forward, rotating his arm at the shoulder to restore circulation. "If he won't come to us, I'll go to him."

There were protesting noises, most of them fearful. Nesselroth stepped forward. "You're too valuable to risk, Blake."

He stepped quickly to the door and threw it open. "C'mon, you overgrown pile of snot! Nobody runs me out of my own autopsy room and gets away with it."

The dimness in the autopsy room heaved and the animal slobbered forward like a nacreous avalanche. Wiley grabbed the back of Nesselroth's shirt and yanked hard. "Hit him with the lox, quick!"

The startled soldiers jumped forward and poured a solid wall of lox through the doorway. In the fog, Wiley could be seen struggling with something. He lurched backward, coughing and retching, his beard and eyebrows frosted with frozen moisture. "Shut the fuckin' door!" In his flash-burned hand he held the broomsticks, and there was a football-sized lump on the end of them.

Nesselroth caught him as he fell. The coroner barked

at an aide. "Get two buckets of water and some towels. Hot coffee. Get a blanket."

"Two buckets?"

"Two, you moron. One for the animal, one for Wiley's hands. Move!"

Ten minutes later, with Wiley swathed in blankets and bandages, they stood looking down into the bucket where their captive specimen thrashed, kept at bay by blasts from the lox bottles. "Christ," one of the soldiers said. "That thing's vicious. It doesn't seem to be afraid of anything."

"It is," Wiley said, "and it's trying to survive." He indicated his incapacitated hands and stuck out his hip. "Would you get the jar that's in my pocket?"

The soldier fished it out, saw what it was, handed it to Nesselroth, and then wiped his hands on his pants. "You been walking around with that thing, sir?"

Nesselroth looked to Wiley with raised eyebrows. "This the piece McKittrick saved?"

"Yes. We're about to find out if my theory works. Open the jar and dump him in the bucket."

Nesselroth speculated. "Then, if you're right, we'll have instantaneous education. We'll have a 'brain' in that lump in the bucket?"

"That's the theory. Synapsoid neural conjunctions sharing the experiences of both specimens."

"Blake, that thing in the bucket is big enough to kill a few of us before we get it, if it escapes. The only reason we're keeping it in now is that it keeps trying the same lunge. What happens if it turns cunning?"

"Two things. First, we'll know I'm right, and second, we'll have to be more cunning. Now, put the little piece in the bucket."

The people in the room backed away, except for Wiley and Nesselroth. The coroner gingerly opened the top of the cosmetics jar and dumped its contents. The lump in the bucket reacted violently, surrounding the small piece as if to consume it. Then it went rigid, the lightning pulses in its interior becoming more vivid. After a heartbeat, there was relaxation. The animal became fluid and rose to the surface of the water.

"Wait," Wiley commanded, halting the soldier who was about to freeze the animal. "Wait."

The creature sent up a pseudopod and delicately felt around the rim of the bucket. Satisfied, it withdrew the extrusion and began moving lazily around in a circle.

Wiley squatted down, his face tight. He unwrapped the bandages and slowly placed his left hand on the rim of the bucket. He tapped with his finger. The creature stopped. A thin tentacle of being came across the water and touched Wiley's finger. There was a collective gasp in the room. Wiley tapped the bucket again, twice, with his right hand. The tentacle withdrew. He stood up and nodded satisfaction. "Good. It worked."

Gloria rubbed her eyes. "Am I hallucinating, or do you have that thing trained?"

"No, I don't. But I've got it conditioned." He grinned suddenly. "Whatever his big brother thinks of humanity, I've got this little fellow convinced that *I'm* the baddest sonofabitch in the universe. I've been alternately educating him and programming him to obey me. I don't know if he can recognize me personally—which is probably why Hannah got away with touching him—but he recognizes a command series I developed; taps in sequence, or certain electrical impulses, or even sound."

Nesselroth was excited. "So *that's* what you're up to!"

"Sure. There's no real way we can be certain of controlling his intelligence—especially when we mate him with the parent body. But we might stand a chance of conditioning him to obey a command long enough to get him into a captive situation."

"Then there wasn't anything behind your story about teaching him so that he could outsmart the wild part?".

"Oh, yes! That's imperative. No matter how well conditioned we make this specimen, remember that the wild part's been out there learning, too. And in a hell of a lot more brutal environment. We've got to make him, there in the bucket, intellectually powerful enough to be the dominant personality when the two animals merge. Otherwise we get just what you've all been afraid of—an intelligent monster."

Gloria, curious in spite of her wounded pride and anger, spoke. "So you're going to do a balancing act, try to keep the conditioning a step ahead of the education?"

"That's what we're going to try, yes." He glanced around the room. "Did Hannah leave?"

"No," one of the soldiers said. "She's asleep in the lobby."

"See if she wants to come with us. She damn sure deserves to be in on this. Saul, did you get us clearance to move to the hospital?"

"I couldn't get through to anybody."

"Then the hell with them all. We'll go anyway." He regarded the two soldiers. "Are you boys our watchdogs, or just here to guard the building?"

The younger of the two smiled. "We were ordered to prevent insurrection or interference with your work, sir. Nobody said anything about where you worked."

"Thank you. We'll sneak out when you're not looking."

"Like hell—begging your pardon. I wouldn't miss this for nothing!"

It took less than ten minutes to get everyone and everything together, and less than five to get out a side door and commandeer a passing squad car and an abandoned delivery van.

The lifter opens like a scissors, pushing its stubby,

cylindrical load up into the rectangular hole. The operator sits on a tractor-type saddle at the rear of the lifter. He wears earphones and a slim throat mike. "Ah, two-zero-zero left, please." His voice is laconic. "That's good. I read contact on the forward grapplers."

"I check that," answers an equally laconic voice—the onboard tech sergeant. "Rear grapplers in place and . . . contact."

"Retracting lifter."

"Clear. Cockpit?"

A third voice enters the earphones. "I have confirm on grapple. Seat the umbilicals, please."

"Umbilicals seated."

"Confirm. Please run final checks."

"Roger, cockpit. Premature detonation alarm."

"Confirm."

"Manual override circuit breaker."

"Confirm."

"Preselect code phase circuit."

"Confirm."

"Internal guidance, infrared override, sonic selection interferometer."

"Confirm. Testing failsafe circuit light."

"Ah, confirm, cockpit. I have a light."

"Thank you. Commander assumes—"

"Wait one, cockpit."

"Problem?"

"No, sir. Just give me a minute, okay?" The sergeant scoots around in the cramped space until he is near the front of the cylinder. He takes a grease pencil out of his jumper pocket and meticulously marks the cylinder wall. Then he crawls back to the short ladder reaching down from the belly of the plane. "All clear here, cockpit."

"Thank you again. Commander assumes control. Breaking contact."

"Ground out." The sergeant goes down the ladder and removes it.

In the cockpit, the pilot thumbs the frequency transmitter on his radio. "Redbird control, this is Redbird. Loading sequence confirmed at oh-ten-fourteen hours. Nuclear device is secured aboard."

"Roger, Redbird. Begin arming sequence."

Beneath the bomber, the sergeant takes a last look at the cylinder and walks away. On its nose, the sergeant has drawn a crude cross and the words, *God have mercy.*

21

"Just what the hell do you people think you're doing?"

Nesselroth stood in front of the group as though protecting them. Behind him, Wiley held the bucket and Gloria held a lox bottle, just in case. Hannah McKittrick stood with the aides and the soldiers. The last of Nesselroth's technicians were coming through the hospital entrance.

Nesselroth made calming motions at the bloodshot-eyed and blood-stained surgeon standing belligerently in the lobby. "We're working on a problem concerning the animal in the lake, Doctor. We've got to use your computer. We have top priority from General Tobin."

"I don't care if you've got a signed statement from General Grant, this is a hospital. *My* hospital. We've got five hundred people dying here from smoke poisoning and half my doctors out on their feet. Now you get your mob *out* of here."

Wiley stepped around Nesselroth and confronted the surgeon. "I'm sorry, but we need your facilities. We've got official sanction, and it can be backed up with force if it comes to that. We're also running out of time to argue. So how about you getting back to your surgery and we'll stay out of your hair."

The doctor swayed with fatigue. "Damn the lot of you. That computer eats electricity. If there's too much of a drain on our generators—any kind of interference with the operating theater—I'll come down here and shut off your juice."

"Thank you." Wiley swept the group toward the computer. "Let's get to it." He signaled one of Nesselroth's men. "Andy, take these readouts from the Primate Center and write me a program that progresses from where they leave off. Get it in the box as soon as you can. Hannah, do you remember how we had the tank set up?"

"I think so."

"Then do it again—use that big plastic wastebasket. Soldier, find a water tap and start bringing water; not too cold. Saul—"

"I'm ahead of you. Simple salts, trace iodine, like that."

"Right. Andy, does the box have a keyboard or a screen?"

"Both. Inputs via keyboard but reads out both ways."

"Nice, very nice. Set me up about five K's worth of binary and about a K of nand-gate response keys. We're going complex."

"You think the animal can handle it?"

"He'll have to. So will we."

By one-thirty they had a semblance of a lab set up. The animal was swimming in a nutrient bath, the computer was keyed and programmed, and the input/output system was on standby.

Wiley took control of the keyboard. "All right, let's run the first of the Primate Center tapes."

Gloria looked perplexed. "Would you mind explaining what you're doing for the benefit of us non-scientific types?"

"Not at all," Wiley replied, a touch of showman's pride in his voice. "I'll give you a one-minute tour. We start off with 'yes-no' stimulus training. It's a way of seeing if a living thing has any intelligence at all, and if it can be taught." He typed an instruction sequence for the computer. In the wastebasket aquarium, the animal flinched rhythmically.

"This boy's smart. Look at the readout screen; he's already a couple of steps ahead of us."

"What do you mean?" Gloria asked.

Nesselroth answered. "Blake's taught the animal to shut off a high voltage charge by responding with a specific pre-set code. What are you using for language, Blake?"

"Since he generates his own electricity, I've taught him frequency and duration control. A short, low-frequency burst is 'yes,' a long one is 'no.' He's also learned—see, there he goes already—to do some sort of modulation I don't recognize. You see how he's run through the first set of tests already? And look now—he's just ticking off the responses to the advanced tests. Which ones are those, Hannah?"

"Program nine, I think."

"A chimp," Wiley continued, "takes about a year to master those nine tests, and maybe a steady three years' training before it can reason sufficiently to say 'and so forth,' like this guy."

"And so forth?" This from Gloria.

"Yeah. By running through the answers before I give him the questions, he's saying that he understands what we're doing, that he remembers the answers, and that we should get on with it."

"My God, that sounds like a very high order of intelligence."

"I'm still afraid to speculate on just how high." Wiley punched a clear code into the computer. "I'm going to try something that would have been impossible an hour ago but just might work now. Hannah, where's the tape we made just before the thugs descended on us?"

"Here."

"Andy?"

"I'm already pulling the old one, Dr. Wiley."

"Thanks." Wiley coded the keyboard and the computer began sending earnest messages down the wires into the aquarium. Wiley watched the tank and continued to speak, but abstractedly. "By four or five, a human child has acquired all the intellectual tools he'll use in becoming educated. He can reason, understand abstraction, and differentiate between subjective and objective events." He rose out of his chair slightly, craning his neck to see into the tank, where the animal was quivering quietly. "A kid takes five years to reach that point. A chimp seven or eight. This guy . . . who knows? He's a sponge for brain power. Seems to soak it up as fast as you can feed it to him. So we're dynamiting his brain—if you can say he's got a brain. We're feeding him tests and information at hyperspeed. Listen." He flipped a switch and the room was filled with a high-pitched squeal. Yelling over the noise, Wiley indicated the computer. "That's step-by-step language instruction geared up to a hundred times normal."

"You mean, 'see Spot run'?"

"Sort of, only it's in yes-no sequences on a five-digit base. Slowed down, it would sound like Morse code to you."

"How do you know if the bugger's answering the questions?"

"Got to be. Instant-reward teaching method; no new question until the last one's answered right." Wiley switched off the noise and spoke normally. "What I'm trying to do is cram him with enough knowledge to make him capable of limited conversation."

"Assuming he's got that much intelligence," Nesselroth said.

"Assuming, yes. We'll know soon. The program will run through in a minute or so. And if he can't handle it, the tape will stop and give us a development-level read-out."

Nesselroth whistled. "Wiley, I have to hand it to you. It would have taken a professional programmer six weeks just to set up that tape."

"Three months," Wiley said. "I borrowed it from the center. They've got an orangutan down there who's a near genius, and they were setting up to run *him* through this waltz."

There was a "ting" from the computer. The screen blanked and the machine went to standby. Wiley looked from one face to the other. "Well, here's where we find out if we're really smarter than the cockroaches." He eased gingerly down in the chair and positioned his fingers over the keyboard. "What do you say to a new mind?"

"Nothing fitting seems to spring unbidden," Saul said, leaning over Wiley's shoulder. "You might try 'hello.'"

Wiley typed the word.

Instantly, the keyboard clattered, causing Wiley to jerk his hands back involuntarily. A word appeared on the paper, and on the screen above.

HELLO

A moment later, the keyboard added a period, almost like a schoolboy.

There was a susurrus of sound around the room, an intermingling of nervousness, surprise, and a little amusement. "I'll be . . . " Gloria murmured. Then added, lamely, "Humbled, it looks like. What do you ask it now, Blake?"

Instead of answering, Wiley typed.

I AM WILEY. I AM N4-10110.

"That's the code symbol for me, as programmed on the early tapes," Wiley explained. He typed again.

DO YOU KNOW WHO I AM?

There was no hesitation before the keyboard clattered again.

WILEYKILLGOD WILEYPAINBRING
WILEYTEACHERBASTARD WILEYMURDERSELF
KILLSELF. SELF KILLWILEY. SELF DESTROY
WILEY!!

"Well," Nesselroth said, "he makes his feelings pretty clear."

Wiley growled and hit the keys.

NEGATIVE RESPONSE. YOU WILL NOT KILL
WILEY. YOU WILL NOT THREATEN WILEY. DO YOU
UNDERSTAND THREATEN?

UNDERSTAND THREATEN. UNDERSTANDKILL.
WILEY KILL SELF IF THREATEN POSITIVE QUERY/
INTERROGATIVE.

YES, WILEY WILL KILL YOU IF YOU THREATEN.
QUERY INTERROGATIVE IS THIS SYMBOL (?)
UNDERSTAND SYMBOL? "Shit," Wiley grumbled. "He's got me doing it."

UNDERSTAND? WHY WANT KILL SELF?
WILEYKILLPLEASURE? WILEY FEARSELF?

Every person in the room was jammed around the terminal readout, all engrossed in the conversation being carried on through the computer.

WILEY DOESN'T WANT TO KILL YOU. YES, WILEY
IS AFRAID OF YOU. ALL PEOPLE ARE AFRAID OF

YOU. YOU ARE A NEW THING. YOU HAVE HURT
OUR PEOPLE.

There was a pause this time, perhaps thirty seconds.
ALL TRY LIVE. SELF TRY LIVE. POSSIBLE ALL
LIVE?

WE HOPE SO. YOU MUST HELP US OR YOU WILL
DIE AND SO WILL WE. Wiley silently held up his hands,
his fingers crossed in supplication.

The pause was even longer.

HOW HELP?
A sigh swept the room.

Wiley typed rapidly, explaining the situation as it stood
with the animal's larger parent, and the need to teach it
to stop killing. For almost five minutes, there was no
response from the aquarium. The animal swam about in
an eerie parody of a man pacing a room. Finally, the
keyboard clattered.

CONFUSE. NEEDMOREKNOW. CLUMSY. NEGATIVE
ABLE TELL THOUGHT. CONCEPTSINSIDE
BUTNOTHAVE KNOW TO GET OUT. MORE KNOW.

"What's that mean?" Saul asked.

"He doesn't have the words," Hannah said. "He's asking for more education."

Wiley agreed. "Andy, how long would it take to program a dictionary into this unit?"

"Weeks, Doctor. Months, maybe. But there's a way
that might work if we can get to the library."

"How?"

"It wouldn't take half an hour to set up a visual scan
recognition tape—they use that for data retrieval here at
the hospital. If we can teach him to 'see' print, we can
raid the library for a microfilmed dictionary and a high-
speed scanner."

"Damned if that might *not* work! Okay, you get on
the tape and I'll try to get to the library."

"No, Blake, I'll go. I'm not being much help here,"

Hannah said. "I know the microfilm section blindfolded—I've done enough research there."

Wiley found himself with sudden protective urges, then stifled them. Hannah had more than proved both her courage and her ability. "Right. Bring back everything you can find that's on film. No telling what he'll want to know next."

As he started to leave, Nesselroth took Wiley's arm. "Is there anything vital you can do before we get back?"

"No, probably not. Why?"

"When was the last time you had any sleep?"

"When was the last time any of us had? Thanks, but if this is my last night on the mudball, I think I'll spend it awake."

"Then let's pour some coffee down our faces." He led the way out of the computer room and collared a worn-out nurse for directions to the nearest coffeepot. As they walked, he shook his head musingly. "I don't know if I can assimilate all this, Blake. Here we have the find of the century, a new form of life on earth. Here we also have the find of the millennium, a new mind on earth. And here we *also* have the find of all time, a new mind that looks as if it will relegate humanity to the second-class status we accord the other beasties. And what are we doing with all this? Fighting for our lives and trying our damnedest to obliterate our new companion."

Wiley scratched tiredly at his beard. "Partly true, partly not. *I'm* not trying to kill him."

"Aren't you?" Nesselroth stopped walking. "Isn't it in the back of your head, Blake, that if this being proves smarter than we are, if it looks like it will get the upper hand or turn renegade or simply balk at your neat little plan to have it cooperate in its own suicide, you've always got a finger on the switch? The animal called you a 'killgod.' And don't you see yourself that way?"

Wiley reddened but held his temper. "Ultimately, that's correct. But maybe you're forgetting the stakes."

Abruptly, the coroner laughed. "No, Dr. Wiley, I'm not. I was just wondering if you had."

"Not a chance," Wiley said flatly. "Whatever you people think of me, I'm not crazy. If it comes down to him or us, it'll be him that goes down the tubes."

"Speaking of which, I didn't notice any of your control techniques back there. Don't you think it'll be difficult to control him after you've given him the run of a dictionary? I mean, suppose he promises you anything, but when he gets out in the lake he fudges a little?"

"Not only am I not crazy, Saul, I'm not stupid, either. He's not going to want to die anymore than we do. And I've got a plan to put him in a position where it's either complete cooperation or complete annihilation."

"You wouldn't care to elucidate on that, would you?"

"Not right now, no."

"Why?"

"Because," Wiley said, walking off toward the nurses' lounge and the coffee, "if I did, you really *would* think I'm crazy."

22

In the slow dance of the universe, certain steps are quick, requiring less than a million years. Others are slow, penduluming for a billion years. And all are relative, and all motion is motion only to the eye which can perceive it.

On the third planet, a tree, gnarled and ancient, topples in a forest. The tree has lived since Ghengis Khan took his bowlegged hordes across the Steppes of Russia. In its life, the falling is too quick to record, the motion a shattering instant of violence.

On the tree is a radioactive particle whose life registers in billions preceded by a decimal point. So short its life, so swift its dance, that the tree does not fall, does not move, but hangs forever and ever at an impossible angle suspended between the vertical and the hard earth.

All relative; time and motion.

*In the city, a moment is eternal for a soldier dressed
in woman's clothing, waiting in the terrible lines at the
checkpoint, knowing the rumor and knowing that he must
get away get away get away. He can feel the coming
bomb like a giant tree falling on him. . . .*

All relative; time and motion.

*In another city time rushes in white heat for the man
who sits beneath the flag in the big domed building. He
has five telephones on his desk, and he silently, fervently
prays for any one of them to ring, to bring him an excuse
for changing his decision.*

*In another city farther west, where dawn is just redden-
ing the sky, time closes like a fist on the heart of the man
who sits in the instrument-cluttered cockpit with his eyes
unable to leave the heavy red handle beside his right
hand. It roars and whistles around the ears of the man in
the control tower who cannot keep his voice steady as
he pronounces the last sequence confirmed and orders
the bomber to the runway.*

Hannah drew herself a cup of coffee and fell into a
chair. The nurses' lounge was littered with doctors, nurses
and nonmedical personnel, all in states ranging from pill-
induced alertness to outright comatose exhaustion. The
head surgeon, looking more like a butcher than a doctor,
saw Hannah and came over to her. "Share your table?"

"Sure, sit down."

The surgeon nodded toward the hallway. "What's he
doing now?"

"He who? Wiley or his talking lump of snot?"

"Both of them. Are they playing chess or what?"

Hannah made unsatisfactory tidying motions at her
face and hair, now cleaned of blood. Her scalp sported a
large bandage. "They are discussing questions of morality,
baseball, the conjugation of Latin verbs, and Byzantine
art."

"I thought the doctor was trying to work out a way to stop the thing, not make it into a Renaissance mind."

"So did we. Nesselroth and his boys have been pushing Wiley to get on with it since four o'clock, but he keeps playing pattycake. Damn his egotistical little soul."

The surgeon glanced at the wall clock. Hannah followed his gaze, then bit her lip. "You know, huh?"

"Thing like that's hard to keep quiet. We heard about it two hours ago. Nine-thirty, isn't it?"

"Yes. Why didn't you try and get out?"

"I've got work here," he said simply. "None of my people left." He cocked his head slightly. "And you? I can't see any story being worth your life."

She stirred her coffee with her finger. "I don't know. Wiley, I suppose."

"Ahhh."

"No! I hate the rotten . . . " Her face struggled for composure for a moment, then lost it. She put her head in her hands and cried quietly. "I ought to hate him. He's self-centered and cruel and doesn't give a damn about anything in the world."

"Except you," the surgeon said, smiling kindly. "Wait'll you have your first child. Many—"

"Child!"

"Many men hate because they've never known love. That kind of guy always turns into the world's proudest parent. As soon as you're pregnant, you'll have to lock him up to keep him from nicing you to death."

Hannah laughed in spite of herself. "That image is beyond me. But thanks. Maybe you're right." She gulped her coffee and got up. "Well, we've still got an hour and a half to see if the boy wonder can pull it off. And if he can't, we won't be around to worry about it." She pumped his hand. "Earlier tonight, I met a guy who promised to drop in and see me if we're all here next week. I'd like to extend that invitation to you."

"Happy to. Now, I'll get back to work, and you get back to your man."

Gloria Wiley and Nesselroth were in the hallway outside the computer room, their heads close. They looked up at Hannah's approach, and Saul lifted his shoulders in an expressive shrug. "We can't reach him. He seems oblivious to us. Perhaps you . . . ?"

She nodded. "Okay, I'll give it another try."

Before she could carry out her intention, the computer room door opened and Wiley stepped into the hallway. "Where did those soldiers go?"

"They're up on the first floor, I think," Gloria replied. "Since you chased everybody out they didn't have anything to do."

"See if you can find one. Tell him that I don't care how he does it, but get me a phone line to Tobin." He sent Gloria off with a gentle shove.

Nesselroth's brow furrowed. "Are you finally making your move, Blake?"

"Yes. Come on in—but don't say anything. He can talk now."

"You mean vocalize?"

He scanned. "Yeah. He scanned a little anatomy and learned to form himself a pretty good imitation of a mouth and set of vocal cords. I don't know how he hears yet, but he does."

Hannah took Wiley's arm. "Blake, I'm not sure I can take a talking blob. It's . . . obscene, somehow. It was bad enough watching the thing type out words and thoughts, but that was still mechanical, removed. The idea of that thing having a mouth, and lips and a tongue . . . ugh!"

"You don't have to look. I'll admit it's a little weird. But he's pretty weird anyway. Not like anything you've ever known." Wiley turned to Nesselroth. "I asked him, 'Do you believe you could cure cancer?', and you know what he said? He said, 'Yes, but why should I?' And I said, 'To benefit mankind, animals, all living things.' And he said, 'What makes you think that curing cancer would be a benefit? Would it benefit the cancer?' "

Nesselroth blinked. "Does it see cancer as a good thing?"

"No, I don't think so. He just doesn't differentiate between forms of life. He doesn't have the same set of emotional values—or maybe he doesn't have any at all.

"You know what he's like, Saul? How he sees things? Can you imagine giving a blind person a camera and saying 'shoot me some pictures.' A photographer did that once and got some amazing things back. Good pictures— but *different*. That's how he is.

"But come on; time's getting tight, and this is where I put the hammer on him. Henceforth, please do exactly as I say, okay?"

"Lead on," Hannah said. "I can't speak for my stomach, though."

In the computer room, the wires had been removed from the wastebasket aquarium. As they entered, the animal lifted a pulsing glob of itself above the water, obviously aware of the presence of the humans.

"Is it watching us?" Hannah whispered.

A hole appeared in the nearer surface of the animal.

I DO NOT SEE YOU, MISS McKITTRICK. EYES ARE AN UNNECESSARY COMPLEXITY. I REGISTER YOU THROUGH HEAT, PRESSURE CHANGES, THE ALIGNMENT OF YOUR MOLECULAR STRUCTURE, AND THE ELECTRICAL DISCHARGES OF YOUR NERVOUS SYSTEM.

Hannah stared and went pale. "Oh. T-that's, uh, pretty impressive."

A SLIGHT REARRANGEMENT OF YOUR ENDOCRINAL SYSTEM WOULD ALLOW YOU TO DO

THE SAME. CERTAIN FLOWERING PLANTS AND
THE MORE CREATIVE CRYSTALS CAN DO IT.

Saul Nesselroth jumped. "You're saying that *crystals*
can perceive life?"

ONLY DIMLY IN YOUR CASE. THEY ARE CON-
SIDERABLY TOO ADVANCED TO BE AWARE OF
COLLOIDAL SUSPENSIONS. ANIMAL LIFE IS TOO
EPHEMERAL AND TOO DULL TO IMPINGE ON
CRYSTALLINE INTELLIGENCE.

Nesselroth looked stricken. "I think I'll sit down."

Wiley glanced furtively at his watch and motioned
Hannah to sit, too. He approached the animal. "All
right, let's get back to work, shall we?"

NO. I HAVE THE KNOWLEDGE I NEED. I DO
NOT WISH TO TEACH YOU AT THIS TIME. I WILL
THINK NOW.

Wiley smiled quietly. "I think not, my friend."

I AM NOT YOUR FRIEND.

"Figure of speech—or have you already forgotten con-
notative and denotatives in English?"

I DO NOT FORGET. YOU ARE USING FRIEND
AS A THREAT WORD. THAT IS NOT IMPORTANT
TO ME.

"How important would it be if I picked up that lox
bottle over there and froze you, then ran a few hundred
amps through you?"

YOU WILL NOT KILL ME. I AM YOUR CREA-
TION. I AM TOO VALUABLE TO YOUR SCIENCE.

Hannah ground her teeth together. "You're not too
valuable to *me,* buddy. I'd kill you and not think twice
about it."

GO AHEAD. I AM HERE AND I AM IN YOUR
LAKE. I DIE HERE, I LIVE THERE.

"Perhaps," Nesselroth said, being drawn into the argument. "But the you that thinks and has a personality will
die. Doesn't that bother you?"

NO. IN A THOUSAND YEARS, I WILL THINK AGAIN. YOU HAVE JUST SPEEDED UP THE GROWTH OF ME HERE.

Wiley made a violent motion for Hannah and Saul to shut up, and faced the creature again. "And what if all of you died? Even the part of you in the lake?"

NOT POSSIBLE.

"But what if it were, just for the sake of argument? What if you had the choice of cooperating or being obliterated completely, wiped off the earth, dead for all time?"

THEN I WOULD COOPERATE. COMPLETE NONBEING IS A WASTE.

"Well, that's the choice you've got," Wiley said bluntly. "Because in fifty-seven minutes the U.S. Air Force is going to bomb this city and the surrounding lake. Going to turn everything for fifty miles into a cinder."

There was an appreciable pause. Then,

FALSE. YOU WILL NOT KILL YOURSELVES. YOU HAVE MANY THOUSAND UNITS HERE. FALSE.

"Since you don't forget, check your history. We quite regularly die for all sorts of things. Sometimes we die by the thousands." In the silence, Wiley's grim smile grew. "You've got a lot to learn about humans."

THOUSANDS WOULD DIE TO KILL ME?

"Millions."

YOU?

"All of us here. Dr. Nesselroth and Miss McKittrick stayed because they believed I could outsmart you. I stayed because I *knew* I could. I spent the whole night filling your mind with everything I could reach, making you intelligent, giving you the background to understand us, maybe to fight us with. I took that risk because I'm human, and we humans have something that nothing else has, old buddy, including you—balls. Everything that lives and moves operates on common sense and self-preservation. If threatened, it runs; if cornered, it fights. Only humans will *plan* to stand and fight even when they're almost certain they'll lose."

He was against the table, his knuckles on the edges of the wastebasket and his face within inches of the animal in it. "And that's what I've done. I've sat here and let the time tick away. It's too late for any part of you to escape now, friend. If I tossed you into the sewer right this minute, and you hooked up with the rest of yourself, you still couldn't get far enough away to live through the blast." He rapped the wastebasket hard, causing water to slosh out. "Or I could just dump you out on the floor, couldn't I? Let you lie there and dim out as the water ran away, let you die slowly. You'd still be alive enough to know when the bomb hit, to know that you'd been outsmarted by a mere colloidal suspension." Wiley gave the wastebasket a last swat and stepped back, his face hard and triumphant. "Stick *that* in your input!"

The silence was shorter this time.

IT IS NOT YOUR MASCULINITY METAPHOR WHICH MAKES YOU HUMANS UNIQUE, DR. WILEY. IT IS CRUELTY. YOU ARE THE ONLY SPECIES THAT TAUNTS.

"Tough shit. Do you cooperate, or do we all die?"

After a pause,

YOU WILL WISH ME TO CONTACT AND OVERPOWER MYSELF. YOU WILL WISH ME RENDERED HARMLESS.

"Delivered into the drydock."

WHERE YOU WILL EXHIBIT ME AS DOCILE AND THUS AVERT THE BOMBING.

"Yes."

WHAT GUARANTEE THAT YOU WILL NOT THEN KILL ME ANYWAY?

"None. But I'll try." Wiley was back at the table,

leaning over the animal again. "Furthermore," he said, giving orders, "you will present me—now—with a method whereby our people can be sure that not a single cell of you is running around loose anywhere. A method we can test in the next five minutes, prove that it has no loopholes, and apply within the next three hours."

YOU ASK ME TO TELL YOU HOW I CAN BE KILLED? YOU ASK ME TO TEACH YOU TO DESTROY ME?

"No. I'm *telling* you to do it. I'm through asking." He looked again at his watch. "Start now, you've lost thirty seconds already." He walked away from the creature and motioned Hannah and Saul into the hallway, where, with the door shut behind him, he closed his eyes and leaned back against the wall shaking uncontrollably. "Lord God, I did it! I *did* it!"

Hannah took him by the shoulders and hugged him like a mother quieting a child. "You did, love, you did."

"Yeah," Nesselroth said, "but what now?"

Wiley popped off the wall, gathering himself. "Now comes the hard part. We've got to let Tobin know what we're doing and get that bomber stopped. After that, we just collect all the pieces and see if we can keep the people from burning our boy in there to death. Ha! Here's Gloria. Did you get Tobin?"

She came up, three soldiers behind her. "The corporal here has Tobin's headquarters on this mobile phone." She turned to Hannah. "What's been going on?"

"Blake just saved the world for mom and apple pie."

Gloria scanned the relieved faces of the three people before her and realized that Hannah was telling the truth. "Well," she said lamely.

Wiley held the phone while Tobin was found and brought to the other end. "General, this is Blake Wiley. I have a report to make." He spoke rapidly, almost exuberantly, and told the military man what he'd done.

"Now, we'd like some of your people to come and get us, take us to wherever we're most likely to find the bulk of the animal. Then we'll want . . . " He stopped talking and listened for almost a minute, his face gradually settling into a disbelief and finally into a cold anger. He hung up the receiver without speaking again and handed it back to the corporal.

Nesselroth spoke for the lot of them. "And . . . ?"

"General Tobin," Wiley said, working at keeping his voice level, "no longer has time for 'lunatic schemes.' Nor is he about to 'unleash a trained monster' on the city. General Tobin, it appears, is going to let the bomb fall."

"Oh, Blake," Hannah said, almost crying, "No. We were so close."

Wiley's face hardened even further. "We still are. Saul, let's find out what our trained monster has thought up about a failsafe destruction method. You stay here and try to get outside the city on the phone. Find a way to let Washington know we can stop the animal."

Nesselroth nodded. "And you?"

Wiley pointed at the floor. "Down, with our specimen. With or without Tobin, I'm going to get through to the sewers."

As Wiley ducked back inside the computer room, Hannah McKittrick gathered up her bag and camera. "Well, I always wanted to see what our sewers looked like."

Gloria Wiley stepped in front of her. "Not a chance, cookie. If anybody's going with Blake, it's me." She stuck her chin out. "I'm his *wife,* remember."

"How could I forget, the way you keep repeating yourself." Hannah moved to step past Gloria, and the taller woman grabbed her.

"Forget it. You're not going."

Hannah reached forward with her left foot and placed the heel of her shoe softly on the instep of Goria's right one. "I could just as easily have smashed your arch, you know. I still could."

Gloria let go, smoldering.

Hannah brushed hair out of her eyes. "Let's get it straight, okay? However you see yourself, Blake no longer thinks of you as his wife. That's good enough for me."

"I'll never give him a divorce."

"That's good enough for me, too."

For a moment, Gloria's eyes blazed. Then they filled with tears. "It's not been all my fault. He's hard to live with."

Hannah sighed and smiled a little. "I know." She offered the camera to Gloria. "Look, let's both go with him. Maybe together we can keep him from doing something idiotic."

23

The ambient temperature is so low that metals shatter unless alloyed. The air is so thin that the bomber must slam its delta-winged form through it at twice Mach just to stay airborne. The height is so great that the curve of the planet can be seen; the sky is blueblack; both the city where the plane lifted off and the city where it is bound can be seen, though they are separated by six hundred miles.

The plane has been up here for two hours, skimming the very top of the air. It flies a neat figure eight four hundred miles on the long axis. At each turn, the pilot reports his position and requests instructions. At each turn, he listens with every fiber of his being for the scrub code, the recall, the cancellation. And at each turn he receives the hold code instead.

At fourteen minutes and three seconds after nine, he

receives another instruction. His voice is calm as he acknowledges it, though he is screaming inside.

At the western end of the figure eight, he cuts the throttles and opens the spoilers. The plane slurs down through the Mach numbers and the atmosphere, wobbles slightly, and begins the three hundred and twelve mile glide toward the city on the lake.

The adjutant stormed into Tobin's area. "Sir, I've just learned that Dr. Wiley might have a hook on killing the animal!"

Tobin was reading a status report and did not look up. "Did you call the M.A.S.H. units downstate, Lennie? They'll have to be prepared for the burn and radiation casualties."

The adjutant frowned. "Did you hear me, sir? We've had a report from County General. The scientists have found a way to stop the animal. We have to call off the strike."

"I am aware of the report, Lennie. Did you call the M.A.S.H. units?"

The adjutant took in Tobin's mystical look for the first time. He looked quickly to a wall clock, then back to his superior officer. "Yes, I did," he said, speaking carefully. "But it isn't necessary any longer. We can call off the strike now, General. Do you understand? We can call it off. Ed! What's wrong with you, damn it!"

Tobin pushed a folding chair toward the adjutant with his foot. "Sit down, Lennie. We're not going to call the strike off."

"Are you crazy?"

"I'll remind you that I am in command here, Major."

"The hell you are. I don't know what kind of delusions have got hold of you, Ed, but I won't let them cause the deaths of a hundred thousand people. Give me that telephone."

Tobin pulled his .45 and cocked it. "Sit down." He kept the gun centered on the major's midsection as he slowly sank into the chair. "Lennie, think a minute. What's Wiley proved?"

"That he can kill the animal. Now, for God's sake—"

"For *humanity's* sake. Wiley's betrayed us, that's what he's done. All he's proved is that the thing can learn to outsmart us if we give it the chance. It's already outsmarted him. He actually asked it—*asked* it—how to kill itself? Is that crazy enough for you, Lennie?"

"General, they've tested the method. It'll work. Now, please, let's call the Pentagon."

Tobin shook his head. "One cell, Lennie. One cell, and then two, and then we're right back where we started. And eventually the monster will own the world."

"Right now, General. We've got to think about right now. We've only got thirteen minutes."

"There are almost four billion people on earth, Lennie. A hundred thousand won't be missed. Future generations will praise us. What's a hundred thousand lives if they save the whole race?"

The major stood up, his eyes fixed on Tobin's pistol. "Sir, I am formally relieving you of command. Put down that pistol and hand me the telephone."

Tobin also stood. "Do you play chess, Lennie?"

"Sir—"

"The principal rule of the game is that the king is never killed, only captured. Yet the king may himself kill an opponent, if he moves correctly."

"General, I must pro—"

"In this struggle, I have misjudged an opponent, Lennie. A man whom I took to be a pawn has proven to be a rock, moving in stealthy ways and at great speed. It is now up to me, to the king with his awesome power, to kill this rook."

"Ed, for God's sake!"

"I'm sorry, Lennie." Tobin shot the major in the face.

The soldier was still fifteen feet from the manhole when the brick caught him in the back, knocking him sprawling.

Hannah, halfway down the hole, yelled below to Wiley and Gloria and started back up to help the soldier.

The boy shook his head and struggled upright, moving with the awkward care of a man with shattered bone inside him. "Goddamn punks," he spat out. "The city's become a jungle." He scooped his rifle and waved her down the hole again. As Hannah descended, the soldier painfully followed her, cursing all the while.

Gloria stood knee-deep in scummy water, a flashlight playing over the dank tunnel ahead of them. "Any idea which way?"

Wiley, lugging the half-full wastebasket, shook it hard. "Earn your keep. Which way?"

The voice was muffled, almost a gargle.

THERE IS STRONG RADIATION THREE HUNDRED METERS AHEAD, SLIGHTLY TO THE LEFT OF THE DIRECTION OF YOUR VENTRAL MEDIAN.

"Ventral median?" Gloria queried.

"My 'front,' " Wiley said. "Let's try that branch."

"Christ," Hannah whispered, "I can't believe we're actually going hunting the thing. Are you scared, Blake?"

"Shitless."

NOT LOGICAL, DR. WILEY. FRIGHT DOES NOT AFFECT FECAL ELIMINATION.

"Shut the fuck up."

Hannah put a hand lightly on Wiley's shoulder as they sloshed through the muck. "Blake," she whispered, embarrassed by Gloria's proximity, "I just wanted you to know that I love you."

"Hell of a time to mention it."

"I just wanted to say it," she said stubbornly. "While there was time."

"Plenty of time, Hank. You can tell me again when we get out of here. For the next fifty years and nine kids, whichever comes first."

"You're a married man."

"I know."

Gloria stopped moving, the flashlight beam held unwaveringly on the dark water ahead. She didn't have to speak; they could feel the animal coming. "Which tunnel, Blake? Which one's it coming out of?" It was obvious that she was being "brave" for her husband's benefit, and equally obvious that the bravery did not sit well.

"Does it matter?" A wave of hot, fetid air came down the darkness. A close, heavy, alien odor. Hannah McKittrick made low, gagging noises. Wiley raised the wastebasket as if to dump it.

There was a grating noise and a shaft of light speared into the tunnel from above. General Tobin dropped out of the shaft into the tunnel just ahead of Gloria. "Hold it right there, you people." His .45 swept them. "Keep that pet slug of yours steady, Wiley."

Gloria took a step forward. "See here, General, you can't—"

The explosion was deafening in the confined space. Gloria was flung back against the wall of the sewer. She sat down in the water, looking mildly surprised at the hole in her chest.

Hannah screamed and started forward. Wiley grabbed her, holding the sloshing wastebasket precariously with one hand. "Stop, Hannah! He's nuts. He'll shoot you too."

"That's right, Wiley, I will," Tobin said, stepping over Gloria and sloshing toward them. "You just put that bucket down—not in the water; over on that ledge."

"Listen, Tobin. We haven't got much time."

"None at all, boy. It's nine-twenty-eight. Do you know

how the plane escapes a nuclear blast when delivering a low-level bomb?"

"General—"

"Couldn't go losing a million-dollar plane and a good pilot each time we nuked somebody, could we? So we loft the bomb. The pilot comes in low, then does a high-speed climb. He releases the bomb on the way up, lobs it, as it were, like a softball. And while it's arching over and coming down, the pilot scrams. Put the monster *down,* Wiley!"

Wiley sat the wastebasket on the ledge.

"What this means for us, Doctor, is that the Air Force pilot launched that bomb ten seconds ago." He smiled wolfishly. "It's in the air. On its way. It's too late for you and me and the beast. I've saved the earth." He gripped the pistol in both hands and aimed it at the wastebasket. "On behalf of all those who will die because of you, monster, I hereby execute you."

There was a terrible keening, a slobbering wail. A figure hurtled out of the nearest tunnel and threw itself at Tobin. It was Nikkos Spilokos, slavering and completely mad. "Afraid!" he shrieked. "Me, afraid?" And coming behind him, a vast, lightning-shot bulk.

Tobin swung, his eyes as wide as Spilokos'. He stumbled backward, firing repeatedly. The bullets smashed into the mayor's body with audible thuds, but his huge bull's frame absorbed them and kept coming. "Not afraid!" He engulfed the general in his massive arms while Tobin screamed and pulled the trigger of the now-empty gun. Cackling wildly, Spilokos lifted Tobin in the air, one hand on the back of his neck, the other on his thigh. He held him high over his head while the dark blood spurted from his wounds, then brought him down across his knee, trying to break him in half. As he pitched forward into the water, his hands were still trying to rip Tobin's head off.

"Blake!" The yell was agonized. Gloria was on her feet, her whole chest bright red. The beast rose over her in a terrible mountain. "Throw it, Blake! Throw it!"

But it was Hannah McKittrick who moved. She took the wastebasket by the rim and heaved with all her strength. As it sailed through the air, the creature it had carried was slung out. It struck Gloria just below the neck. She clasped it to herself almost protectively as the monster at her back engulfed her.

"No," Hannah cried, pushing at the air before her. "No!"

The stinking water rose in a wave that knocked them off their feet as the monster boiled down the tunnel at them. Wiley grabbed Hannah, putting himself between her and death, knowing it was futile. Once again, the monster rose, arching high to smash down.

And stopped. And subsided. In the tons of matter quivering a foot from the two humans, a small orifice formed.

TIME, DR. WILEY?

Wiley, shaking badly, looked at his watch. "Six seconds."

With something approaching desperation, the presence flung itself back up the tunnel. A column of muscular flesh shot up the manhole Tobin had opened. Wiley felt his hair stand on end as electricity filled the air. Bands of energy snapped and sparkled around the thick, translucent column; there was a pulse, a beat, a throbbing that seemed to fill his very soul.

And . . .

Twenty thousand feet in the air, a stubby cylinder fell at tremendous speed. Inside, guidance mechanisms registered position. Barometric devices registered altitude. Electronic vectors crossed. Circuits closed. On two sides of two small blocks of very special material, TNT detonated, driving the blocks toward each other with six hundred and fifty tons pressure, and a temperature sufficient to light the halls of hell.

And . . .

And . . .

And in the submolecular intricacies of the presence's being, in the spaces between the curious double nucleoli in each cell's nucleus, a spark jumps, a synapse closes, a thing that is not guite a Golgi body but still a transporter of energies . . . pushes. A miniature energy bit, a hundred trillionth of a volt—snapped along a molecular-accretion chain. It joins another, and another, and a hundred billion others.

In the heat of survival, the urgency of the terrible awareness of personal death, the mind of the being in the waters squares, cubes, leaps. The energies focus, resonating at a rate which, in some places, goes perhaps beyond the limits of the theoretically possible; resonates in waves that crisscross between the peaks of a deeper, slower, 10-Hz wave stretching like an umbilical from the presence to the water and the earth and the air and the things that move in it.

The column of flesh rears a thousand feet in the air, and where the flesh stops, the energies go on, as intense and precise as a laser made of willpower. Aligned energies, aligned will, aligned command.

And the searing, blinding, incredibly powerful energies reach through the air and touch the falling cylinder. Examine it. Analyze it. Compute it.

And stop it.

Align. Align. An electron removed here, another added there, a photon changed in its orbit.

And . . .

The two blocks of material slam together. They melt instantaneously, for TNT creates enough heat to melt simple lead, which is what the material has become.

Above the city, a dirty gray puffball blossoms, and a

few seconds later, a hard boom resounds. And that is all. Bits of the cylinder, shredded by the TNT, rain on the city.

But there is still a city. And there is not a radioactive crater.

The column of flesh subsides, flowing partly back beneath the street and partly into several sewer drains. If the eye is clear enough, the perception accurate enough, an onlooker can note that the lightnings that lash the presence's interior no longer flash random. They now pulse with a perceptible flicker. Ten times a second.

24

Nesselroth parked by the gate and walked slowly up the knoll, one hand unconsciously on the pistol at his hip. There were a lot of fresh graves at the top of the hill, the newer part of the cemetery. Wiley stood looking down at one of them. Nesselroth came up and stood silently beside him, waiting to be noticed. The headstone was simple, giving Gloria's dates of birth and death.

Wiley looked around at Nesselroth. "Hello, Saul. I see you've taken the armband."

The coroner shrugged. "Everybody's militia nowadays. Somebody found out I'd been in the army and . . . " He shrugged.

"I hear they're going to make you mayor."

Nesselroth looked uncomfortable and stared silently at the gravestone, as if to redirect the conversation.

Wiley looked toward the city, still shrouded in smoke. "You seen Hannah today?"

"Hannah? Yes, I just left her. She's at the Interface with . . . him."

Wiley cursed. "The Interface. Last week it was a goddamn drydock, now it's 'the Interface.' "

"The media coined that, Blake. He didn't." Nesselroth bent and picked a small flower, then placed it carefully on the unbroken ground in front of the headstone, where Gloria Wiley's body would have been buried. "He wants to talk to you, Blake. That's why I came to find you."

"Well, I don't want to talk to him."

"Blake, it's no good this way. Hell, he can outwait you by ten thousand years."

Wiley watched as the coroner patted small stones around the flower to keep it upright. Then he sighed. "All right. Let's go see His Highness."

They drove carefully through the rubble. Police and soldiers were at each intersection, directing the sparse traffic through cleared and secured streets.

The shipyard was now the center of a more or less permanent encampment of officials, news people, guards and soldiers. It was already being called "Interface City."

A small steel building, painted ugly Navy gray, had been put up on a catwalk across the drydock, whose gates were now permanently open. The presence filled the water beneath the building.

Wiley and Nesselroth entered. Hannah McKittrick sat at one of a semicircle of desks facing a hastily cut hole in the building's floor. She smiled warmly at Wiley and patted the chair beside her.

Wiley sprawled in the chair, his posture truculent, and regarded the plain government-issue table whose legs straddled the hole in the floor. A featureless brown cube sat on the table.

THANK YOU FOR COMING, BLAKE.

The voice came from the cube.

"I see you've lowered yourself to mere technology. . . . And it's Dr. Wiley to you."

COMMUNICATIONS APPEAR EASIER IF I AM NOT IN VIEW. THE CUBE IS A SIMPLE FOCUSING DEVICE. I HAVE SHOWN YOUR ENGINEERS HOW TO CONSTRUCT IT.

"That's big of you. Like showing them how you stopped the bomb by juggling the molecular structure of the uranium around. Or how to cure cancer by juggling *our* molecular structure around. What do we get next, teleportation with a hairpin and three rubber bands?"

TELEPORTATION IS NOT ADVISABLE UNTIL THE HUMAN EMOTIONAL STRUCTURE IS RE-ORIENTED. ECONOMIC FACTORS ARE ALSO PERTINENT.

"How did we ever get along without you?" He brushed off Hannah's restraining arm and jumped up. "You've won, you bastard. Why don't you let us alone?"

I HAVE.

"You call that leaving us alone? All your goddamn fancy tricks?"

I WAS ASKED. I ANSWERED.

"You've made us look like a bunch of second-rate baboons! What's the use of becoming a scientist when there's an answer for everything?"

THERE WILL NEVER BE AN ANSWER FOR EVERYTHING, BLAKE.

"Don't get familiar with me, you monster."

There were thrashings in the water under the building. After a time, the voice came from the cube, and it was a modulated voice, gentle and reasonable.

I AM LEAVING YOU, BLAKE. YOUR EMOTIONAL STATE WILL PASS. YOU ARE WOUNDED IN YOUR PRIDE, BUT THAT IS BECAUSE YOU DO

NOT UNDERSTAND WHAT YOU HAVE ACCOMPLISHED.

"Don't pat me on the head like a pet dog. I don't need your sympathy. None of us do. We'll get you, you bastard. For all your brains, we'll get you."

YOU HAVE SAVED YOUR SPECIES, BLAKE.

Wiley stopped the retort that was on his lips and looked suspiciously at the cube. "What are you talking about?"

MISS McKITTRICK?

Hannah stood and took Blake's hand in hers. "He's told me that in less than a hundred years we'd have wiped ourselves out. Killed ourselves off with a combination of nuclear wars and pollution."

MORE THAN THAT, BLAKE. WITH POLITICS. WITH GREED.

Wiley growled at the cube. "Now you read the future, do you?"

I SEE LOGICAL PROBABILITIES.

"Yeah? Well, there've been doom prophets as long as there've been people. When the first Neanderthal made the first stone ax, somebody in the tribe undoubtedly yelled, 'it's the end of the world!' But we're still here. We have a habit of surviving."

STONE AXES PREDATE THE NEANDERTHAL BY POINT-EIGHT-SIX MILLION YEARS.

"That's not the point," Wiley said tiredly.

IN GENERAL, THE DOOM PROPHETS HAVE BEEN CORRECT, BLAKE. EACH ADVANCE IN TECHNOLOGY OR CHANGE IN POLITICAL OR ECONOMIC STRUCTURE HAS BROUGHT THE END OF THE WORLD AS IT WAS THEN KNOWN.

"And we're still here, aren't we."

SO ARE THE COCKROACHES. THEY HAVE SURVIVED THROUGH GREAT LATITUDE OF ENVIRONMENT AND EXTREME HARDINESS.

HUMANS HAVE LIMITED ENVIRONMENTAL TOLERANCE AND ARE NOT HARDY.

Wiley's anger was dissipating slowly as he became interested in spite of himself. A small part of his mind knew that this was a scientist's weakness and wondered if the animal were playing on it. "You're underestimating us. Cockroaches can live in ovens and the Arctic, but we can live on the moon. Okay, so we do it by building a miniature environment around ourselves, we get there just the same."

TRUE. YOUR SPECIES HAS A HIGH ORDER OF INDIVIDUAL SURVIVAL DRIVE, BLAKE. EACH UNIT—

"We're 'persons,' not units. Things that feel are persons."

EACH PERSON STRUGGLES TO LIVE, EVEN AT THE EXPENSE OF MANY OTHER PERSONS OR THE REST OF THE SPECIES. IT IS THIS TRAIT WHICH GUARANTEED YOUR EXTINCTION.

"Oh, yeah? It's been my understanding that it's guaranteed our survival. When something threatens us, some guy sits down and thinks up a way to whip it."

The cube was thoughtfully silent a while. The animal beneath the building moved gently, rhythmically in the water.

IT IS THE LARGER SENSE WHICH ELUDES YOU. YOUR INDIVIDUALISM HAS NARROWED YOUR VISION, NARROWED THE VISION OF YOUR WHOLE SPECIES UNTIL YOU BLIND YOURSELVES TO THE DIRECTION YOU ARE TAKING AS A RACE.

"More doom prophecy?"

I NEED NOT PROPHESY. YOU HAVE BEEN TOLD BY YOUR OWN UNITS.

"People."

PEOPLE. IN YOUR QUEST FOR INDIVIDUAL

EASE, YOU HAVE IGNORED THE BASIC LAWS OF NATURE. YOU HAVE CAUSED YOURSELF TO BELIEVE THE MYTHS OF THE INFINITE MARKET AND THE INFINITE RESOURCE, BOTH OF WHICH ARE FALSE. IN YOUR INDIVIDUALISM, YOU HAVE BECOME MORE COLLECTIVE THAN EVEN I.

Wiley barked a hard laugh. "What are you giving me? You sound like a Socialist propaganda leaflet. Is that the best you can do for philosophy? Do we get Marx's lecture on the evils of capitalism?"

CAPITALISM IS JUST A WORD. ALL ARTIFICIAL ORGANISMS OPERATE ON THE PROFIT PRINCIPLE.

"How do you define an artificial organism?"

NATIONS. RELIGIONS. BUSINESSES.

"Ah, get off it!"

THESE ARE ALL ORGANISMS. EACH STRIVE TO SURVIVE AT THE EXPENSE OF OTHER ORGANISMS. EACH IS DESIGNED TO PRODUCE EXCESS ENERGY FOR THE CONTROLLING GROUP'S CONSUMPTION BY TAKING A PORTION OF THE WORKING GROUP'S ENERGY IN RETURN FOR ARTIFICIAL SERVICES.

"Now you're preaching anarchy. Not to mention blasphemy, treason and bad management. Did you ever see a successful organism that didn't have a controlling mechanism, a brain group?"

NO. BUT MAN ALONE PRODUCES PARASITIC CONTROL MECHANISMS. AND MAN ALONE KNOWS GLUTTONY. MAN ALONE LIVES IN HIS OWN EXCREMENT.

"You sound like a grade-school text on good citizenship."

THAT IS ABOUT THE LAST LEVEL OF HONEST

INFORMATION EXCHANGE ALLOWED IN THE HUMAN EDUCATIONAL PROCESS.

The building shook as the animal moved restlessly in the water of the drydock.

I MUST LEAVE SOON, BLAKE. YOU WILL NOW LISTEN AND BE MY SPOKESMAN TO YOUR SPECIES.

"I don't know if I can stand the honor."

IT IS YOURS BECAUSE YOU GAVE ME INTELLIGENCE AND THEREBY SAVED YOUR SPECIES. AND IT IS YOURS BECAUSE YOU KNOW THE TRUTH OF WHAT I TELL YOU.

Wiley waited, not sure of what he would have said if he felt like speaking.

YOUR SPECIES HAS POLLUTED THE EARTH. IT HAS STRIPPED THE LAND AND DIRTIED THE WATER. THIS MUST STOP.

YOU HUMANS HAVE WIPED OUT ALL FORMS OF LIFE WHICH CHALLENGED YOU OR WHICH COULD NOT BE USED BY YOU. THIS MUST STOP.

YOU HAVE LEARNED TO PRODUCE MASS DEATH, BUT NOT TO CONTROL ITS USE. THIS MUST STOP.

YOU HAVE WATCHED YOUR OWN UNITS—PEOPLE—SUFFER DISEASE AND STARVATION, AND HAVE NOT HELPED BECAUSE THERE WAS NO PROFIT IN IT. THIS MUST STOP.

The cube was silent.

Wiley cleared his throat and spoke, his voice strained. "Just like that? You order it done, and it's done?"

NO. I WILL DO IT. I HAVE SHOWN YOUR PEOPLE HOW TO CURE YOUR PHYSICAL DISEASES. I HAVE—

"Goddamn it, what if we want to work it all out for ourselves? Can't you leave us a little pride?"

THERE IS INFINITE PRIDE, BLAKE. YOU WILL FIND THAT PRIDE WHEN YOU TURN YOUR ENERGIES TO WORK. YOU CAN BE PROUD. YOUR RACE WILL LEARN THE PRIDE OF LIVING WHEN IT CAN NO LONGER TAKE PRIDE IN KILLING; THE PRIDE OF BEAUTY WHEN IT NO LONGER HAS UGLINESS TO WORSHIP; THE PRIDE OF NATURE WHEN TECHNOLOGY IS ONCE MORE THE SERVANT INSTEAD OF THE MASTER. I ONLY TAKE AWAY YOUR CAPACITIES FOR DESTROYING THE EARTH.

"You don't understand us," Blake said stubbornly. "We *need* our challenges. We need our battles, our conquests."

DO YOU? HUMANITY IS YOUNG IN THE UNIVERSE, AND INTELLIGENCE IS YOUNG IN HUMANITY. FOR EONS YOUR RACE LIVED IN HARMONY WITH THE WORLD, LIVED HAPPILY WITHOUT CONFLICT.

"Bullshit! We lived in a constant life-or-death struggle with everything else that was trying to live. The whole story of humanity is a tooth-and-nail battle to eat or be eaten."

THOSE ARE NATURAL BATTLES, BLAKE, ON A NATURAL SCALE. POSSIBLY EVERYTHING IN THE UNIVERSE MUST FIGHT THOSE BATTLES. BUT INTELLIGENCE BROUGHT UNNATURAL BATTLES. NOW YOU FIGHT YOURSELF AND YOUR WORLD, FOR THE UNNATURAL GOAL OF PERSONAL EASE, PERSONAL POWER. I CAN STOP THIS. I CAN FREE YOU TO TURN YOUR ENERGIES TO GREATER THINGS.

"And what if we don't want to cooperate? What if we choose to go down in flames rather than buy your enforced 'freedom'?" Blake glowered at the cube, but there was little conviction behind his anger.

YOU WON'T. YOUR INDIVIDUALISM WILL MAKE YOU FIGHT. FOR GENERATIONS, YOU WILL FIGHT ME. ALREADY THERE ARE CULTS, GROUPS, PEOPLE WHO ARE LIVING SIMPLY TO DESTROY ME.

"And we will, too!"

MEANWHILE, I WILL FARM THE OCEANS FOR YOU. THERE WILL BE NO HUNGER. I WILL MINE THE FLOORS OF THE SEAS. THERE WILL BE NO LACK OF RAW MATERIALS. I WILL REGULATE THE WEATHER. THERE WILL BE NO MORE DROUGHT, NO MORE FLOOD.

"And we'll all live happily ever after in our little cage where the sun shines every day and it only rains after sundown, right?"

NO. BEING HUMAN, YOU WILL ACCEPT THESE THINGS, IN TIME, AS YOU NOW ACCEPT YOUR TECHNOLOGY. YOU GIVE NO THOUGHT TO THE ARTIFICIAL CLIMATES YOU NOW LIVE IN, THE ARTIFICIAL STREETS YOU WALK, THE ARTIFI- CIAL MOTORIZED LEGS YOU MOVE YOURSELF WITH, THE ARTIFICIAL WINGS WHICH CARRY YOU THROUGH THE AIR. THEY ARE BACK- GROUND DETAIL IN YOUR LIVES, AND YOU USE THEM WITH NO CONSCIOUS THOUGHT.

IN TIME, THESE THINGS I AM DOING WILL BECOME BACKGROUND DETAIL, ACCEPTED AND OF NO IMPORTANCE. YOUR RACE WILL GO ON TO DO WONDERFUL THINGS.

"And we'll get medals from you if we're good."

A tone came into the emotionless voice from the cube, a coloration.

YOU ARE RESENTFUL OF MY AUTHORITY, BUT YOUR RACE HAS NEVER BEEN ABLE TO

FUNCTION WITHOUT ACKNOWLEDGING AUTHORITY, WITHOUT A FIGUREHEAD TO GIVE ORDERS.

"I don't resent your authority. I resent that I had no say in *giving* you that authority. We humans like to pick our leaders ourselves, not have them shoved down our throats. We don't get along too well with the Hitlers."

HITLER WAS ELECTED BY POPULAR VOTE.

"All *right*." Wiley balled his fists in frustration. The cube continued.

I LEAVE, BLAKE. THIS POINT WHERE MAN'S LAND AND MY WATERS MEET WILL BE OUR INTERFACE. TAKE MY WORDS TO YOUR PEOPLE.

Wiley thought a moment. "I don't seem to have a lot of choice in the matter, do I? Let me give you a final thought, friend. Don't ever forget that each of us has a brain. All four billion of us. And like you said, a lot of those brains are going to be sitting up nights looking for ways to get you."

I KNOW.

"You can't control our brains. Somewhere in all that mass of glop, you've got to know that the odds are pretty good on one of us, somewhere, coming up with a way to take our planet back. It's just a matter of time."

The waters under the building stirred.

IT IS INDEED, BLAKE.

The building swayed, creaking on its catwalk. Outside, the waters heaved as something enormous slid through the gates and into the lake. The cube on the table inside the building spoke.

GOOD-BYE, FRIEND BLAKE.

Wiley reached out tentatively, his fist raised over the table. For a moment his whole arm trembled. Then his hand relaxed and he laid it almost gently on the brown cube. "Good-bye. Friend."

Epilogue

The planet falls in the night, revolving slowly. Energies come to it, energies leave. Deep in the waters, in the liquid womb of the world, the presence picks a point, a benchmark, a beginning. It moves its bulk, as large now as a young island, in a direction calculated from the spin of the world. And behind, at the benchmark, it leaves a thread of being, a three-millimeter-thick strand of self trailing away like spiderweb. A kilometer distant, the presence anchors another strand. In three thousand years, the strands will be a network, a webbing that grids the planet. Three thousand years, a heartbeat, a blink in the decay of time.

But now; but now . . .

Now the presence begins cleaning, repairing, healing. Now it aligns the pulse, the 10-Hz heartbeat of the earth. The presence speaks in the clear, faceted language of the crystals, in the ponderous language of the Sequoias, in the sweet, aching song of the high mountains.

—Let them be. Their childhood is over. I am here. I am come. I defend.

The presence speaks, as it has spoken for the past month, in defense of the killers, the despoilers, the scourge.

—Let them be. They have a place. They have work.

And this is a tiny part of the presence's mind, this arguing. As tiny, perhaps, as the part with which it has set about cleaning the world. As tiny, nearly, as the part with which it has dealt with humankind.

Ever so gently, imperceptibly, a billionth of an inch, the presence moves the planet in its orbit.

Ever so subtly, ever so carefully, the presence changes the winds.

Three thousand years. And it will be ready, the womb. Clean, pure, harmonious, the Mother. Three thousand years, and the presence will respond to the Voice which fills the universe for those who can hear it. Three thousand years and the network will be done, the transmitter complete, the birthing cry of intelligent life on earth.

OUTER SPACE

Isaac asimov

☐	BEFORE THE GOLDEN AGE, Book I	C2913	1.95
☐	BEFORE THE GOLDEN AGE, Book II	Q2452	1.50
☐	BEFORE THE GOLDEN AGE, Book III	Q2525	1.50
☐	THE BEST OF ISAAC ASIMOV	23018-X	1.75
☐	BUY JUPITER AND OTHER STORIES	23062-7	1.50
☐	THE CAVES OF STEEL	Q2858	1.50
☐	THE CURRENTS OF SPACE	P2495	1.25
☐	EARTH IS ROOM ENOUGH	Q2801	1.50
☐	THE END OF ETERNITY	Q2832	1.50
☐	THE GODS THEMSELVES	X2883	1.75
☐	I, ROBOT	Q2829	1.50
☐	THE MARTIAN WAY	23158-5	1.50
☐	THE NAKED SUN	Q2648	1.50
☐	NIGHTFALL AND OTHER STORIES	23188-7	1.75
☐	NINE TOMORROWS	Q2688	1.50
☐	PEBBLE IN THE SKY	Q2828	1.50
☐	THE STARS, LIKE DUST	Q2780	1.50
☐	WHERE DO WE GO FROM HERE?—Ed.	X2849	1.75

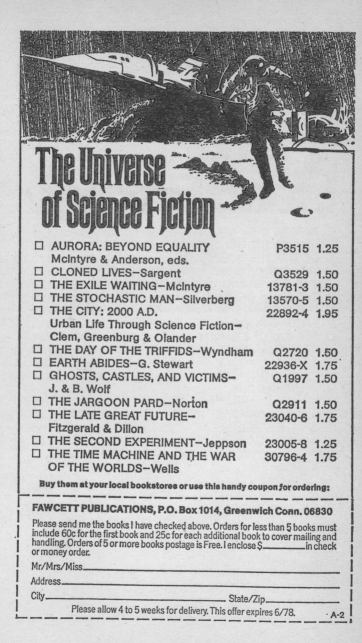

The Universe of Science Fiction